MEDDLESOME MONEY

A COZY CORGI MYSTERY

MILDRED ABBOTT

WINGS OF INK PUBLICATIONS, LLC

MEDDLESOME MONEY

Mildred Abbott

for
Nancy Drew
Phryne Fisher
Julia South
and
Alastair Tyler

Cover, Logo, Chapter Heading Designer: A.J. Corza - SeeingStatic.com

Main Editor: Desi Chapman

2nd Editor: Ann Attwood

3rd Editor: Corrine Harris

Recipe and photo provided by: Rolling Pin Bakery, Denver, Co. - RollingPinBakeshop.com

Visit Mildred's Webpage: MildredAbbott.com

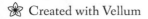 Created with Vellum

For probably the hundredth time that morning, I glanced out the front windows of the Cozy Corgi Bookshop to the luxury home furnishing store across the street. A Closed sign still hung on the front door of Cabin and Hearth. It was the first time since I'd moved to Estes Park over a year and a half ago that Anna and Carl had failed to open, at least without letting me know they were heading out of town—and that wasn't a possibility. With it being July Fourth, our little Colorado mountain town was at the pinnacle of tourist season—no way they would skip that.

Rising from where he was napping in the morning sun a few feet away, my chunky corgi, Watson, stretched his tiny front paws with a big yawn and then plodded my way to prop himself up on the window ledge and peer over.

"Sorry to wake you. There's nothing interesting to see." I grinned down at him in apology. "I can't even take you over to Anna so she can make Carl get you a treat."

Watson's foxlike ears perked up, and he gave a little hop, which was dangerous considering he was balancing on his hind legs. Ever ungraceful, he crashed back down to all fours, managing to scrape his nose on the wall on the way down. After a sneeze, he looked back up to me with an expectant yip.

I realized my mistake instantly. "Good grief, I said your favorite word, didn't I? I was pointing out that Anna and Carl *aren't* over there to get you your treat."

Watson yipped again, and his nub of a tail began to wag frantically.

"Okay, that's proof I need another dirty chai. My caffeine intake isn't keeping up with the number of tourists." I started to turn to Ben to let him know he'd need to handle the bookstore for a few minutes while I took Watson up to the bakery, but at that moment, the front door opened and a fresh wave of tourists entered. Among the group was a family with two young children—a girl carrying a stuffed animal with the head of an elephant and the body of a bumblebee, and a boy dragging one with the body and tail of an alligator, the arms and legs of a teddy bear, and the head of a corgi.

The sight was enough to distract Watson from his treat, and he gave a growl toward the corgi intruder.

Not heeding Watson's warning, the little boy thrust the corgi-alligator-bear toward Watson, bopping his already abused nose. "Look! He's got your face!"

Watson yelped in alarm and was in such a hurry to get away that his nails scrambled over the hardwood floor for a few seconds, before he caught his grip and tore off across the bookshop, up the stairway, and vanished into the bakery.

Shaking my head at his disappearing act, I grinned at the little boy. "Corgis without alligator bodies aren't very brave."

Nonplussed, the boy merely shrugged and picked his stuffed animal up off the floor.

Three days before, my brothers-in-law had opened a stuffed-animal store next door to the Cozy Corgi. Judging from the constant stream of bizarre stuffed animals wandering around downtown, it seemed their *Imagination Station*, as they called the build-a-stuffed-animal-from-various-body-parts   in the back of their store, was a success.

With another glance toward Cabin and Hearth's Closed sign and a quick wish that Carl and Anna weren't hurting as badly as I knew they were, I refocused on the tourists and helped Ben sell a host of books over the next hour or so.

It was well after lunch before we had a lull in the steady stream of tourists. The afternoon thunderstorm helped a bit with that. As I rounded the corner of the stairway into the bakery, a flash of lightning illuminated the sky outside of the second-story windows. A middle-aged redheaded woman typing away at her computer flinched at the following crack of thunder, peered outside, and then began typing once more. Besides her, and Watson sleeping under a nearby table, the bakery was empty.

Katie grinned at me from behind the counter. Though she looked frazzled, her voice was cheerful as she spoke. "I think we're going to nearly double our sales from last Fourth of July. Nick and I were barely able to keep up." She nodded over to Ben's twin, who was pulling out a tray of scones from the oven. "Of course, the article in *The Chipmunk*

Chronicles didn't hurt business this morning. Everybody was here to get the latest scoop."

I internally winced for Anna and Carl again. "Same thing happened yesterday when Delilah was the focus. I'd rather have a little less business than see people we care about—"

"Excuse me." The redheaded woman appeared beside me at the counter and thrust her coffee mug toward Katie. "May I have another refill?"

"Of course." Katie's smile never wavered, but knowing my best friend as I did, I could see the annoyance in her brown eyes. "Can I get you anything else, Bridget? We just pulled our blueberry-and-white-chocolate-chip scones out of the oven."

"Goodness no." The woman patted her flat stomach. "No carbs, remember?"

"I do." That time Katie's smile seemed a little more forced. "But as a baker, I try to block out those kinds of words." She waited until the woman had taken her coffee refill and settled back in front of her computer again before she leaned closer to whisper, "I've always hated those coffee shops and bakeries that have a minimum purchase required before they give out a Wi-Fi password or put time limits on it. But..." Her gaze flashed toward the woman, then back. "She was in here yesterday for hours. And again today. And both times only paid for coffee. And she drinks a whole cup about every five minutes. I've never seen anyone down so much caffeine so quickly. She's even more addicted than you are to your dirty chai."

"I didn't think that would be possible." I was tempted to look over my shoulder at the woman but refrained. "I don't blame you for not wanting to put limitations, but if she's really drinking that much coffee, surely she wouldn't blame you—"

Katie shook her head. "It's just part of doing business, and that's a good thing about tourists. No matter how wonderful or annoying they might be, their time is limited. She can't be here more than another day or two."

"You're probably right." I leaned against the counter and grinned at her while I waggled my eyebrows. "And... speaking of caffeine addiction..."

"One dirty chai coming right up." Katie didn't miss a beat as she headed toward the espresso machine. "And I'm willing to bet I can talk you into a freshly baked scone?"

That time before I answered, I did check over my shoulder to make sure we weren't being watched before I patted my own stomach in a mocking manner. "Absolutely. *I* definitely do carbs, even if it shows."

"And that's why we get along so well."

In less than a minute, Katie and I settled in at Watson's napping table, with the dirty chai, a hot chocolate, and two blueberry-and-white-chocolate scones.

Though he grumbled at being woken, Watson emerged to plop down beside my chair and peer up at me with plaintive chocolate eyes. He received a large chunk of scone with a fat blueberry in the center for his trouble. After gulping it down, he repositioned himself in front of Katie.

She tossed him a large chunk as well. "But no more, you've already gotten three of your favorite doggy T.R.E.A.T.S. from me."

"*Three!*" I gaped at her, nearly choking on my scone.

Katie shrugged one shoulder as she took a bite and spoke with her mouth full. "In my defense, he was terrified when he came storming up here. They seemed to make him feel better."

I glowered at Watson. "You heard the lecture Dr. Sallee gave us yesterday about your weight. You're supposed to lose five pounds."

Watson blinked up at me innocently, but it was

Katie who came to his defense. "I'm pretty sure our doctors would tell us to lose a good ten or fifteen, so I don't think either one of us should cast aspersions on our furry mascot."

Chuckling, I refocused on Katie. "And that's gracious of you to have stopped at ten or fifteen."

She shrugged again. "Well... that's only because I plan on having a second scone before I return from my break. An act of self-love in which I'm certain you'll join me."

"I'd like to pretend otherwise, especially since we have a feast planned for the picnic this evening, but I'm sure you're right. How can I refuse fresh-baked —" A motion out the window caught my attention. The sidewalks were mostly empty, thanks to the downpour, but a shadowy figure stood by the front door of Cabin and Hearth. I leaned forward, acci- dentally bumping my forehead on the window. "Oh, maybe that's Carl. I tried calling him and Anna—" Another flash of lightning cut me off as the figure was illuminated when he turned around. "Gerald Jackson." Despite myself, I leaned forward again and received another knock on my head for the effort. "Apparently he's not been able to get ahold of them either."

Proving she was just as caught up as I was, Katie

didn't make a joke about me bumping my head twice as she looked from Gerald to me. "No way that's a coincidence. Bet you anything he's panicking since he's clearly the next feature tomorrow." Katie pulled a copy of the paper out of her apron and spread it out. "I've not had a chance to read it fully. *Not* that I need to, from all the secondhand speculation I got today." She flipped a few pages to a column titled "A Little Bird Told Me," pointed to the very bottom, and read aloud, "Make sure you check out the gossip tomorrow, where we take a look at how a certain lawyer not only manages to stay out from behind bars, but even has a thriving law practice."

"Yeah. That's about Gerald, no doubt." I looked out the window in time to see Gerald give a final knock, then turn and storm away. "I have to admit, I've always wondered how he manages to stay in business, but I hadn't contemplated him doing anything illegal... well... at least not too much. He always seemed more incompetent than sinister."

Katie hummed. "I probably shouldn't admit it, given how angry I am for Carl and Anna, but I'm curious about what Birdie Sutton will tell on Gerald tomorrow. Whoever Birdie is, even though she's a gossip and mean... she seems factual."

For a moment, I thought I noticed the redheaded

woman cock her head as if she was listening to us from over Katie's shoulder, but then she stood and carried her mug over so Nick could get her another refill. I refocused on Katie. "I'd like to disagree with you, but I can't. The things she said about Carl and Anna today were true, but..." I scanned the article as I spoke. "...it's clear she takes pleasure from causing pain. And really, most of this didn't need to be reported anyway. Everyone knew about the problems Anna and Carl's son caused at Christmas. There was no reason to make it sound so salacious. Besides, he's a grown man. They're not responsible for his choices."

"I agree." A flush rose to Katie's cheeks as she pointed to a line in the middle. "To call Carl henpecked. Well... that's just offensive. To Carl and to Anna. Even if Anna does get a little... emphatic with him sometimes. And to make fun of their repeated attempted campaigns to get on the town council, making them sound... incompetent."

I started to lower my voice to respond, then waited until the woman returned with the coffee and got back to typing. "I have to admit, I am worried about what Anna's reaction is going to be at finding out about Carl investing so much money in Gerald's schemes... not that the article named Gerald, but I bet that will happen tomorrow. I've tried calling them several times today. No one answers."

"This is probably horrible to say after what we were just discussing, but..." Katie winced. "...you don't think Anna would actually... hurt Carl, do you?"

"No. Of course—" I started to shake my head, then paused, considering. *Did I?* There was no doubt that Anna would be furious; I couldn't blame her. It would've been hard enough to find out your husband was investing money in risky ventures behind your back, but even worse to have it announced so publicly. "No. I don't think she would. In fact, I imagine she's more hurt than angry."

"I'm sure you're right." Katie didn't sound like she quite meant what she said. She tore off another large chunk of her scone, then chewed it thoughtfully for a few moments. "I have to admit, I'm dying to find out who this Birdie Sutton character is. No one seems to know. But she came out with a bang. Her first article was only yesterday and more talked about than anything else I've ever seen printed in *The Chipmunk Chronicles*." She snorted. "Although, really, why she started with Delilah Johnson and all her affairs is beyond me. It's not like any of that was a secret. Delilah admits it freely; she's not embarrassed about them at all." Katie scowled, her feelings about Delilah evident.

"True, but it was more than that." Even as I spoke, I started to make connections between what had been written about Delilah, and Anna and Carl. "It was almost like she was making a case that Delilah shouldn't be allowed to own a business in Estes Park. Not only because of the moral failings of her affairs, but insinuated that her Pink Panther Club hurts the good nature of the town and was bordering on delinquent behavior." I poked the article. "Just like with Anna and Carl. Sure, it's an embarrassing amount of dirt, but the theme is the same. Indicating they're not the type of people that should be allowed to operate a business. And it sounds like that's going to be repeated tomorrow about Gerald."

Katie cocked her head and nodded. "You're right. That's interesting."

Another thought hit me. "I don't know how I didn't think of this before. Tomorrow is about Gerald Jackson." I tapped the paper again. "*Gerald Jackson.* He owns part of the paper. How in the world do you think that works?"

Katie's eyes widened. "You're right again! Oh,

Fred, I know it's not a murder, but you gotta look into this. There's a story here, obviously."

I laughed. "Look into what?"

"Well, who Birdie Sutton is, obviously." Katie *tsked*. "I guarantee you, there's more here than meets the eye. Clearly whoever she is, she's got a vendetta and a long list of targets."

"You make it sound so covert." I laughed again. "I doubt it will be all that hard and won't require much digging. Did you forget we have a friend at the *Chipmunk Chronicle*?"

"Athena! Of course! What's wrong with me?" Katie reached across the table and swatted at me. "Pull out your cell, call her right now."

Before I had the chance to decide if I wanted to do that or not, the redhead stood once more. I assumed she was heading back for another refill of coffee, but instead of walking toward the counter, she turned toward Katie and me and then stopped beside our table. "Let me save you a call." She stuck out her hand toward Katie. "*I'm* Birdie Sutton."

Watson scooted from under the table to under my chair, taking shelter from where the fabric of my broomstick skirt fell around him.

Katie gaped at her, staring from the woman's

hand, to her face, and then back to her hand again. "I thought you said your name was Bridget."

"It is." She left her hand outstretched for a few more seconds, then shrugged and let it fall. "Birdie is just my nickname."

"But you're visiting. You're a tourist." Katie cranked around in her chair, gaping toward the computer. "You sat in here all day yesterday and today, just typing and..." She returned to Bridget. "You wrote the article about Anna and Carl in *here*?"

"I never said I was a tourist or that I'm visiting. That was your assumption." Bridget looked toward me. "No need to call Athena Rose. I'm a new employee at the paper. I moved to town last week, and this is my first week on the job."

Before I could think of what to say, Katie stood. "You wrote the article about Anna and Carl in here, in *my* bakery?" That time, as she repeated the sentiment, she sounded furious.

Bridget merely cocked her head, causing the sharp edge of her sleek bob to caress the shoulders of her expensive blouse. "I'm sorry, do you have a problem with me reporting facts?"

"Facts?" Katie's voice spiked. "Anna and Carl are our friends. They're dear, sweet people. And you're trying to rip them to shreds."

At her raised tone, Watson shifted, and I felt him poke his head out from under my skirt before giving a growl.

Bridget spared him a glance but refocused on Katie. "I heard you and your business partner here, just moments ago, acknowledge that everything I wrote was true."

"And cruel." Katie bit out the words.

For whatever reason, Bridget looked at me as if expecting me to come to her defense. "I've heard of your reputation, Winifred Page. You've been known to dig around for... facts."

I stared at her, completely caught off guard at the comparison.

"You need to leave." Katie's whisper was barely audible. "Now."

Bridget looked back at her, raising a perfectly manicured hand toward her chest. "Excuse me?"

"I said *leave*." Katie's voice rose again, and she pointed toward the computer and then at the stairs. "Get out of my bakery. You're not welcome here."

For a second, it looked like Bridget was going to argue. Instead she lifted her chin, strode over to her computer, closed it, slid it into a leather satchel, and walked haughtily toward the steps.

Trembling, Katie yelled after her as Bridget

began to disappear down the stairs, "And another thing, it's rude to sit in a bakery for hours and only order a coffee." She started to sit back down, but then straightened once more. "And if you ate a carb every once in a while, I bet you'd be a nicer person!"

By the time we arrived at the fairgrounds by the shores of Lake Estes, the thunderstorms had given way to a bright, cloudless blue sky. What little snow remained on the peaks of the surrounding mountains glistened in the early evening sunlight. The earth and grass were still damp, but no one seemed to mind. It didn't even soak through the countless blankets spread over the meadow, turning the wide-open space into a large patchwork quilt.

Though there were easily thousands of people in attendance, there was an effortless, cheerful feel. The murmur of children laughing and playing overarched the hum of adult conversations, and the gentle breeze mixed the heavenly scent of pine and the aromas of grilling hot dogs and burgers around us.

As I sat on a blanket, my hand in Leo's while he joked around with Katie and Paulie, Watson wedged himself between our legs so his head rested on my knee and his hip on Leo's calf, and I decided the best part about Estes Park was that every holiday was my favorite. Halloween was charming, with all the kids and families dressed up as they wandered through the downtown while storeowners handed out treats outside their shops. At Christmas, the little town, without fail, transformed into a sparkling winter village. And the Fourth of July? Between the beauty of the mountains, the camaraderie of the crowds, and the fireworks that would soon be glistening in reflected glory over the surface of the lake, it was all pure perfection.

Leo looked over at me and laughed, breaking my reverie.

"What?"

He grinned. "You and Watson just let out simultaneous sighs of contentment."

"Did we?" I hadn't even realized I'd made a sound.

"Sure did. It was lovely." His honey-brown eyes twinkled as he leaned nearer to kiss me on the cheek. "And I quite agree." He pulled back and ruffled the fur between Watson's ears.

Watson groaned happily, and without opening

his eyes, twisted so he lay on his back, wedged between our legs, so he could get belly rubs.

Leo obliged, as did Katie.

Paulie's two corgis scampered over at the sight, clearly wanting to get in on the action. Flotsam skidded to a stop, bumping into my leg, and pressed his nose to Watson's, while Jetsam took the opposite approach, launching onto my lap and licking the nearest of Watson's back paws.

Though the heavy corgi knocked my breath from me, Watson didn't bother opening his eyes. He merely gave a warning grumble toward Flotsam and flicked his hind leg bopping Jetsam on the nose.

Having finally developed a soft spot for the crazy corgis, after catching my breath, I motioned at Flotsam, and half a second later he pounced upon me as well, then all was lost to frantic paws and licking tongues.

Watson issued a grunt that clearly communicated he found the display quite below his level of dignity.

"Good Lord, Fred," my uncle, Percival, screeched over Flotsam and Jetsam's whimpers of happiness. "You're creating a tornado of corgi hair, and we just laid out all the food."

"Oh, hush," Gary chided. "*You* didn't make any of it."

"That doesn't mean I want to be picking out dog fur from between my teeth." Percival scowled at his husband. "Besides, it's disrespectful to the ones who did make it. Just look at all this food Katie brought. She clearly spared no effort. She even made hand pies for dessert, and they don't need an icing of dog hair."

"Don't worry about that." Katie laughed, reached across Leo, and rubbed Jetsam's flank, intentionally increasing the fur flying around. "With Watson in my life, I've made sure all my recipes are compatible with dog hair."

Percival's scowl deepened.

My mom chuckled as she and my stepfather continued to unpack food from the picnic baskets. "I'd like to pretend you're kidding, but—" She narrowed her eyes at me. "—from the looks of it, we really are going to have a side order of dog hair with everything."

"And hopefully this doesn't disappoint you." Katie cringed just a bit, continuing to address Percival. "But they're empanadas, and only some are dessert—apple pie filling for the Fourth, of course.

Most are traditional mincemeat, beef, candied fruit, and—"

"Describe them later!" Nearly choking on all the hair, I managed to look over at Paulie, as Flotsam bounded up and down behind me getting tangled in my hair, and Jetsam licked slobber over my ear. "Can you help me out? I should've known better."

"Oh, sure. I'll try." Paulie hopped up and hooked each of his hands in their collars struggling to pull them away. "Come on, boys. This is why we don't get invited very many places. If you'd only learn to—"

Jetsam cut off whatever Paulie was about to say by hopping up and shoving his nose in his daddy's mouth.

Paulie sputtered and looked over at Leo. "Can you help me? Please."

Leo scampered to assist.

Katie swatted him on his hip as he stood. "Smokey Bear to the rescue!"

"I'm not promising anything." Leo scooped up Flotsam, who thrashed in delight at the embrace. "I've met mountain lions that are easier to corral."

The entire family, and some other observers a few blankets over as well, paused to watch the two men try to get the corgis under control, each offering advice or simply laughing. Even Percival struggled to hold back a grin under his furrowed brow while he grumbled about straight people and their "children."

Once Leo and Paulie secured Flotsam and Jetsam's leashes to a spike in the ground a few feet away, the rest of the food was unpacked and everyone dived in. Even though—with my stepsisters and their husbands and kids present—there were sixteen of us, not counting the dogs, there was such an abundance of food, there would no doubt be leftovers.

As the family filled their plates, people gathered in various little clusters over the blankets. Mom and Barry sat close to Leo, Katie, and me.

"Okay, these little meat empanadas aren't half bad," Percival called over to Katie from the other side of the blankets. "I might have to have a few more of those."

"I can't take all the credit." Katie thumbed over at Leo. "It's his grandmother's recipe. Although I made a few of my own... adjustments."

Leo leaned close to her, keeping his voice low. "Think we should let them know there's suet in them?"

"No, definitely not." I shook my head adamantly, then reconsidered. "Although... his reaction would be priceless. It might turn him into a vegetarian like Barry."

"You have to be kidding me." Katie looked up suddenly, staring across the meadow, the humor leaving her expression.

The rest of us followed her gaze and didn't have any trouble spotting what she'd seen. A large band of women wove through the families gathered around on blankets. Each of them was dressed in skintight white halter tops, red leggings, and silky pink jackets that read *Pink Panthers* in white lettering on the back. Though the women came in every shape and size, there was a high number of them who could have passed for sultry Barbie dolls. A tall, stunning redhead led the group.

"Say what you want about Delilah Johnson," Percival practically purred. "She's not about to let anyone tell her what she should or shouldn't do. And she enjoys rubbing it in everyone's faces with style."

"I don't know if I'd call that style."

At Katie's criticism, Percival looked over with a raised eyebrow. "My darling little baker, you know that I adore you, and not just because you provide me with sugary happiness, but the embossed fat pigeon waving the flag on your T-shirt would suggest you may not want to cast stones."

Leo chuckled and earned himself an elbow to the stomach.

"Don't encourage him." Katie pulled back her elbow and tilted her chin at Percival. "Whimsy is more stylish than clothing that looks like it's painted on." Katie growled again, though seemingly at herself this time. "Although, as a feminist, I support Delilah and her group's right to wear whatever they want. *Without* getting shamed for it in the newspaper. But... still..."

Watson sat straight up suddenly and let out a giant bark toward the group of women, clearly just having noticed them.

As one, they all turned toward us. Though a couple of them waved, Delilah motioned them onward and then headed our direction.

"Seriously, Watson?" Katie grumbled under her breath. "Just because I support her wearing whatever she wants, doesn't mean I want it shoved in my face while I'm trying to eat."

Ignoring her, Watson barked happily once more as Delilah drew near. He always liked Delilah, but his reaction was unusual. Typically such excitement was reserved for Barry, Leo, and Ben.

"Well, hello there, handsome." Delilah knelt in a sultry twist of her body and spoke in tone that matched. She reached out to stroke his head. "Good to see you, too."

Watson allowed the caress for a moment, then ducked from her touch and peered desperately around from one side to the next as he whimpered.

Leo chuckled. "Oh... he's looking for the boys."

Of course he was. Now it made sense. While Watson had grown to tolerate and even care for Flotsam and Jetsam, he'd had an instant love affair with Delilah's three rescued Basset hounds.

Not looking offended in the slightest, Delilah cupped his face. "I'm sorry, sweetie. Zuko, Kenickie, and Putzie aren't as brave as you. They stay home during the fireworks."

Watson pulled free again and gave one final, searching glance for his Basset friends, then settled back between my legs with a dejected sigh.

I rested my hand on his hip in sympathy as I addressed Delilah. "Watson's not the biggest fan either. He'll shelter under my skirt. I've noticed he does better when he's with me than if I leave him at home."

"Not my boys," Paulie spoke up with a laugh. "I'll be taking them home before the show begins. They go a little insane as soon as fireworks start."

Delilah arched an eyebrow. "And that's saying

something for those two." As she stood, she looked over her shoulder, spotting where the rest of her Pink Panthers were setting up their picnic. "I should get back, but it's good to see you all." With a wink and twinkling of fingers toward the group, she whirled and made a deliberate show of slinking through the crowd. When she was far enough away to have to raise her voice, she called back over her shoulder. "Oh, and if any of you want an autograph on your copy of my featured article, just say the word, I'm only charging a minimal fee for the honor."

"Oh my Lord, I love her," Percival practically howled.

"I do have to admire her spirit." Mom turned from watching Delilah weave through the people and whispered in concern, "She's kidding about the autographs, though, right?"

"I wouldn't count on it." Katie scowled at Delilah's retreating form.

"I hope she's serious. Besides"—Percival nodded sagely—"she's making lemonade out of lemons. We should take notes. It might be one of us next."

"You're not wrong." Barry sounded atypically serious. "Yesterday Delilah, today Carl and Anna, tomorrow Gerald it seems. Could just as easily be one of us the day after that."

Gary nodded his agreement. "It is a shame that such divisiveness is being spread through the paper in this day and age."

"It is horrible." Mom refocused on the Pink Panthers. "It brings out the worst in people. I was in the grocery store today and couldn't believe the things people were saying about Carl and Anna. *Locals*, at that, people who should know better."

"I'd forgotten that Athena was out of town. I was hoping to get the inside scoop about Birdie Sutton tonight." Katie rolled her eyes. "Or should I say *Bridget?*"

"Bridget?" Mom had started to take a bite but paused with the empanada lifted halfway to her mouth. "Is that her real name? How did you find that out?"

"She was in the bakery today. Yesterday as well, it turns out. Fred and I met her." Katie huffed out an angry breath. "It seems she was using my bakery to write her horrible articles."

"Really?" Leo sat up a little straighter, and at the motion, some of the meat slid out from his sandwich.

With sharklike reflexes, Watson lunged and scarfed down the large mouthful in one gulp.

"Careful, buddy. You're liable to take off someone's hand." Leo laughed, and nudged Watson with his leg.

Watson only stared up at him expectantly.

Proving to be the softy that Watson knew he was, Leo pulled out another slice of meat and tossed it to him before looking at me. "You didn't tell me you'd met the suddenly infamous Birdie Sutton."

"I think I tried to block it from my mind. Although you should've seen Katie." I grinned over at her. "She was filled with righteous indignation. Kicked the lady out of the bakery, all the while recommending the woman eat more carbs."

Katie wriggled her shoulders. "And I stand by it. The woman was waif thin, and clearly hungry. It's no wonder she's cranky."

"We tried to get ahold of Anna and Carl all day." Mom glanced over at Barry as she spoke. "Even went by the house. I'm worried about them."

"I tried calling too." I debated for a heartbeat, then decided I wanted to see what reaction I'd get. "I also noticed Gerald making an attempt. He was knocking on Cabin and Hearth during a thunderstorm."

To my surprise, neither Barry nor Percival rushed toward his defense as they typically would. If anything, Barry grew even more serious. "I'm sure

Gerald is in a panic over what might be written tomorrow. The way the article made it sound, it seems like she's going to reveal some pretty incriminating stuff."

"And so far, while it's been framed in a mean and gossipy way, Birdie hasn't said anything untrue." Percival exchanged a wary glance with Barry. "While I'm worried, I have to admit I'm a little curious what we're going to find out about our friend tomorrow."

It was a little too similar to the conversation Katie and I had earlier that day.

"Did she say where she's from?" Mom looked back and forth between Katie and me. "It seems suspicious that she arrived on the scene and instantly began this drama. It feels intentional, like she's got a hit list that she's checking off one by one. And I've never heard of Birdie, or Bridget, Sutton, for that matter. So... why?"

Leo smiled warmly at my mother. "I've heard you say many times Fred got her detective instincts from her father, but look at you. It sounds like you've already got a theory."

Mom flushed and waved him off; she was clearly pleased. "I wouldn't say a theory, just an observation. And an obvious one at that."

"Oh my Lord." Percival's shocked whisper drew everyone's attention, and we followed his gaze. "It seems Anna took a page out of Delilah's playbook, which is an interesting turn of events, considering how much she can't stand the woman."

Sure enough, Anna Hanson was clearly making a show to be seen. Though she and her husband were short, neither were small people, both rather round and hard to miss. But there was no chance anyone would fail to notice her as she plodded over the meadow with her chin in the air and clothed in enough fabric to upholster several bedspreads. She'd chosen a red, white, and blue caftan that streamed behind her in the breeze, fluttering as if she was the embodiment of the American flag. Weaving his way behind her, clearly uncomfortable, Carl was equally conspicuous in a large red and white suit and a star-spangled top hat shoved on his bald head. With his ruddy cheeks, round spectacles, and fuzzy white beard, he typically reminded me of Santa Claus, but at the moment, he channeled a jolly Uncle Sam.

Anna halted in her stride as her gaze swept over us. Relief seemed to pass over her features, and she changed direction and headed our way.

Not missing a beat, Mom stood as Anna approached, and was her typical loving self by wrapping the larger woman in her thin arms. "We're so glad to see you, dear. We tried to call you all day."

It looked like Anna was about to break for a heartbeat in Mom's embrace, before she glanced around as if remembering where she was, then hardened once more as she straightened. "We had to retreat and lick our wounds for a little bit. I wasn't planning on showing my face for months, but then an hour ago I changed my mind. I'm not going to let some stupid little gossip columnist make me ashamed in my own town." She swatted at her husband who'd just arrived beside her. "I told Carl, I said, 'Carl, we're getting dressed up, and if people want a show, well, we'll give them a show.' Carl's suit is a little tighter than the last time he wore it, but we made do."

Carl patted the gold button straining at his belly as he glanced around as if he expected someone to attack. "Don't worry, dear. If the suit explodes, it will just give them more of a show, won't it?"

Anna scowled. "Don't give me attitude, Carl. I'm done with you. I can't handle any more of your scandals."

Carl didn't answer back, but his gaze flicked to me, his bloodshot eyes looking as if he'd spent the day crying. He turned away and took a long swig from his thermos.

"Do you mind if we join you?" Anna refocused on Mom and scanned the rest of the family. Her bravado faded and her voice trembled. "If you'd rather not be seen with—"

"Nonsense!" Barry threw an arm around Anna's shoulders and pulled her in close. "Look at the feast we have. What's it for if we can't share it with those we love?"

A tear slid down Anna's cheek as she nodded.

For the second time, Watson left his place between Leo and me, padding over to Anna and rubbing against her leg in a near catlike fashion.

Anna choked out a sob and knelt, cupping Watson's face like Delilah had done, but pressed a kiss to his forehead. "Oh, my sweet little baby. You know Mama needs some love, don't you?" Both of her hands stroked him almost hungrily.

Watson sat and allowed himself to be pawed.

Knowing Watson as I did, I wasn't completely sure Anna was right. Watson was often attuned to people's distress and frequently offered comfort, but he also saw Anna as a human-sized treat dispenser. In truth, I was willing to bet his response to her was a combination of both qualities.

"Carl," Anna barked over her shoulder. "I put some treats in the picnic basket. Hurry up and get one."

Yep, sure enough.

As the sun began to set about half an hour later, Paulie took Flotsam and Jetsam home, and Anna joined my mother and stepsisters at the other side of the group. Zelda and Verona had brought some crystals with them, and Mom launched into making a necklace for Anna, choosing stones that would offer comfort and healing.

Clearly, Carl had been waiting for Anna to be distracted, and though he'd been in midconversation with Percival, he peered over at me, his voice jittery. "You were right. I should've told her. We'd been so close over the last month or so, after the explosion downtown. But now..." He twisted to gaze at Anna, sighed, and seemed to deflate. "She feels betrayed and lied to."

Katie patted his knee, and I knew I should offer some sort of comfort, but he wasn't wrong. It was exactly what I'd warned him about. "Please tell me you kept your promise, that you didn't use any of your retirement savings."

"I didn't. I swear." Though sincere, a flash of defiance showed in his bloodshot eyes. "But she'll see. It doesn't matter what that stupid article said. Gerald's investments will pay off. *They will!* And you'll see too. That investment I made in your name is going to make you wealthy beyond your wildest dreams."

It took an exorbitant effort not to groan.

To my surprise, Percival came to my defense. "Really, Carl, you need to be careful. We don't know what's going to come out about Gerald tomorrow. And I know neither of us wants to think anything bad about—"

"It will be all lies," Carl bit back and took a drink from his thermos. "Someone's out to get Gerald. Out to get me, clearly. Why else would this happen?"

"Carl, come on, it's—"

Carl leaned closer, grabbing my forearm, cutting Percival off. "I think it's the Irons family. Whoever that Birdie woman might be, she's clearly in league with them."

Despite the ridiculousness of the claim, at the name of the organization that was responsible for my father's death and a host of illegal activities in Estes Park, ice settled in my gut.

Apparently feeling the same, Leo flinched beside me. "Carl, why—"

"I bet that's why they're after Delilah as well.

Maybe she's a secret agent, here to spy on the Irons family, try to bring them down." As he spoke, Carl's gaze shot over my shoulder, flicking from person to person. "Maybe they're watching us right now."

I opened my mouth to respond, but couldn't think of a thing to say.

Percival didn't give me the chance as he leaned around Carl, snagged his thermos, and then sipped it before narrowing his eyes at Carl. "How much of this have you had today, Carl? Between this and the stress, I think it's scrambling your brain. You sound positively paranoid."

Carl snatched the thermos back with a glare, and hissed at Percival, "Keep your voice down. Anna thinks it's beer."

Ignoring him, Percival looked at me to explain, though I'd already caught on. "It's Gerald's home-made kombucha. And while we know I have no problem with it, Carl's displaying the signs of having too much. Paranoid, jittery, bloodshot eyes. All that's left is the munchies."

"That isn't true," Carl hissed again, and dared to glance at Anna. "It doesn't even affect me anymore."

Gerald Jackson was notorious for his homemade kombucha, which he infused with cannabis. Though I told myself I did it for Anna, part of me was aware that I was simply irritated at Carl for springing the Irons family out of the blue on me. I leaned closer to him and gave a hiss of my own. "Really, Carl? You're going to deceive Anna on kombucha now? I suggest you pour it out, because I'm *done* keeping secrets for you."

"You wouldn't dare." Carl sounded truly offended, almost hurt.

"Try me." I motioned toward Anna. "You said yourself how much closer you two have been since the accident. You think this is going to help you get back on track?"

Carl hesitated. "Fine." He took a ridiculously long swig, then held the thermos over the edge of the blankets and poured out the little that remained onto the grass. "But it's *not* affecting me, and I'm *not* paranoid. You mark my words, Winifred. The Irons family is all around us right now." He stood, wobbling a bit. "In fact, I'm going to prove it." With that, he took off into the crowd.

"What is it?" At the commotion, Anna looked around, and her eyes went wide as she saw Carl disappearing. "Carl? Carl!"

Percival sprang up. "Carl was just saying he wanted to get some kettle corn from the vendors. Which I think is a great idea." He flashed Barry a meaningful stare. "Care to help? We'll need some more arms to carry enough to feed us all."

Barry sprang into action, as did Gary.

Night had fallen, and the fireworks had just begun when they returned, Carl in tow, *without* any popcorn. Percival claimed they'd been sold out. Within minutes of sitting down, Carl passed out on the blanket, snoring over the explosions of the fireworks. He was always a little left of center, but nothing about Carl that evening was typical at all.

With Watson sheltering contentedly under my broomstick skirt, I snuggled against Leo and tried to lose myself in the beauty of the fireworks sparkling through the night sky, causing the mountains to glow, and doubled in size by being mirrored over the surface of the lake. I almost managed it, the majority of me settled into the serene beauty and contentment of the moment, but some little part of me kept mulling over Carl's words and strange behavior. And though up to that point the "A Little Bird Told Me" column had been nothing more than a mean, salacious form of gossip, certainty settled over me that it was going to take a darker turn than anyone expected.

THREE

Watson looked back at me quizzically as I halted in the doorway of the Cozy Corgi the next morning. I'd expected to see the bookshop already bustling, especially since I was running about half an hour late. Leo, Watson, and I had taken a leisurely stroll through the forest outside my house before he reported for a double shift of park ranger duties. I'd texted Ben to let him know, confident he could handle the morning crowd, as he always handled everything.

The day after the Fourth of July was typically as busy as the day itself, but not a soul was present... not even Ben. All the lights were on, as was the soft piped-in background music. I peered into the mystery room. He'd even opened the window and lit the fireplace, as he knew I loved.

Proving I needed a dirty chai, or two, to combine with the caffeine from the tumbler of coffee I'd had, I didn't catch on until Watson let out an annoyed huff and finished waddling across the bookshop and cantered up the stairs to the bakery without waiting for me. I finally realized where everyone was. Though it was only the smell of fresh yeast, cinnamon, and sugar that hinted of life, there was barely any sound coming from upstairs. For a ridiculous moment, I wondered if I would be walking into a mass crime scene—some horrible accident that happened just as the bakery had opened for business. I shoved that notion aside. Watson hadn't displayed any of his typical signals when trouble was afoot—no pausing, laying back of ears, or warning grumble—just his typical annoyance at his mother.

As I followed in Watson's footsteps, it wasn't until I reached the top of the stairs that I finally heard the hushed murmurs, right before I turned to see the bakery nearly filled with people. For a second ridiculous moment, I had a flashback to my surprise fortieth birthday party from a little over a month before. Though no one yelled surprise, as I stepped farther into the space, all eyes turned and looked at me.

Annoyance forgotten, Watson was frolicking in his typical joy around Ben, where he stood on the opposite side of the counter speaking to Katie and

Nick. He bent, giving a quick caress to Watson's muzzle before straightening, tucking his long straight black hair behind his ear and motioning me to join them.

I offered a wavering smile to the breakfast crowd, most of whom were locals, though I didn't spot Anna and Carl among them. "What's going on?" Despite myself, I heard an accusatory tone in my words as I addressed Katie and the twins.

Ben started to answer, but was cut off when Watson, having not received nearly enough attention from one of his idols, reared up and shoved Ben's thigh with his forepaws.

As Ben sank to his knees to truly greet Watson, Katie pushed the paper on the counter toward me. "Today's 'A Little Bird Told Me.'" She tapped the bottom of the page. "Skip to the end."

There was only one explanation, and as I read the brief sentences, I wondered how I hadn't seen it coming. Or... judging from my sense of inevitability, maybe I had. Barry and Percival had suggested as much the night before.

Don't miss tomorrow's edition, where we explore how a certain bookseller, who peddles pastries topped with dog hair, was forced out of her own publishing company. We'll question how she's allowed to interfere in countless police investigations, and explore her dark romance with a dangerous mobster who has ties with her father's death.

No... I hadn't seen *that* coming. I stared at the last three words. *Her father's death.* Maybe the rest made sense, judging from what Birdie Sutton had written about Delilah and Carl. The reporter, or gossip columnist, whatever she was, pedaled in scandal and embarrassment, but to use my father's murder... To imply that I'd knowingly had a relationship with...

My shock transitioned to fury.

"I'm going to kill her." I hadn't realized I'd spoken out loud until the words reached my ears. Flinching, I looked around—all eyes were still on me, though I didn't think I'd been loud enough for anyone at the tables to hear.

"Fred," Katie whispered, leaning across the counter and squeezing my arm. "You've not done anything wrong, we both know that. It'll be okay, no matter what she writes."

I looked at her, confused for a moment. "Not done anything..." Then it clicked. That was the point of Birdie Sutton's articles so far—to cast judgment, to condemn, to embarrass. I scanned what she promised to say about me the next day again. With that point of view, which should have been obvious from the beginning, I supposed, I felt better. Katie was right, I hadn't done anything wrong. And Birdie Sutton could twist the truth to make it as embarrassing as she wanted to, or at least she could try. None of that was a secret. The whole town knew about my relationship with Branson Wexler. They also knew about his connection with the Irons family. There'd been several articles in *The Chipmunk Chronicles* over the months with that revelation. And as far as being pushed out of my publishing house? That wasn't a secret either, and I'd been the victim, not the perpetrator.

Watson, probably feeling my emotions raging, had left Ben and wedged himself against my leg.

I looked down as I felt his weight against me, met his concerned, warm brown eyes, and something settled within me. I'd already faced the betrayals from my ex-husband, ex-best friend, and a police sergeant who'd promised I'd always be safe with him. I'd lost my hero father in the line of duty. I'd hit reset on my life and built something beautiful and more wonderful than I could ever imagine. I'd faced down more than one murderer and come out on the other side. Was there a chance some scandalous, gossip-filled article about my life could hurt me? Not likely.

Reaching down, I scratched Watson's head and then straightened, smiling out to the crowd as I raised my voice. "Sounds like a certain bookseller you all know is going to be the star of tomorrow's headlines. Meet me here in the Cozy Corgi Bakery the same time tomorrow morning for a live reading of whatever it says. We'll make a celebration out of it. Free dirty chais for everyone! And bring your friends." I pointed down at Watson. "Though, you'll be responsible for collecting your own dog hair to put on the baked goods."

With that, the tension in the bakery broke. People whooped, cheered, and laughed. A sense of strength and peace settled over me. I turned to see both the twins staring at me with identical expressions of openmouthed wonder. Katie simply beamed. "I love you."

I laughed, leaned against the counter, and smiled back. "I love you too. But next time, call or text and give a girl a warning, would you?"

"I di—" Katie's eyes narrowed, and she looked back and forth between the twins, as if trying to remember. "Good Lord, I didn't, did I? I guess we were just too..." She finished by motioning toward the article.

I laughed again. "It's okay. I can't blame you. Maybe it was better this way, reading it in public and not having to wonder what everyone was thinking."

Nick was still staring at me, and his voice was a whisper. "You're really not worried about whatever she'll say tomorrow?"

I shrugged, not having to consider. "No. I don't think I am. I don't have any secrets, not anymore. And from what we've read so far, while she puts a scandalous spin to everything, Birdie doesn't say anything that isn't true." I gave a knowing grin to Katie. "I think I'll channel my inner Delilah Johnson and simply own whatever the truth is. I can't imagine people will have a problem with it, but if they do"—I shrugged one of my shoulders—"then who cares?"

"And again, I have to say that I love you." Katie shuddered as well, though I got the impression it was more for effect. "But I'll *never* compare you to Delilah Johnson." Before I could comment on that, Katie continued, growing a little more serious. "You may want to read the article before you get too confident in what Birdie Sutton will say tomorrow. Either she's willing to stretch the truth more than we thought, or Gerald Jackson isn't exactly the bumbling idiot we assumed."

"Really? It's that bad about Gerald?"

Katie nudged the paper farther toward me. "I'll make you a dirty chai as you read, a double."

"And I'll man the bookshop." Ben gave a brief but firm squeeze to my shoulder, and his dark gaze met mine, communicating a world of trust and support. "Let me know if you need anything?"

"I will. Thank you." I watched him disappear down the stairs and felt a warm glow as Watson stayed by my side instead of following. "Katie? Do you mind getting Watson one of his favorite all-natural dog bone treats while you're at it?"

Watson gave a happy yip and a quick little twirl at my feet.

"Yep, that's right. Don't forget your mama pays for your love and loyalty with food." I grinned down at him and then refocused on the "A Little Bird Told Me."

My beautiful, dear gossip-loving little chickadees, has Mama Birdie got a story for you today, just like I promised.

Now you know me, I don't name names, so you will

have to fill in the blanks, but luckily, I know how astute you are and that you won't have any trouble at all figuring out who our dirty little lawyer might be.

One likes to think that in this complicated, often confusing world, there are a few things that are black-and-white, good and evil, right and wrong. A beloved, trusted, long-term fighter of justice and defender of the weak should be just such a person. And indeed, for decades, this individual has been seen as just such a being. A moral, glowing beacon in the darkness, if you will. Though it pains me to share this with you, my little chickadees, many of you have placed your faith in the wrong keeper of justice.

As I like to do, I'll start off with the good and the true. This unnamed lawyer does, in fact, have a law degree and a license to practice in his field. He—and yes, I give you that clue, this individual is a man—has licenses, credentials, certificates, and everything else up to date and in good standing. And that, my little ones, is where the good news ends, and in fact, may even be tarnished by the end of this tale.

Your Mama Birdie has uncovered that this purveyor of liberty has taken advantage of the blindfold that covers Lady Justice's eyes, doing dark, evil, and manipulative deeds where she cannot see. So much

so, that I struggle with knowing where to begin. So…
I'll roll the dice. And we land on…

Addiction and relations with drug dealers. Yes, you
read that right. This man who's sworn to uphold the law
flaunts the will of the very town he serves by engaging and
dealing in illegal and dangerous substances. While our
colorful state of Colorado has legalized the use of marijuana—which many consider a dangerous hallucinogen—
our town has taken the moral high ground and not
permitted it to be sold within the city limits. Given that, it's
a fine tightrope this lawyer walks. Perhaps his activities are
not illegal in the truest sense of the word, yet they cause
this humble reporter, a seeker of truth, to question. Are the
suppliers of this substance aboveboard or are there direct,
easily traceable ties to the dark and dangerous underbelly
of our society? It is common—though often unspoken—
knowledge that this lawyer uses this controversial
substance in an addictive, nearly constant manner,
sipping it in liquid form while meeting with clients,
researching cases, and even whilst in the midst of a courtroom. I ask you, is this altered state of being what clients
expect when they pay his significant hourly fee? When
they put their legal fates in his impaired hands?

You only need to roll the dice a solitary turn to
stumble upon the next revelation. There are many civil

servants who unfortunately must work more than one job to make ends meet. How many teachers do you know who are forced to work weekends and holidays to keep a roof over their heads while having the responsibility of enlightening young minds?

Rest assured, little ones, this lawyer is not such a civil servant. The salary he brings in annually could supplement the income of a host of educators and yet… can the search for wealth be satiated? In this case, no. Perhaps, this individual's connection to the grimy underworld of drug dealers is what led to his dalliances with bookies, money launderers, and racketeers. For this lawyer, it matters not if you are stranger, client, or friend, he'll have an "opportunity" to share with you. Something that sounds glittering and special, something that promises high dividends and returns. But be warned, my little chicks, when you hand over your hard-earned cash, make sure you kiss it goodbye, because those promised pots of gold will never appear.

As you know, I won't lie to you, so I'll merely ask some questions, aroused as I lifted rocks looking for fat, juicy worms to feed my little ones. Is this lawyer robbing Peter to save Paul? Has he gotten in too deep to the scourges of our underworld and is now unable to dig his way out? Will he steal your money while making promises, because he fears for his very life? Perhaps. Perhaps.

Let me offer you one final morsel upon this delicious platter, my little chickadees. And this one may have the most question marks yet. As I told you at the beginning, this particular lawyer is in good standing. The credentials and licenses all have dotted i's and crossed t's. But... I'm not sure how this could be, for you see, I've uncovered proof that this lawyer has taken the trust and faith of his clients and knowingly, nay, willfully, stabbed them in the back. Let me ask you this, and though I know the answer, I'll let you arrive at your own conclusions. Are those payoffs from insurance companies (multiple ones throughout the decades, I might add) slipped into this lawyer's back pocket when he intentionally loses a case for his clients? Does their loss of promised insurance payouts mysteriously find a way into this lawyer's wallet? Could it be that while the high rate of losses would indicate this lawyer—while seemingly well-meaning but rather incompetent—is intentionally losing cases and claims in order to receive payments under the table?

And the biggest questions of them all, my little chickadees? Could it be that these three rolls of the dice are not truly three rolls at all? Is it too farfetched to wonder if this lawyer hasn't stumbled into relationships with the dark and dangerous elements of our society that operate in shadows? Could he, perhaps, be one of the masterminds behind it all? Again, I only say perhaps. As always, I leave it up to you to determine where the truth lies. It is merely my job to deliver the delicious facts. It's up to you what you do with them.

Don't miss tomorrow's edition, where we explore how a certain bookseller, who peddles pastries topped with dog hair, was forced out of her own publishing company. We'll question how she's allowed to interfere in countless police investigations, and explore her dark romance with a dangerous mobster who has ties with her father's death.

I don't know how long I stood there or how many times I read the article. But each time it sank in a little deeper. What Birdie Sutton had written about Delilah and Carl had been embarrassing and scandalous, but none of it was illegal. And it was all true. If the implications around Gerald Jackson were also true, there was landmine after landmine embedded in her gossipy tidbits.

Finally, I looked up and met Katie's expectant gaze.

"Well?" She lifted her eyebrows questioningly.

"I don't think I would've ever dreamed of this in my wildest imagination. But..." I wasn't entirely certain until I spoke out loud. "This would explain a lot. A lot."

Katie bit her lower lip as she nodded, before she answered, "Yeah. I was thinking the same thing."

FOUR

Within half an hour, Watson and I had joined Ben
and were doing our jobs in the bookshop. As I
assisted customers, I let the questions Birdie Sutton
asked roll around in my mind, or rather the implications of those questions. I'd never given much
thought to where or how Gerald had purchased the
cannabis he used to make his kombucha. By this
point, though the selling of it was still illegal in Estes,
it was common enough across the state that no one
blinked twice. There'd be no reason for Gerald to use
illegal means to get his supplies. But in the cases of
Delilah and Carl, nothing Birdie had claimed had
been inaccurate. That led me to believe there was
something to her claims about Gerald.

That was a dangerous path to wander down,
however, considering I was the topic of the next
column. I might want to withhold judgment on the

validity of her accusations of Gerald until I saw the ones tossed my direction. But the way Birdie had tied it together with Gerald's investment schemes lent some weight to the accusations. How many times had I expressed my own concerns about what he was up to in that arena? And though I never would've thought of it on my own, the possibility of Gerald intentionally being incompetent in his cases for nefarious reasons almost made sense. In a way, it had been almost too easy to dismiss him as a small-town bumbling-idiot lawyer. But what if his actions were darker than that?

And the part I really didn't want to think about, but yet couldn't keep my mind from mulling over? Birdie Sutton hadn't said anything directly about the Irons family, but her implied claims about Gerald, and her hint of what she was going to reveal about Branson and me in the following column, clicked with Carl's paranoid ramblings from the night before. It all seemed too far-fetched, too ridiculous, though... even without all the details, something about it fit together far too easily.

Pondering the possibilities made me less effective with the customers, and I was certain I was coming off distracted and slow. In the same length of time Ben practically cleared out the children's book section with the families of tourists who came in, I only managed to sell two books.

Some relief was provided when most considerations of Gerald were swept away as an elderly man debated the merits of the biographies of Michelle Obama and Nancy Reagan with me for nearly twenty minutes. It was a welcome distraction. Just when I thought I'd talked him into purchasing both, he set them aside with a shake of his head. "You know, politics can be exhausting. My granddaughter was reading a series a few years ago, about this young girl who had to pick between a vampire and werewolf. That might be less stressful. Do you have whatever that is?"

It was such a one-eighty, it took me a second. "Do you mean the Twilight series?"

"I don't know." He grimaced as his brows knitted, and then he brightened. "I think I remember her saying something about the vampires sparkling in the sunshine."

I couldn't help but laugh. "That's them. Would you like me to get the first one for you or the entire series? There are four books altogether."

"Let's do the whole thing!" He patted my hand as if doing me a favor, but as soon as I turned around, he called out to me once more. "Actually... I just remembered. That very same granddaughter got me one of those"—he waffled his hands in the air—"electronic book thingies."

"A Kindle?"

He nodded enthusiastically. "Yes. That's it. I promised her I'd use it, and I haven't yet. You sell books for that here?"

"No. Sorry." This wasn't the first time this had happened. "If you turn on your Kindle and connect to Wi-Fi, you can purchase your books from right there. They'll download to your device."

"Oh good. Do you think they'll have those sparkly-vampire books?" He looked skeptical.

"I'm sure they will." As he left the Cozy Corgi, my gaze flitted to where Watson napped in the sunshine. I was certain he'd disagree with me, but his job of mascot was a lot simpler.

Before I had a chance to assist another customer or get lost in more speculations about Gerald, Anna Hanson burst through the front door, strain easily visible behind her wide eyes. Finding me instantly, she made a beeline my way, proving how focused she was by not even glancing toward Watson's snoring form.

"Fred." She grasped my hands between both of hers over the counter before I could offer a greeting. "I need your help. Do you have a few minutes?"

"Of course..." I glanced around at the milling customers. "Do you want to go somewhere private?"

She considered and then focused on the mystery room. "Actually, no. I know it's July, but I just can't seem to get warm. I think it's stress." She released me and headed that way without waiting. "Let's sit in front of the fire. That sounds nice. And honestly, at this point with everything public, what does it matter if a few tourists overhear?"

I followed Anna, and when she sat in my typical spot in the corner of the antique sofa beneath the portobello lampshade, I settled at the other end. As Anna stared into the crackling flames, I waited. I had a feeling I knew what this was about, but it would be far too easy to make things worse between her and Carl if I was wrong.

When she finally met my gaze, though they didn't fall, tears glistened in the corners of her eyes and her voice trembled softly. "I owe you a thank-you."

It was good I'd waited, that I hadn't anticipated what she'd say. "You do?"

She offered a brief smile and then refocused on the fire as she spoke. "Carl was... strange last night as we left the fireworks display." She chuckled, but still didn't look back at me. "Strange, even for Carl. When we got home, he passed out on the bed, didn't even bother getting between the covers. But then he woke up around four this morning and was... well... he was a wreck. An absolute wreck." Finally, she focused on me again. "He confessed everything. I thought he already had after we read that horrid smear job yesterday, but there was more. He told me you knew about his... *investments* with Gerald."

I started to reply, but hesitated. I'd known this moment would come in one form or another, and I'd dreaded it. Anna's accusations and fury that I'd kept it from her. I simply nodded and prepared to receive a tongue-lashing.

Instead she reached over and grabbed my hand again. "He told me you kept questioning him about where he was getting the money to give to Gerald. You told him you'd inform me if you thought he was hurting our retirement or our joint savings."

I nodded again.

"Thank you." She squeezed my hand again, and a tear fell before she released me. "You're a good friend. Thank you. From both of us."

I wouldn't have predicted that, not in a million years. I had done what I thought was right, trying to walk the balance of supporting both Carl and Anna, but if I'd been in her shoes, I might've been angry to not have been told instantly. "I... take it Carl was honest with me? *You're* still financially secure?"

She nodded, and her gaze flicked over my shoulder, and then seemed to follow something as she smiled gently.

The soft clack of Watson's nails on the hardwood floor behind me announced his presence and explained Anna's reaction. He hopped up on the matching ottoman, stood on the very corner, and looked expectantly at Anna.

"Oh... dear boy." She stretched out both of her chubby hands and squeezed Watson's face. "I didn't even think. I didn't bring any of your treats."

He whimpered at the word.

At the sound, another tear rolled down her cheek, and she released him. "I'll go get one. I'll be right back."

I leaned over and gently took her arm, holding her in place. "He's fine, Anna. He's had several this morning already."

Watson looked my way, betrayal clear in his eyes, proving once again he understood quite a bit more than I sometimes gave him credit for.

"Don't be rude. You've had plenty." I narrowed

my eyes at him and patted the spot on the ottoman closest to me. "Just sit here, take another nap. You can dream of as many treats as you want."

He straightened slightly at the repetition of his favorite word and let me know I'd pushed things too far by spinning around, hopping off the ottoman, and then lifting his muzzle in the air as he strolled out of the mystery room. He paused at the base of the steps, looking back at me, his expression clearly stating, *Nice attempt, Mom, but just try to stop me,* before tearing up the stairs at breakneck speed into the bakery.

"Do you think he'll ever forgive me?" The genuine worry in Anna's voice over possibly causing irreparable damage in her relationship with my corgi was almost funny.

"Don't worry. *You* won't be the one he holds a grudge against." I refocused on her, letting Watson win the battle of eating too many treats. "You said you needed my help. What's wrong?"

Anna stared at the empty steps for a few more seconds, and then finally turned to me. "I'm sure you read the article about Gerald Jackson this morning?" She didn't wait for confirmation. "It's obvious what that horrible woman is doing. She's setting us all up like domino pieces, ready to flick her finger and watch us all fall."

It was a different analogy than what I'd been considering, but as I pictured it, it seemed apt. I hadn't tied what Birdie had written about Gerald and what she promised to write about me the following day back to Carl, but with Anna sitting in front of me, I couldn't help but see the strings being woven into a noose. However, the theory didn't entirely work. "If that's true, what about the article on Delilah? There was nothing about Gerald or the investments in that."

"Like Delilah matters." She waved me off, clearly unconcerned. "Carl insists, even now, that there's nothing nefarious about Gerald's investments. And I know my husband. I believe him. Or... more accurately, I believe *he* believes that. While he's not an idiot, he's not the sharpest tool in the shed, and he's as trusting as he is squishy. Gerald Jackson could convince him to buy magic beans and Carl wouldn't pause to blink."

Unfortunately, I followed Anna's meaning perfectly. "So if Gerald's investments—or whatever they are—aren't how he presents them, Carl could be taken down in the fallout."

"Exactly. No one's going to believe Carl's innocent, that he didn't know." Her gaze darkened, as did her tone. "Especially when you put together that he's been buying that horrible kombucha concoction Gerald makes. It makes Carl look like he's nothing more than one of Gerald's cronies, involved in swindling and part of some underworld drug kingpin sort of situation."

I had to bite the inside of my cheek to keep from laughing at the thought of either Carl or Gerald being some sort of kingpin. Although... hadn't I just had a similar thought myself? That if what Birdie Sutton wrote was true, we'd all been vastly underestimating Gerald. "I don't think anyone could believe such a thing about Carl. Surely. But if you're worried about it, maybe the two of you should go to the police, talk to Chief Dunmore or Susan. Proactively tell them about everything that's gone on. That way you're in good standing."

"Maybe." Anna's tone contradicted the sentiment, made it clear she wasn't considering going to the police. "I'd feel better if you looked into it."

"Looked into what?"

"Gerald, of course." Anna stared at me as if that should've been obvious.

I started to point out that no one had died, that there hadn't been a murder, those were the only things I looked into, or... *interfered* with, according to Birdie.

Before I could think of how to respond or even fully process her suggestion, she leveled her gaze on me again. "It's for your own benefit too. Like I said, she's setting us up. Clearly there's some connection between Carl and me, Gerald, and *you*. Maybe others, depending on who she writes about next. But you can't tell me the people she's picking are all random. There's a reason." She scowled, though seemingly at herself. "Maybe even Delilah. I'd hate to think Carl and I are connected to her in any way, shape, or form, but who knows what evil deeds that woman has been up to?"

My first instinct was that I wasn't connected, but clearly I was, and not just because Carl had purchased some sort of investment in my name from Gerald. That hadn't been hinted at in Birdie's column. As much as I wanted to slough the whole thing off as one of Anna's crazy schemes, I couldn't. In a way it was too similar to what I'd already been thinking. And Anna was right. It wasn't random. I could feel it. There was a purpose behind every person featured in the "A Little Bird Told Me" column. Besides, I was the focus of whatever Birdie was going to write tomorrow, but we didn't know who was next. If Gerald was somehow at the center of it, he was part of a large good-old-boys club of people who had grown up together in this town. And that included Barry and my Uncle Percival. Maybe they were lined up to be under Birdie Sutton's magnifying glass and poison quill.

There wasn't really even a decision to be made, and I'd already been mulling over the possibilities. "Okay. I'll look into it."

By the time Watson strolled back down the steps, licking his lips as he darted a quick side-eye my way to make sure I was watching, before making a show of finding exactly the right position in the beam of sunshine flowing through the front windows of the Cozy Corgi, I'd given up even pretending to be a bookseller. I remembered functioning without Ben Pacheco as I'd wandered off to look into this or that murder while leaving Katie in charge of the bakery and the bookshop, but I couldn't recall how either one of us had done it. As I rifled through the options of how to begin investigating Birdie Sutton, Ben cruised his way through the tourists, helping them find the perfect novel for their vacation, answering endless questions about Estes Park—the logical and asinine alike—and paused every now and then to bend down and press his forehead between our mascot's ears and elicit franticly happy wags from Watson's nub of a tail.

My first inclination was to approach Gerald. Though our relationship had started off benign when he'd first acted as my stepfather's lawyer—however incompetent, when Barry had been accused of murder—things had grown strained between us to the point of Gerald nearly being hostile when he saw me. Not that I made any effort whatsoever to get into his good graces. Still, after the "A Little Bird Told Me" about him that morning, I wondered if he'd like the idea of me diving into the situation, that he might hope I'd help clear his name. I disregarded that quickly. First and foremost, I couldn't see Gerald putting any trust in my ability, no matter my reputation. Even more so, the article rang true, and if so, the last thing Gerald would want would be me poking my nose in it.

Delilah was an option. She'd probably welcome me looking into it, not that she'd been embarrassed by anything Birdie had said about her, but still... Gone were the days of Delilah holding details and information over my head like some scandalous game. She had more than proven that she respected my amateur sleuthing, and had even trusted me with her own secrets, which I'd been surprised she possessed, considering how she flaunted her private life. Still, Anna was right. There had to be a connection between the subjects of Birdie's reputation kill list, but I couldn't picture Delilah involved with the things implied about Gerald. Delilah's vices lay elsewhere. Or... maybe that was simply what I wanted to believe because she'd become a friend of sorts.

There was nothing for it, I needed to hear it all directly from the horse's mouth. Birdie Sutton was anything but subtle. It was something we had in common, so I might as well let my natural inclinations lead the way. The question was, where would she be? Up until the day before, she'd been using Katie's bakery as her workspace. That implied she didn't enjoy being at *The Chipmunk Chronicles* or hadn't hit it off with her coworkers. Maybe she was writing from home, wherever that was, or... she'd simply traded one coffee shop for another.

Watson didn't resist when I fixed the leash to his collar, but kept his head turned away, refusing to acknowledge my existence, despite having been put in a cheerful mood, thanks to Ben.

"Oh, come on. A little exercise isn't going to kill you." I stood, holding the other end of the leash and stepping in front of his face, only to have him turn the other direction. "You had endless... things you love, but that I can't say... this morning. You're going to be in a huff all day simply because Anna said that favorite word of yours and I didn't rush to get you one that very instant?"

Again with the side-eye.

"You're being ridiculous." I couldn't help but snort out a laugh. "Come on."

Watson followed, but at a pace that would've brought him dead last in a snail marathon. By the time we crossed the street and made it halfway down the opposite block, I recalled a lesson I'd only learned a billion times before. Watson was a grump, a spoiled one, and though I wasn't sure what his life was like before he'd appeared out of nowhere to more or less proclaim me his human, he was obnoxiously spoiled and entitled. That had been in his personality from nearly the moment we met, but I'd done nothing to discourage it. When Watson and I were passed by a woman using one hand to push a stroller containing a set of triplets and her other to hold tightly to a screaming toddler who wanted to be carried instead of walking beside the mini caravan, I gave in. "Fine. I'll get you a treat at the Koffee Kiln. Will that satisfy his majesty?"

Watson peered up at me again, and I could swear one of his eyebrows rose.

"Yes, I said treat." I popped my fist on my hip and leaned closer to him, forcing the stream of tourists to part around us. "*Treat*! Let's get you a treat."

With that, all was forgiven. Watson let out a happy yip and sprang into super-corgi speed. He darted around and practically dragged me the rest of the way to the Koffee Kiln.

I felt a little better when we finally overtook the woman with the stroller and the screaming kid. Though I paused at the front door of the Koffee Kiln, with Watson demanding entrance, I didn't get the chance to whisper a prayer that Simone Pryce would be working and *not* Carla Beaker. Sure enough, the unwhispered supplication went unanswered, and Carla peered from behind the espresso machine, her green eyes bright and happy under her blond bangs, only to transition into a scowl.

It was the greeting I expected from Carla. And at a glance around at the people drinking their afternoon coffees and espresso martinis while painting various pieces of pottery, I cursed myself for not putting a hand to the window and checking for Birdie that way. She wasn't there. So not only had I irritated Carla by reminding her that I existed, I'd done it for nothing. I took a step backward, ready to retreat and make both Carla's and my day a little better. Watson whimpered and pulled at his leash, determined to get to the pastry counter. Interacting with Carla was the second-to-last thing I wanted, so to keep Watson from returning to his version of a temper tantrum, I crossed the shop and forced what I hoped appeared to be a genuine smile at Carla. "Good morn... er... afternoon."

Still scowling, Carla emerged the rest of the way from behind the espresso machine. "Really? We're doing this? I don't blame you for being tired of Katie's watered-down coffee and her subpar baking, but things tend to go better when we keep our distance from each other, haven't you noticed?" She flicked her wrist over her shoulder toward the hallway leading to the back room. "I promise, there're no dead bodies here for you to find."

I should've at least taken the time to come up with a plausible excuse of why Watson and I had come to the Koffee Kiln, in case Carla was present. Since I didn't, my foot-in-mouth disease was true to form as I blurted out the first thing that came to mind. "Barry said you turned down his offer of investing into your idea of an Estes Park museum."

Impressively, Carla's scowl turned colder. "I don't need charity from you or your family. Thanks."

Her voice lowered so she couldn't be overheard by the closest tables. "Although it's not really charity, is it? Though you package it that way. Your family would get to pretend it was doing something benevolent while you sat back and enjoyed watching my mother-in-law treat me like an even lower form of dirt than she currently does."

Though I bristled at the accusation, I wasn't tempted to retort back. I despised few people as much as Ethel Beaker. If I had her as a mother-in-law, I'd probably be in the same mood as Carla all the time. "I promise that wasn't the intent. It was clear how much you wanted to do it, and Barry and Mom think it would be a great addition to the town."

Carla flinched, barely enough to be noticed. Maybe she heard the sincerity in my voice, because she blushed slightly and her tone went flat. "What can I get you, Fred? Let's get this over with. There's no reason to drag it out and have that dog's hair cover my patrons' food and pottery."

I decided to take the out. There was nothing to be gained here anyway. Sparing a quick glance into the case, I ordered on instinct. "I'll take one of your chocolate-espresso scones. You were right, the one I had before was amazing—" Carla flinched again and practically beamed. "—not at all dry like the ones..."

My words petered out pathetically as Carla's scowl returned. "Sorry. I didn't mean to..." For a second I started to offer a defense, remind her that her previous scones had literally been dry enough to kill people.

She merely grabbed one of the chocolate-espresso scones and stuffed it in a bag. "You're getting this to go."

"That's perfect. Thank you." At the sound of the rustling of the paper bag, Watson whimpered in anticipation below me, and I realized my mistake. My overly fluffy corgi already shouldn't be having another treat, much less chocolate or espresso. "Oh, could you add in a blueberry scone? Watson loves those, and since it has blueberries, I can pretend it's sort of healthy."

For a moment it looked like Carla was considering taking back the already packaged scone and kicking me out of her store at the unintentional reminder that my dog had always been more of a fan of her baked goods than myself.

Before Carla could say anything, or take the scone away, Simone emerged from the back room, carrying a brightly painted ceramic vase. She halted midstep when she noticed Watson and me. Her beautiful dark eyes flicked from me to Carla and back again. "Well... this promises to be exciting." There was a touch of humor in her tone. "Carla, do I need to prepare the pottery for World War III, or are you going to refrain from exploding?"

"Oh, shut up, Simone. I'm just fine." There was no anger directed at Simone, but Carla continued to glare at me.

The humor left Simone's voice, and she turned to me in concern. "Is everything okay? If you're coming in here—"

"Everything is fine, Simone." That time Carla had a bite to her tone. "Fred's just here to stir up drama. As always. Go deliver that horridly painted thing to whoever is responsible for it."

Simone's nostrils flared and daggers shot from her eyes. "I swear, Carla Beaker, I love you, but you sure make it tempting to shove you in the kiln." A little humor returned as she continued on her way. "Probably not the best thing to say in front of Estes Park's super sleuth, but still." Though she winked as she passed me, I almost thought I caught a note of mockery. I was probably just projecting from Carla.

"All right, let's just get this done." Carla snagged a blueberry scone and stuffed it into the bag like it had offended her. She held it out to me with a hiss. "Don't bother paying, just leave. Don't even think about asking for your favorite drink. You'll just have to go back and enjoy Katie's lackluster white chocolate mocha. It's what you deserve."

Carla had never been able to remember that I drank dirty chais, but in a miraculous event, I refrained from reminding her. However, there was no way in the world I was accepting free scones from Carla. Though we both knew the offer was merely to get me out of her sight quickly and not from the goodness of her heart, at some point in the future, such an action would be thrown back in my face and she'd probably claim I'd taken advantage. Tucking the bag of scones under my arm, I made quick work of digging my billfold out of my purse and handing her a credit card. "No. I insist."

Once more she nearly refused, and once more she glanced at the tourists before snatching the card from my fingers and jamming it into the credit card reader. "You know—" Her voice returned to a whispered hiss. "—I almost considered dropping by your overpriced bookshop yesterday to give you a warning about today's little announcement that you're the star of tomorrow's smear piece. I'm glad I didn't. In fact, I'll probably frame Birdie's article and display it by the register." Withdrawing the card, she turned the screen toward me. "Don't forget to tip."

Out of spite, I started to type in a ten-dollar tip just to be obnoxious, then froze as the implication of her words sank in. With my finger paused over the signing screen, I met Carla's green eyes. "You knew I was going to be featured?"

"Sure did. Bridget is my wicked mother-in-law's new neighbor, and they've become quite the BFFs." To my surprise, a blush returned to her cheeks, and it seemed she'd interpreted my words as an accusation instead of simply surprise. "Oh, don't give me that look. I don't *owe* you anything. The truth would've come out about what happened in the back room without your interference. And I for sure don't owe you, or your family, anything for trying to invest in the museum. *That* was more of a desire for you to stick it to Ethel than really help me."

I couldn't stop myself. "Do you know who's going to be the subject of the article after me?"

Carla started to shake her head, but caught herself, though not soon enough. "Of course, but I'm not going to tell you. I can't believe I even considered giving you warning." She slid the credit card toward me and swiveled the screen back around before I could sign. "I only considered it because I can't stand Bridget any more than Ethel, but I'll enjoy *whatever* she has to say about you tomorrow."

Unable to make my body work, or my mouth, I stood there gaping at Carla. The excruciating visit to the Koffee Kiln hadn't been a waste after all. If memory served correctly, I knew exactly where Bridget Sutton lived, or at least, close enough.

"Seriously, Winfred, what are you doing?" Carla shoved the credit card closer to me. "Take this, the scones, your fat dog, and leave. From now on, remember what I *thought* was our unspoken agreement. I stay on my side of the street, you stay on yours."

I turned and walked toward the door, Simone and the tourists painting their pottery little more than a haze beside me as Watson pranced at my feet in anticipation. So Birdie had moved to town and instantly gotten chummy with Ethel Beaker. Maybe *that* was where she was getting her information. I paused, gripping the door handle, some of the article about Delilah flitting through my mind. The accusations that her Pink Panthers were a detriment to the town. I'd heard Ethel say just that. Called it gang behavior, in fact. No way was that a coincidence.

A loud throat-clearing brought me back to the moment, and I glanced over my shoulder to see Carla glaring. Without waiting, I exited, and only made it a few yards back down the sidewalk before pausing and tearing off a bit of the blueberry scone when Watson's whimpering suggested he was near a nervous breakdown. As I finally returned to his good graces, an Ethel Beaker-shaped piece clicked into place in the "A Little Bird Told Me" puzzle. When it did, it only highlighted how many other pieces of the puzzle there would be to turn over. If Ethel had provided Birdie with the gossip around Delilah, and it only made sense she would have had a hand in whatever was going to be said about me the next day, then what part had she played in Gerald's revelations? And how did she have access to all he was allegedly involved in?

I brought my volcanic-orange Mini Cooper to a stop at the entrance of the mini-McMansion development that occupied the cliff overlooking Mary's Lake. Ethel's house was the queen of the McMansions, larger and sitting in the premier spot at the end of a limestone driveway. In fairness, considering she had a butler—an *actual* butler—maybe Ethel's home qualified as a genuine mansion, no Mc about it. The other mansions, Mc or otherwise, that surrounded Ethel's were smaller and less grand. With the amount of space between them, the development didn't have that many to choose from. One of them, if Carla was accurate, belonged to Birdie.

I hit the gas, then instantly stomped on the brake, earning a glare from my corgi copilot as he had to catch himself to remain upright on the passenger seat.

"Sorry, buddy." I offered him a quick pat on the head in reparation, and since he didn't duck out of reach, I assumed that with his tummy still full of blueberry scone, all was forgiven. Refocusing on Ethel's house, I considered. There was no guesswork to where she lived, and if they really were newly formed best friends, perhaps that was where Birdie was writing her articles. Something about that didn't sit right. Friends or not, I couldn't see Ethel Beaker allowing her home to be treated as a workspace, even if she did get the privilege of whispering gossip in Birdie's ear about the people she despised. And though I hated to admit it, the prospect of facing both Birdie and Ethel—and, I might as well be honest, the butler—all at the same time, was more than I cared to attempt.

Making my choice, I pressed the gas pedal once more, gentler that time as to maintain Watson's newly acquired cheerful disposition, and drove slowly through the development, hoping Ethel wouldn't notice my car.

I'd like to say it took superb sleuthing skills to determine which house belonged to Birdie. That I had to consider the cars parked in the driveways to decide which one suited her personality or something equally as clever. But people who lived in mansions of any variety didn't typically leave their vehicles strewn in their driveways, not when their garages were practically little castles of their own. No, it was much more obvious than that. Even mansions had mailboxes, and each one had a last name in decorative wrought iron, boasting who lived there. All of them, save one. The tiniest—still four times the size of my cabin—mansion at the end of the road, the one *without* a view of Mary's Lake. If Carla was right and Birdie was a neighbor, that was the only option.

I started to leave Watson in the car after I parked in the driveway but decided one grumpy episode was enough for the day, so I reaffixed his leash, and he joined me as I strolled up the brick—not limestone—sidewalk to the front door. That time, I took a few moments before ringing the bell, not so much to whisper any prayers, but to take a few deep breaths, clear my thoughts, and do my best to ensure my foot-in-mouth disease would pretend to be in remission for a while.

When there was no answer to the bell, I pressed my ear to the door, thinking maybe I could hear the retreating clack of a butler's shiny black shoes after looking through the peephole to see a redheaded woman and her dog. There was no sound. After another few moments, Watson let out a bored groan and curled up on the welcome mat—though it didn't technically proclaim the word *welcome* on it. It seemed Watson didn't detect any signs of life either.

I rang again and waited.

Then a third time.

Still no answer, and clearly there wasn't going to be. Either Birdie wasn't home, or she wasn't going to allow herself to be disturbed.

Maybe I'd have to face Ethel Beaker and her butler after all.

Proving my cowardice, I decided before I attempted that drastic measure, though I was already there, I'd check in at *The Chipmunk Chronicles*.

When I turned to go, Watson issuing another groan as he was forced to stand, I noticed a gap in the curtains of the large picture window at the end of the porch. While I preferred the terms sleuthing, or *looking into things*, I hadn't been accused of being a snoop for no reason. You could learn a lot about a person from a glimpse into their home. Chances were low I'd learn too much about Birdie. Being new to town, she probably hadn't done much in the way of decorating, but why pass up the chance?

Watson was already headed toward the sidewalk, but followed me toward the window without much more than a grunt.

Like I'd wished I'd done at the Koffee Kiln, I covered my eyes with my hand, pressed my hand to the window, and peered in. Though I'd been wrong and the vestibule under the sweeping staircase was completely decorated, I didn't notice any of the items. My deductive skills were proven true. Judging from where her body lay on the marble floor, the home did belong to Birdie Sutton. And from the large dark pool of blood surrounding her, the brief but scandalous run of the "A Little Bird Told Me" column had come to an abrupt end.

The internal debate over whether to break in and check on Birdie or call the police barely took ten seconds. It was easy to see that Birdie was beyond any help I had to offer. From the broken position of her body, I was willing to bet she hadn't suffered. I used the moment it took to retrieve my cell phone to send a beseeching thought heavenward—*let Officer Brent Jackson be sent out.* I didn't have it in me to deal with Susan Green's condescending insinuations.

"Estes Park Police Department, is this an emergency?" a young man answered the phone.

I hesitated. "Not exactly. I've discovered a dead body, at least she appears to be beyond help."

"Is this Winifred Page?"

"Yes, it is. I—" For a second, I was thrown off. "I'm sorry, how did you know?"

"We don't get many calls about dead bodies, and when we do, they're from you." He didn't wait for me to respond. "Hold on one second. Officer Green wants all your calls to go to her. I'll put you through."

"No, wait... I—" The hold music cut me off, but it was gone again before I could get my bearings.

"I've been expecting this call any day now," Susan's harsh voice grumbled on the other end of the line. "What's it been, four weeks? Maybe five?" She didn't wait for me to answer. "Who is it, and where are you?"

I balked. "What do you mean you've been *expecting* this call? It's not like I'm arranging to stumble across dead bodies on a schedule. This isn't routine."

"Isn't it?" Susan gave what I interpreted as an intentionally bored affect. "Just skip the dramatics, Fred. Just tell me who it is and where you are."

Opting not to argue, I gave in. "I'm at Birdie... er... Bridget Sutton's home. She's dead."

"Birdie..." Surprise caused Susan's voice to spark. "You don't say? Interesting timing. And you're at her house, you said?" Once more she didn't wait for an answer. "Did she die in front of you this time, or did you break in and discover her body?"

"Neither." I wasn't sure if I was more annoyed or amused that she knew me so well. And I had to admit, clearly from our conversation, this indeed had become routine. "I'm on her porch. I can see her body through the window."

That time, it was Susan who hesitated. "Really? You see a body and *don't* break in to the rescue. It must be clear she's past such help." She sighed. "Bridget moved into the development overlooking Mary's Lake, right? I'll be right there."

Susan hung up before I could confirm.

Watson and I were seated on the top steps of Birdie's porch, his head in my lap, as the police cruiser pulled around the corner and up the brick driveway. Proving that I should have been more specific in my supplications, Brent Jackson emerged from the passenger side, giving me a solemn yet cordial greeting, followed by Susan.

She smirked as she made her way up the steps. "Don't you find it interesting that you're the subject of tomorrow's column, and here you are with the body of the writer? Handy."

Somehow that aspect hadn't sunk in during the

quarter of an hour we'd waited for them to arrive. And though my temperature spiked at the accusation, I couldn't deny how it looked. Talk about motive. Even so, I glared at Susan's muscled form as she and Brent reached the bottom of the steps. "Can we skip this part, Susan? I didn't kill Birdie to stop her article and then call the police station. For all I know, it's already written, submitted, and will come out on schedule."

She rolled her eyes exaggeratedly. "It should be *me* asking *you* to skip this part. Unlike many people I can name, I'm not an idiot. That's part of why I've instructed that all your calls be directed to me. You're nosy, intrusive, a bit of an annoying know-it-all, but you're smart, and as much as it kills me to admit it, you have killer instincts. The one thing you're *not*, is a murderer." She shifted her narrowed glare from me to Watson. "And *you* are still a fleabag."

Watson started to growl at her, but was distracted by Officer Jackson, who pulled a small dog bone out of his pocket, offered it to Watson, and then ruffled the fur between his ears.

Susan cast a surprised glare at Brent. "*Seriously?*"

He shrugged one shoulder as he continued to pat

Watson, who was too busy chowing down the object of affection.

Focusing on the house, Susan did a brief scan, then headed directly toward the window at the end of the porch, not needing any explanation. She let out a hiss as she peered inside. "Ah. I see what you mean. Ms. Sutton's beyond anyone's help."

In a matter of only a few minutes, a couple more police cruisers pulled up, the scene was secured, and they had the front door opened. Watson and I stayed on the porch at Susan's directive, as the police went inside.

Watson watched the officers go back and forth for a while, sitting at attention, ears perked and nose twitching, but after a bit, he curled up against me and fell asleep.

Susan had thrown me off. I supposed, in a way I'd thrown myself off as well, not even considering how the situation appeared—me finding her body only a few short hours before her scandalous article was to be printed. Not that it would have changed what I'd done. I couldn't just load Watson back in the car and simply drive away. But still, I should've considered how it seemed with me being present at the scene.

A few months ago, Susan would've taken the opportunity to cuff me and take me in without a second thought—and enjoyed every moment of it. Actually, that wasn't true. It was a lot longer ago than a few months. It was back in the days when she'd had Chief Briggs and Sergeant Wexler over her. Things had changed in the police department, and between the two of us as well.

Proving that to be true, a little while later, Susan stomped back onto the porch and received a growl from Watson for waking him. "Stuff it, fleabag." She motioned toward the porch and addressed me. "Tie up the mutt, then come on in."

I gaped at her. "Excuse me?"

"You heard me. Secure the fat hamster or shove him into your car, whatever, but I don't need a bunch of corgi hair all over my crime scene." She sneered. "For once."

"You want me to come in?"

"Fred." With simply saying my name, Susan sounded like an exasperated teacher getting ready to explain the directions for the billionth time. "You just happen to be on the porch of the very woman who's written three scandalous articles about prominent members of the community. You're the subject of the one being published tomorrow. Do you expect me to believe you came out here to deliver cookies?"

I didn't answer, not that she gave me a chance.

"To most people, it would look like you came out here to beg her to not publish anything about you. And while there's a million things I find obnoxious about you, you're not the type to snivel, beg, or bribe." Susan crossed her arms, the motion causing the uniform to strain from the flexing of her shoulders. "You came here to snoop, probably to question Ms. Sutton on her motivation, where she's getting her information, or figure out how to stop this, right?"

Though we'd historically driven each other crazy, I admired both Susan's intelligence and her directness. Maybe never as much as in that moment. I merely managed to nod.

"Right, so I would be acting the part of an idiot, which we've already established I am *not*, if I thought you would turn, walk away, and not look back. *Especially* now that there's a dead body added into the equation. For you, it's practically like Christmas in July."

"I don't enjoy—"

"Keep telling yourself that." She waved me off and leveled her stare at me again. "That's another reason I've instructed your calls to come to me. I've already spoken to Chief Dunmore about it, and he agrees. We can't keep you from snooping, and really, we'd be fools to want to. As I pointed out multiple times, and hopefully I won't need to again, I am *not* Briggs or Wexler. I have nothing to hide, and I will use every tool at my disposal to keep this town safe and get to the bottom of things, even if that means accepting your help from time to time, which, I've already proven to you I'm willing to do. So can we agree to not go through this every time? We both know you're not going to keep your nose out of things, so as long as you keep in mind that *I'm* the law and you're simply a smarter-than-average busybody who's useful to the police, we can both cut dancing around this from now on." She sniffed. "As long as you continue to be *useful*, that is."

Still I stared, and as was typical in most interactions with Susan Green, had to battle whether to be flattered or insulted.

"Now you're just wasting my time." She shrugged again. "Do it or don't. I'm not going to send you an embossed invitation."

Before she'd disappeared inside, I'd already started tying Watson's leash to a post. Once finished, I leaned close. "Sorry, buddy. I don't think now is the time to push the limits. I'll be back soon." With a quick kiss on his nose, I stood and followed Susan inside.

Bridget Sutton might not have had a butler, but her home was grand enough to qualify for one, more so than I'd been able to tell from the window. The sweeping staircase that led from upstairs looked like something out of *Dynasty* or from the *Titanic*. A glimpse through the three doorways that broke off from the foyer revealed rooms of opulence, indicating a ton of money. My first instincts that Birdie hadn't had time to settle in had clearly been completely off the mark.

"This is crazy. It's like she's lived here forever. Although I suppose, if she lived somewhere similar before, she simply could've moved everything and recreated it here. But... what kind of reporter or columnist has this kind of money? It's not like she was a household name."

"Not even close." Susan nodded her agreement, and I thought I saw approval at my assessment. "I checked her out after the first article on Delilah. She's moved around a few times—Cincinnati, Olathe, Santa Fe, to name a few. Always gossipy or society-type *reporting*." Susan made air quotes around the word. "But nothing that ever caught fire, nothing that looked like it would have brought in the money required for this. Although maybe she was the type born with a silver spoon." Susan smirked. "Or struck oil, like *The Beverly Hillbillies*. But she wasn't a sweet, innocent Elly May."

Despite the dead body, I nearly laughed. I always forgot about Susan's love of old television shows. I couldn't picture her watching *The Beverly Hillbillies*. But at the mention of Elly May, I finally looked toward Birdie's broken body. Though it had been obvious from the window she hadn't been in need of rescuing, up close other details were clear. The pool of blood in which she lay was dark red and didn't glisten at all. There were a few shards of thick broken glass scattered around, but none on her. "The blood's dry. She's been dead for a while."

"Yeah." Susan nodded again and once more crossed her arms as she studied the body. "I'm thinking at least twelve hours, probably more."

Birdie was clad in a seafoam-green nightgown. A few feet away lay a fuzzy blue slipper. I scanned the rest of the marble floor. "There's only one slipper."

That time, a smile, albeit a small one, accompanied her expression of approval, and she pointed upward. "It's up there, a few feet away from the railing, right in front of the doors that lead to the bedroom."

I glanced up, just able to make out the edge of the twinkling chandelier through a doorway. I looked back and forth from Birdie's body to the curved mahogany banister that ran along the landing and then spiraled down the steps. "She fell. Or was pushed."

"Duh." There was no real venom behind the word. If anything, it was nice to have Susan sound like Susan again.

"Did you find evidence of someone else being present?" I peered toward the bedroom once more.

"No. An empty bottle of wine in the living room, but only one glass." Susan gestured through the doorway on the right. "Or drawing room, salon, I don't know—whatever rich people call that."

I pointed out a couple of shards of glass surrounding Birdie's body. "Maybe she was holding the other glass."

Susan started to shake her head, then paused, considering. Voices of other officers drifted in from another room as she knelt beside a piece. "Maybe, though it's pretty thick to be a wineglass." She stood again and spoke over her shoulder as she headed through the doorway. "Let me go check the other one. I didn't notice it being abnormally bulky, but maybe..."

Instead of following, I inspected where Birdie must've fallen from. The railing appeared intact, not like she'd been shoved through it. Maybe thrown over? Or tripped and fell over? Was that even possible? I wasn't amazing with spatial relationships, but I estimated the height from railing to floor to be around fifteen or sixteen feet. Enough to do damage, but not necessarily lethal. Although, from the appearance of it, Birdie landed on her head, and again, I figured it had been a quick death. Almost mercifully so.

For the first time, a wave of nausea rose as I studied her broken body, and I turned away and focused through the open front door. I felt a bit better as I caught sight of Watson straining at the end of the leash, trying to peer in.

He gave a demanding bark as he caught my eye, clearly offended at being left on the porch.

I started to call out an apology, but something glistening under the narrow ornate table beside the main door caught my attention. I walked toward it and knelt as Susan reentered the vestibule.

"Not a match. The wineglass is thin." Her voice perked up. "What did you find?"

I reached for it and then paused halfway, catching myself just in time before I left my own fingerprints. It was another thick shard of glass, this one with ridges. I started to answer Susan, but paused as something about the ridges seemed familiar. Narrowing my eyes, I leaned a little closer, and it clicked. "It's part of a jar." I looked back at her. "The glass has ridges on it, kind of like how you screw the lid on a Mason jar of jam or pickles."

Susan joined me, knelt, and peered under the table before giving a grunt of affirmation. "Maybe so. But since it shattered, it indicates she either fell with it or it was thrown over somehow, and I don't see any pickles rolling around or splattered jam." She grimaced and glanced over at the body. "Although, I suppose certain types of jam would be hard to differentiate from—"

I sucked in a gasp, cutting her off, a thought arriving at random out of the blue.

"What?" Susan whipped back around, looking at me as if I'd just solved something. "What is it?"

I hesitated for a second, feeling like I was making an accusation, but I wasn't. At least I didn't think so. Before answering I inspected the broken ridges a final time, then spoke in a whisper. "If it is what we think it is, I've heard that Mason jars are often used when making kombucha."

Susan didn't miss a beat, and as she spoke, she gave a growl that Watson would've been proud of. "Gerald Jackson, today's star of the 'A Little Bird Told Me' column."

SEVEN

"You know—" Leo leaned to snag the remote from the arm of the sofa, causing Watson to shift in his sleep to keep his muzzle resting on Leo's thigh "—it indicates you're living a spectacular life when your day-to-day events are more exciting than what's on television." He hit a button and the set went dark.

"Considering what we're watching, I'm not certain that's a good thing." I didn't bother to keep the teasing from my voice. "Maybe if it was a comedy or a romance, but it's probably not desirable to be more exciting than a murder mystery."

As he resettled, Leo snagged my foot, pulled it into his lap, and began to rub. "Oh, come on. In all fairness, anybody's life is more exciting than what we were just watching. There might've been a murder, but it hardly qualified as a mystery. Obviously the husband killed the wife."

I took a second to groan as Leo's thumbs sank

into the arch of my foot, before responding. "Considering you're providing this little bit of heaven right now, I probably shouldn't disillusion you, but it wasn't the husband."

"What do you mean? It was clearly the husband." Sure enough, he paused in the foot rub. "Who do you think it was?"

Wriggling my toes, I pulled Leo's attention back to my foot before providing my answer. "It was the daughter."

"The daughter!" Again, his fingers paused. "She was seven, maybe eight."

I merely shrugged.

That time he kept rubbing while he responded, "Well, that's dark. And more interesting than I gave it credit for. Now I kinda want to finish it."

Opening one eye, Watson shifted again, repositioning his head under Leo's elbow so we were getting massaged at the same time.

Leo grinned down at him before refocusing on me. "How do you know it was the little girl?"

"Didn't you notice the music changed in the past couple of scenes every time the daughter came into the room? It was subtle, but foreboding."

He glanced back at the black TV screen as if in accusation, then back at me once more. "If only that could happen in real life, it would make you even quicker at solving murders." His honey-brown eyes twinkled teasingly. "Or is that how you do it? You hone in on some frequency the rest of us can't hear. Was there ominous background music when you noticed the glass from Gerald's kombucha jar this afternoon?"

"Hardly." I chuckled at the thought while simultaneously relaxing deeper into the cushions with the foot rub. "Although there might as well have been, for how quickly Susan went from bagging the glass to bringing in Gerald for questioning." Even with the massage, I grimaced. "She didn't let me join in on that. I knew it was too much to hope for."

Leo merely gave one of his gentle grins. "Either way, I knew you two would fall in sync one of these days. I always said Susan was the only one who was ever supportive when I'd call to report poaching. The two of you might be as different as night and day, but you're both fanatical about justice."

He wasn't wrong, but I couldn't help but grimace again. "That's just it. I'm not sure this is justice. The whole thing was a little too easy, too obvious. Gerald was the feature of Birdie's latest smear job, and then hours later, she's dead, surrounded by glass from a Mason jar?"

"There's that honing in on the background music the rest of us can't hear again. Susan saw the glass too, but *she* didn't look at it, snap her fingers, and proclaim '*Mr. Jackson*, in the foyer, with the kombucha.' *You* did."

"That's not exactly how it went down." I chuckled again. "Besides, even if it was one of Gerald's Mason jars, that doesn't prove he was there. Maybe she got it while she was investigating him. We don't even know if it held kombucha yet. And beyond that, talk about jumping the gun. There's no real proof Birdie was murdered. She might've fallen."

"How does someone fall off their own balcony?" Leo scrunched up his nose. "Is that what it's called in a big house like that? Well, either way, maybe she might trip and hit her head on the railing, but would she flip over?"

"True. But it's still too soon to—" My cell buzzed on the coffee table, and it was my turn to lean forward. I snagged it, expecting not to answer, but when I saw the name Athena Rose, the obituary writer for *The Chipmunk Chronicles*, on the display, I angled the screen so Leo could see and then answered. "Hey! How's New York?"

"I flew in this afternoon." Athena sounded

winded. "I got into town an hour ago. I planned on spending the night in Denver, but when I heard about Gerald, I drove straight home, or to the office, rather. I've not been home yet." She kept going before I could interject. "Speaking of homes, may I pop over to yours?"

I flinched but responded smoothly enough. "Now?"

Athena might've sounded winded on the phone, but when she stepped into my cabin less than fifteen minutes later, she looked picture-perfect from her flawless makeup to her stilettos—as always. Athena gave Leo and I both hugs, but pulled back quickly to grin affectionately down at Watson, who was frolicking at her feet. "I won't even pretend to assume you're excited to see me." She placed her whimpering designer bag on the floor and out popped a teacup poodle who was little more than a white fluffball.

The two dogs made a speedy show of happily sniffing and circling each other before promptly sauntering over to curl up together on the hearth, even though there was no fire.

"Poor Pearl is exhausted." Athena sighed at the

picture the dogs made. "She hates flying. But she loves New York. *Just* like her momma." She winked one of her thick false eyelashes. "Best shopping in the country."

Athena was equally as different as night and day from me as Susan, but in a completely different way. The thought of going on a shopping spree in New York sounded like my idea of torture.

Leo gestured toward the cranberry-hued dress she wore. "Is that your new outfit? It's beautiful."

Laughing, Athena swatted at him. "It's *one* of them, and thank you. It is, isn't it?"

"Should we join Watson and Pearl?" I motioned toward the seating area. "Would you like hot tea or anything? I also have some of Katie's brownies left over from—"

"Goodness no, but thank you." Athena cut me off, her heels clicking over the hardwood floor as she made her way to the armchair beside the sofa. "Odessa took me to a different fancy restaurant after every show. I've eaten more and stayed up later than I have in years, which is a deadly combination. I need to rein it in if I want to keep fitting into my new wardrobe."

Following her, Leo and I settled into our places on the couch, but abandoned the foot rub. "How is your granddaughter? What show is she in now? Not that I'll have heard of it. Percival is the one in the family who keeps up with the musicals."

She didn't answer for a moment, and for the first time a shadow passed behind her green-brown eyes. "She's still not herself. I think I mentioned to you before, Broadway has changed her. I can still see my sweet girl in there, but..." She shook her head, cleared her throat, and whatever emotion had arisen left. "You don't need a recap of New York, that's not why I'm here. Paulie has kept me up to date with everything going on. Before I went on the trip, I heard the announcement that Bridget Sutton was joining the staff, but I didn't meet her. Hadn't even heard of her, not that I read her sort of drivel. I couldn't believe you were going to be the star of tomorrow's column, but when I got off the plane and heard she'd been killed, *and* Gerald arrested..." She shrugged. "Well, I had to get back."

"That's all speculation, at least at this point." Given what Leo and I had just been talking about, I felt a little silly saying so. "We know Birdie is dead, not *necessarily* that she was killed, and Gerald was simply taken in for questioning, not charged with anything."

Athena gave an acknowledging shrug. "I suppose

I am making it sound a little more outrageous than it is, considering Gerald's already released, but you're still looking into it, right?"

Leo and I leaned forward as one, but he beat me to it. "Gerald's been released? Already?"

"I thought, from what I heard, Susan practically dragged you into the investigation. Gerald was released before I even got back to Estes." Athena narrowed her eyes at me. "You're telling me she didn't tell you?"

Stupidly, some part of me was a little insulted that Susan hadn't. But that's exactly what it was—stupid. Susan didn't owe me anything. "Technically, no, she didn't bring me into the investigation. She is just allowing me to"—I gave a shrug of my own—"do my thing, I guess you could say. But I have to admit, I'm impressed that you have fresher gossip than I do when you barely got back into town."

"Don't feel bad, dear. I have my sources." Athena chuckled, but didn't elaborate as she leveled her stare on me again. "You *are* going to look into it, aren't you?"

I hesitated, but then checked myself—I trusted Athena fully. "Honestly, I was technically checking into Gerald's investments, not Birdie's... death."

Athena caught on without any further explanation. "I should've expected as much. After what was written about Anna and Carl. But now you have two things to investigate." The corner of her smile turned wicked as she retrieved her purse from the floor, placed it in her lap, and dug out a piece of paper. "Actually, *three* things. This is why I came over."

I took the slip of paper and started to read down the list of handwritten names. "Why? What is...?" By the time I got to my name, I didn't need to ask any longer, and I twisted it slightly so Leo could read it.

He hummed a knowing sound and read the names aloud. "Delilah Johnson, Carl Hanson, Gerald Jackson, Winifred Page, Simone Pryce, Myrtle Bantam, Percival Oswald, Angus Witt, Susan and Mark Green, Marlon Dunmore."

Athena sat in silence as Leo and I continued to stare at the list. A billion questions ran through my brain, and for one second a chill of dread filtered through me, then gave way to anger. Finally I refocused up at her. "Birdie's 'hit list,' if you will. How did you get this? Was it scheduled at the paper?"

She snorted a laugh, somehow making the sound elegant. "No, dear. You know little Tucker? Well... he's snoopy too and good with a computer. He's just a gofer around the office, but... like I said, I have my sources, and I keep them well paid for their morsels."

That time Leo snorted out a laugh, an ungraceful one, proving he was feeling similar to me. "Well, Athena Rose. I probably shouldn't be surprised, but I am. And impressed."

Athena waved it off as if it was no big deal. "Most of the time, not too much comes from it, honestly. But with Ethel being part owner of the paper and her hating my guts, it pays to have feelers out in case she's gunning for my job again. Though I'm too small potatoes to trigger her radar most of the time." She flicked her french-tipped nails at the list. "Speaking of, I'm almost insulted my name's not on there. Clearly she didn't think I was worth the effort."

"Ethel." I whispered the woman's name like a curse, then cocked my head at Athena. "This is the second time I've heard that theory. You think the 'hit-list' was from Ethel? That Birdie was just doing her bidding?"

"I hadn't put that much together until I got the list from Tucker. But that's a veritable who's who of Ethel's most hated. Granted, I didn't know she had a problem with Myrtle Bantam or the new police chief, but the rest are obvious."

One of the things Leo, Katie, and I had wondered about as we had dinner at Habaneros earlier in the evening returned to the surface. "Where did Tucker find this? Was he able to get the next articles as well? Have you seen tomorrow's edition?"

"He snuck into Brian Smith's, er... the editor's computer, but this is all there was. Brian has always been in Ethel's pocket, so I'm sure she didn't worry about him spilling the beans of who was on the list, not to mention that it was going to do amazing things for paper sales, but Tucker said there weren't any future articles." Athena hadn't needed an explanation for my concern, and she ended with a soothing tone. "From what it looks like, Bridget didn't send her articles to Brian until early evening. He's been holding up printing for them. I guess Ethel didn't trust him *that* much. You don't have to worry. Bridget died before sending him whatever she wrote about you. Tucker said they're having Rhoda Biggler expand her town news section to take its place. She'll be covering Bridget's death, of course. And who knows, probably Gerald's arrest as well."

"Thank goodness." Though maybe it was self-absorbed, relief filtered in. And then, to my surprise, so did a flicker of disappointment. "Although, honestly, I was curious what she'd say. Katie, Leo, and I were throwing out all sorts of ideas this evening. I wasn't afraid of anything she might dig up." I laughed. "In fact, I'm supposed to stage a reading of it at the bakery in the morning. But I was curious... and maybe... a little hopeful. If what she wrote about Gerald is true, then Bridget Sutton proved she can do an in-depth investigative report. I thought... hoped... she might have unintentionally unearthed something about Branson and the Irons family connection that would offer some more light on Dad's murder and help bring the right people to justice."

"Oh." Athena leaned forward, patting my knee, just as Leo slipped an arm over my shoulder. "I didn't even think about that, dear. Here I was only thinking it was good news there was no article."

By the unlit fireplace, Watson lifted his head from where it had been resting on Pearl's hip and eyed me questioningly. I gave him a quick smile, and after a second, he settled back down with a grunt.

Feeling warmed by his concern, I looked back and forth from Leo to Athena. "Well, chances are high she'd already written the article about me, so it's gotta be somewhere. Either on her laptop or... if the theory is correct... maybe Ethel has it."

"I don't know if I can help with that. Tucker's able to snoop around on the paper's network, but..."

Athena cringed. "I don't think I can ask him to go digging around on Bridget's or Ethel's personal computers, whether he's able to or not. That's a whole other ballgame."

Another shot of disappointment—I hadn't even realized some part of me had been thinking that very thing. Then another question that had been thrown about over dinner came back. "Returning to Ethel, here's something else I don't understand. If this does all tie back to her, or even if it doesn't, how did this get published in *The Chipmunk Chronicles* when Ethel and Gerald are both majority shareholders? I know Ethel thinks she's all-powerful, but surely there'd be some legal consequences for going behind Gerald's back."

Athena flinched and cast me a quizzical expression. "I could've sworn I told you..." She considered, then shook her head and gave another shrug. "I guess not. But when all that happened with Violet attempting to purchase Gerald's and Brody Bridges' shares before she died several months ago, Ethel approached Brody not long after. As you know, he was looking to sell."

"She bought Brody's twenty percent," I finished for her. "So now Ethel's the majority stakeholder with sixty percent to Gerald's forty."

Athena nodded. "Exactly."

"Hmmm," Leo murmured beside me, pulling my attention. "That broken jar might just belong to Gerald, after all."

I started to nod but shifted it to shake halfway through. "No, that doesn't make sense. Why wouldn't Gerald go after Ethel instead of Birdie?"

"Ethel didn't write the article." Leo looked as if he was debating, then trudged ahead. "Maybe it's insulting to say, but Gerald doesn't strike me as overly bright, never has. Perhaps he hasn't put together Ethel was the mastermind behind the 'A Little Bird Told Me' column."

Before I could respond, Athena jumped in. "Gerald isn't the brightest star in the sky, but he's more with it than people give him credit for. Him pulling his weight back in the day is the only reason I kept my job when Ethel and her deceased husband, Eustace"—she rolled her eyes—"the Lord rest his miserable soul, were gunning for me."

"And even without *that* endorsement—" I smiled crookedly at Athena. "—there's no way I can believe Gerald would be so stupid to show up on the very day Birdie's article came out, kill her, and leave one of his broken kombucha jars to implicate him."

"All right, when you put it that way, that is a lot

for anyone to swallow. So, then, what?" Leo grimaced. "A setup? Someone planted that jar to set up Gerald?"

I forced a sardonic laugh. "Trust me, there's no ominous special-frequency music only I can hear with a theory that indicates Gerald. If someone went to all that trouble, surely they'd be a little more subtle so it wouldn't appear like a setup."

Leo considered again, then shrugged once more. "Which brings me back to Gerald. Sometimes the most obvious, and stupidest, theory is it. Haven't you seen those Darwin awards? They're endless. People do dumb stuff all the time, especially in a rage-filled fury."

"Well, I suppose that's true." Athena almost sounded convinced, and then cocked her head at me quizzically. "Wait a minute? You can hear ominous music that no one else can?"

EIGHT

The bakery was as crowded as expected the next morning, even without me doing a live reading of what would've been my feature in *The Chipmunk Chronicles*. Everyone milled about, clustering around various tables, reading Rhonda Biggler's report on Bridget Sutton's death and Gerald Jackson's arrest as they drank coffee and devoured pastries. Interestingly enough, it said nothing about his subsequent release. That detail was shrugged off easily enough, the assumption being the paper had gone to print before Gerald had gotten out the night before. Maybe that was true, but with the growing speculation Ethel was behind it all, it only seemed one more check mark in that pile of evidence.

Katie noticed me approach as she finished up with a customer and sidestepped behind the espresso machine, starting to work on my next dirty chai—my third of the morning. She managed a loud whisper over the hiss of the milk steamer. "Everyone is speculating about Birdie and Gerald, and I've moved on like it's old news. I keep coming up with what might've been written about the people on Birdie's hit list." She wiped some foam from the back of her hand onto her apron, from which a walrus sporting glittery false eyelashes and a tiara peered over the top.

At the sight of another example of Katie's outrageous T-shirt wardrobe, I realized I'd gotten dressed so quickly that morning in my hurry to get to the Cozy Corgi so I could fill Katie in on Athena's visit, that I'd not paid any attention to which skirt I'd pulled on. For my birthday, Katie had given me a collection of broomstick skirts, each with a silly animal or pastry embroidery.

I didn't have time to check before she kept going. "Some of them don't take too much imagination. Maybe it's because our last police chief was so crooked, but it wouldn't surprise me if Marlon Dunmore had a few skeletons in his closet. Some others always seemed a little... *mysterious* isn't quite the right word, but something. And Percival..." She chuckled affectionately as she poured in a shot of espresso. "Well... I doubt you'd even have to squint to discover something salacious in your uncle's past, though I'm sure he would refer to it as fabulously scandalous."

I laughed along with her. "You're probably right. I'd say he'd have the exact same attitude as Delilah. Shrug it off and say people were just jealous they didn't live as free and exciting a life as he does."

She slid the steaming cup of happiness toward me. "But Myrtle and Angus... what's scandalous about bird watching and knitting?"

"Really?" I'd started to take my first sip, which was always the best, no matter how many dirty chais I'd had, and leveled a stare at her. "We've had murders in a bird club and a knitting club, both of which you were there for."

She waved me off. "That's different. Myrtle and Angus didn't commit the murders. The two of them are like cozy old grandparents."

Once more, my first sip was interrupted so I could cock an eyebrow at Katie. "*Myrtle* is cozy?"

Katie started to nod, then considered before she acquiesced. "All right, *prickly*. She's like a prickly old grandparent. Still, nothing exciting enough to write a column about."

I leaned forward on the counter. "Don't forget I was supposed to be today's exposé."

"Good point." Katie grinned. "You're about as

scandalous as your earth-tone wardrobe, especially compared to Percival. Maybe that list doesn't mean anything. There's clearly a wide range."

I scowled as I finally took the first sip, then let out an involuntary groan as the spiced caffeine touched my tongue and seemed to flow over my entire body. "I might find you insulting if you didn't give me the elixir of life every day."

"Every *day*? Try every half hour."

"Fair enough. The dirty chai isn't why I came up here. Though it made it more than worth the trip." I chuckled, took another sip as I glanced over the patrons filling the bakery before lowering my voice toward Katie. "Have you overheard anything? About Gerald or Birdie? Ben and I are only having tourists come in wanting to buy books downstairs, or attempt to take a picture with Watson."

"I'm sure *attempt* is the operative word there." Her brown eyes twinkled at me. "And don't forget, you're here to sell books, remember? Not stock up on gossip." She laughed at my expression, then grew serious. "No, to answer your question. There are wild theories flowing around, but nothing that sounds partly true. You know how it is with Gerald. Half the people, mostly members of the good-old-boys club, think Gerald can do no wrong.

The rest simply think he's an idiot—a *harmless* idiot. And nobody knew Birdie. *But...*" Her gaze flicked over the tables. "Even the members of the good-old-boys club are wondering what they've missed about Gerald all this time. I've not heard any good theories, but it seems like people are willing to believe what Birdie wrote about him, at least mostly. Even so, from what I can tell, the general consensus is that Gerald doesn't have it in him to kill someone. That he's being set up for Birdie's death."

"Maybe so." Taking another drink of my dirty chai, I considered the theory I'd been mulling over between book sales. "I'm not fully convinced Gerald *isn't* capable of murder, and while I wouldn't have pegged him as a mastermind, or anything, I still can't believe he'd be so stupid to show up at her house, kill her, and leave remnants of a kombucha jar. And if we look at the past subjects of the column, I don't believe Delilah or Carl are murderers."

Katie narrowed her eyes. "*I* can see Delilah killing."

I liked Delilah Johnson more than Katie did, but I shrugged my agreement. "I suppose I can as well. But not for this. I think the only thing that might have upset Delilah about the article was that someone was *trying* to upset her. She didn't care a bit about what was shared."

Katie made an expression like she'd just tasted sour milk but didn't make any more comments about Delilah. "Don't forget you were next up on the list. Maybe you're the one who shut Birdie up and framed Gerald in the process."

"That's exactly what I'm getting at." I laughed as Katie's eyes bugged in surprise. "Well, no, not me specifically. But someone else on the list. If Athena was able to get her hands on it, then it's feasible someone else did as well and knew what was coming their way."

"So someone else on that list may have taken Birdie out before she had the chance to air their dirty laundry." Her brows knitted. "Again, I can't picture most of the people on that list having dark enough secrets they'd be devastated about, let alone kill over." She shook her head before I could respond. "Although I guess that's the nature of secrets, isn't it? I should know that better than most."

"Exactly. If someone seems sweet and benign, and it's all a farce, one that everyone's bought into, that's even more reason to shut Birdie up. Someone like Delilah wouldn't really care. She had a reputation to begin with. But someone else on the list..."

Katie cocked her head. "You're not looking into Gerald's investments anymore, are you? You're investigating the murder."

I supposed I was. I'd slipped into that mode without even realizing it. "Maybe, but remember, we don't have confirmation that Birdie was killed. And if she was, who said I can't look into both her death *and* Gerald's financial schemes? Even if he's not the one who killed her, it doesn't mean they're not connected."

"Fred?" Ben emerged from the stairs and rounded the corner, Watson trotting along at his heels in typical adoration, and handed me the phone, while covering the mouthpiece. "This is Angus. He wants to know if you have time to go down to Knit Witt."

I gave a knowing glance to Katie. "Speak of the devil." No way was this unconnected. Turning back, I took the phone. "Thanks, Ben."

Though the tourists had thinned slightly since the Fourth, the sidewalks were still filled with late-morning shoppers. Watson glowered at every person we passed, clearly irritated that he had to bother to weave in and out of feet and strollers instead of taking a straight shot like we could during the off months.

Unlike the Cozy Corgi's grumpy mascot, I found the brief walk refreshing. I loved Estes Park all of the time, no matter the season—with the shops' mix of 1960s mountain-style log cabin motifs, and a few modern updates here and there, the downtown was always charming. Nestled in a slight valley, the surrounding peaks always towered over the town, making it feel sheltered and hidden, despite it being a tourist trap. Though it looked like a magical Christmas snow globe in December, I loved the brightness and abundance of life summer brought. The trees lining the streets full of verdant green leaves and offering shade, while the planters and scenic sections scattered throughout the sidewalks were overflowing with flowers, bushes, and decorative grasses.

I'd be lying if I didn't admit I also enjoyed knowing it wasn't all pretty mountains, charming shops, and blossoming flowers. That, just like everywhere else, every single person within each one of the stores had their own story, their own histories, and their own secrets. Most of them were harmless, at least relatively so. But there were a few secrets, maybe more than a few, that weren't quite so benign.

Maybe Birdie Sutton stumbled across just such a secret, and it got her killed.

I started to walk in when Watson and I arrived at Knit Witt, but found the door locked. For a second I wondered if I'd misunderstood Angus, if he'd wanted me to meet him at his home, but then his lean figure became visible through the glass as he approached the door, and I understood.

After a turn of the deadbolt, Angus opened the door and ushered us in with one of his typically warm smiles. "Fred, Watson, so good of you both to make time." As soon as we were inside, Angus shut the door and locked it again, before taping a piece of paper facing out. Though backward from where I stood, with the light filtering through, I could read his writing, *We'll be back in ten minutes. Thank you for your patience.* "I hadn't gotten a chance to hang that before you arrived."

I'd spoken to Angus in his shop about cases a couple of different times, and he'd never closed up before. This time must truly be different.

Before I could comment, Angus pulled a dog treat out of his pocket, knelt, and offered it to Watson. I couldn't help but wonder if so many of the shopkeepers had kept dog treats on them at all times before Watson. Probably not.

Forgetting his bad mood brought on by the traffic on the sidewalk, Watson snagged the treat, his nub of a tail wagging happily, and trotted off. He took a second to glare at me over his shoulder when he came to the end of his leash, but the hop returned to his step soon enough when I released him. He continued to the spot he'd occupied last time we were here—next to a gorgeous knitted display in the corner—and curled up to the nearly lifelike baby fawn. By this point, I thought Watson had a favorite spot in every store in town.

It was only as Watson trotted past, without so much as a glance his way, that I noticed Gerald Jackson standing stiffly at the counter. I knew he and Angus were friends, but I'd never quite been able to wrap my brain around it. Seeing the rotund lawyer, with his unruly eyebrows knitted over an irritated expression in the middle of Angus's spectacular shop, modern and sleek with shiny mahogany floors and ceilings and filled with lush yarns of every color and material, only accentuated the dichotomy. Angus was a kind, classy, reserved grandfather-type figure, sort of what Katie had referenced only a little while before. Gerald was... well, cannabis-infused kombucha, outlandish investment schemes, and felt like the used-car-salesman stereotype version of a lawyer.

Angus hadn't mentioned Gerald would be present, not that he'd explained anything. He'd simply asked me to come down, that he had something to discuss about Birdie. From Gerald's expression, I wondered if he was surprised at my arrival. Clearly he wasn't pleased by it. I looked from him to Angus, deciding to skip over any pleasantries or small talk, especially if he planned on sticking to the ten-minute promise he taped to the door. "What's going on?"

"Just wanted to discuss some details about Birdie, like I told you on the phone. I promise, you're not going to be ganged up on." Still smiling, Angus crossed the store, motioning for me to follow, then took a seat in one of the chairs that made up the circle he used for knitting demonstrations.

I chose one two seats down from Angus and near Watson, who'd finished his treat and was already napping with the knitted baby deer.

Gerald remained where he was, merely straightening his glasses before crossing his arms over his chest and resting them on his upper belly.

Angus cast a reproachful glance toward Gerald, then refocused on me as he leaned both elbows on his knees, somehow managing to both make the motion elegant and assuring. "Rumor mill has it you discovered Ms. Sutton's body yesterday and were present with Officer Green at the scene." He didn't wait for confirmation, as it was clearly not needed, and infused an even more soothing tone in his voice. "My question is, why you were at Ms. Sutton's home to begin with. Not that any explanation is required or that I'm entitled to one. My guess is you either wanted to speak to her about the article that was supposed to be published today about you, or to ask her about what she'd written connecting Gerald and Carl." His smile increased. "Although it could be both, I'm placing money on you wanting to help out the Hansons."

Angus was typically blunt, in his way, which was something I normally respected and put me at ease. This time, with the subject matter, the memory fresh of Birdie's dead body next to a broken Mason jar, and Gerald scowling a few feet away, I was thrown off. I took a moment, glancing back and forth between the two men, trying to determine the smartest route. I always felt safe with Angus, at least I thought... and I didn't exactly feel cornered, but I didn't exactly *not* feel cornered either. Unable to truly process through what the best tactic was, I defaulted to my normal, the one that matched Angus, even if I rarely pulled it off as gracefully as he did.

"Well, you know me, I like to be blunt, so here it is." I started by looking at Angus, but then, feeling somewhat defiant, refocused on Gerald and held his gaze. Despite myself, I heard a level of defensiveness in my voice. "We've spoken before about your investment schemes." I raised my hand when Gerald opened his mouth. "I know, you don't appreciate me referring to them as *schemes*, you didn't before either. I spoke to you about my concerns that you were taking advantage of Carl, among other things. So yes, that was why I went to talk to Birdie yesterday. Because, as I predicted to both Carl and to you, his involvement with your *schemes* landed him in hot water."

With every word, Gerald looked like he wound tighter and tighter, and when I finished, his voice was practically a bark. "You might want to turn the accusal in your tone back around on yourself, missy. I wasn't the only one getting featured in that horrid woman's column. If anything, you're the one who should be under the microscope. You might've killed her so your secrets weren't aired to the public."

I bristled, but before I could speak, Angus had

already jumped in, sounding a bit exasperated. "For crying out loud, Gerald, get a grip. We both know Winifred didn't murder anyone. Making such outlandish claims doesn't do any good. We didn't ask her here to attack, but to request her help."

"*You* asked her here." Gerald glared at Angus. "This was *your* idea. Not mine."

"True, I did." Angus didn't rise to Gerald's accusation. "It's for your own good." He ignored Gerald's sputtering and looked to me. "I don't know if Carl came and asked for your help or if you simply dove in because he and Anna are your friends, but I'm... *we're* asking for your help. Gerald's got himself into a bit of a mess."

I blinked, surprised. This was even more blunt than I was used to from Angus. "A mess?" I dared to glance toward Gerald but didn't let it linger. "And why do you need me?"

"We don't." Gerald bit it out.

For the first time, I saw a crack in Angus, and he glared over at his friend, then stood, dusting off his slacks. "Fine. If you're going to fight me on this, then have it your way. I tried to warn you against some of the investments you insisted upon, and you can see where that got you. You're my friend, but as they say, you can lead a horse to water, but..." He shrugged.

I wondered if Angus would be so willing to let it go if he knew about the list, that an article about him had been scheduled to be published in four days.

"I respect Winifred, her intelligence, her honor, and her ability. She could help, but that's your choice. But I *did not* invite her here to have to deal with your insolence and rudeness." Angus turned back to me, the smile finally a bit forced. "Forgive me, Winifred. I shouldn't have bothered you and Watson. I just thought—"

"Fine!" Gerald smacked his hands on his thighs, making a loud crack and causing Watson to yelp from behind me. As Watson came to sit beside my chair, Gerald seated himself across from me in the circle, and though he continued to glare, began to speak. "I went to Birdie's house the evening of the Fourth. I hoped to talk her out of publishing the article about me."

Beside me, Angus sat and folded his hands in his lap in a satisfied manner.

"That viper was alive when I got there *and* when I left." Gerald tilted his chin. "You've made it very clear you have a low opinion of me, but no matter what you may think, I am not a murderer."

I was too shocked to respond, or to do anything more than to continue to stroke Watson's head where he sat beside me and continued to look back and forth between the men. Of all things, I'd not expected that. I hadn't been fully convinced Gerald had been at Birdie's home, but even if I had been, I never would've guessed he'd admit it, especially to me.

"Don't give me that look." Gerald's aggressive tone died a little, leaving him sounding more defensive and annoyed than furious. "You can say what you want about going to visit her for Carl, but everyone in here, probably even the dog, knows you also hoped to get that article about yourself stopped. I didn't do a thing that you didn't do."

"Did you take her a kombucha?" I wasn't sure how far I could push Gerald. When I first met him, I'd written him off as a scatterbrained, small-town lawyer who was more Barney Fife than anything, though with less charm. And while some of that could be true, I discovered he had a temper and a tendency to dig in his heels when pushed, and what seemed to be more than a passing issue with seeing women as capable or equals.

He didn't answer for a second, casting another accusing glare at Angus, and huffed out a breath. "I did. Several of them. Thought they might... soften her up a bit."

So it had been a kombucha jar. "Did one of them break before you left?"

"No. She—" Gerald sneered. "—refused to even try it, acted like she was too good for the stuff. Clearly didn't keep her from sampling it once I'd left."

I started to question him again, the detail of the broken jar hadn't been in the paper, yet Gerald hadn't seemed surprised or confused by the question. Before I could, Angus gave an encouraging motion with his hand. "Tell it all, Gerald. You've gone this far."

Gerald crossed his arms once more, and for some reason, his glare settled on Watson. Finally, he let out a defeated exhale and looked at me, though his gaze flicked away quickly enough. "I also offered her some investments of her own. And yes, I know you probably call that a bribe. Fine." His gaze came back to me again. "I tried to *bribe* the woman with *investments*, not schemes as you say, but *investments*. Free, on her part. She had nothing to gain but possible millions."

That didn't surprise me, not in the slightest. And it not only made sense with what I knew of Gerald, but made his story believable. "So you thought you'd soften her up with kombucha and then talk her into either changing what she wrote about you, or not publishing at all, by—" I had to adjust what I'd wanted to say, insulting Gerald in the moment wouldn't help. "—giving her free access to make a lot of money."

It had been the right choice. Gerald looked a little surprised and then softened. "Exactly."

"She refused that too?"

Gerald's lip curled, and arrogance highlighted his tone. "She had the same deficit as you. Absolutely no vision. Unable to see that to gain, one has to take risks. Although, in her case, there wasn't even any risk on her part." The arrogance fell away again, letting the defiance return, and ushering in a bit of desperation. "But I didn't kill her. Besides, even if I was a murderer, which I'm not, what good would it have done? Nothing's accomplished by killing the messenger."

"Gerald..." Angus had a warning in his tone. "We talked about this."

Ignoring Angus, I stayed focused on Gerald, certain I understood his meaning. "You see Birdie as a messenger? For whom?"

Also ignoring the warning, Gerald met my gaze again and didn't bother trying to hide his scorn. "You have to ask? I thought you were supposed to be good at this."

I tilted my chin as he had moments before. "Ethel Beaker, you mean."

Though he tried to hide it quickly enough, I caught the surprised admiration that flashed behind his eyes. "Obviously."

"So if you were going to kill anyone, it would be Ethel?"

"Exactly." At Angus's groan, Gerald winced and hurried on. "Well, no. I wouldn't kill Ethel, and I'm not going to. I was just merely confirming that Birdie was clearly doing Ethel's dirty work. Even a moron could see that. Ethel hates Delilah, Carl, and me. You as well, you were up next."

"You hate Ethel right back, don't you?" For once I felt like I could push Gerald without him retreating. "She stole your majority ownership of the paper."

"Yes, she did. And yes, I do. I hate her." There was no deceit, nor any shadow in his eyes. "And while I won't shed tears on the day of her funeral, I won't be the one responsible for it."

"This gets us nowhere," Angus broke in, retaking the reins of the conversation. "Ethel is beside the point." Again, I wondered if he'd say such a thing if he knew of the list of names and his placement on it. "If Ms. Sutton was merely doing Ethel's bidding at the paper, and I agree that is the most likely scenario, there's no reason to think Ethel would harm her. Ethel didn't kill Birdie. Why would she?" Angus focused on me again. "That's why we need you, Winifred. Susan Green, though she struggles with temper and temperance, is a good officer, but given her feelings about Gerald, she'll have lack of motivation to look past the obvious."

Angus wasn't someone a person interrupted, but I couldn't help myself, and I motioned toward Gerald. "He was out within hours. Not even held overnight."

"Not that the paper said anything about *that*, of course. Made it sound like I'd been booked."

Angus ignored Gerald's outburst entirely. "That's true, Gerald was out swiftly, *despite* Officer Green's protestations. Which brings me back to why he needs you. Obviously you and Gerald hold no great fondness for each other, which is a shame, as I can see such wonderful qualities in both of you, but that's beside the point as well. Although, it isn't really. One of your qualities, Winifred, is that you can look past your personal prejudices to find the truth. So, only you can be trusted to help clear Gerald's name."

It wasn't the first time I'd been flattered at sincere praise by Angus, and it took me a second to remember the unspoken elephant in the room. "There's a problem with all this."

Angus merely cocked a brow in question.

"You're assuming Birdie was murdered. Gerald is saying she was still alive when he left her home. There's no sign of forced entry or struggle, other than a broken kombucha jar. For all we know, if Gerald didn't do it, Birdie had some type of accident and fell to her death. When the autopsy comes in, Gerald's name may be cleared by default."

Gerald interrupted again, even though he'd been the subject of our meeting, somehow it had become between Angus and me. "That's exactly what I was telling you before you insisted on calling—"

Angus let out a dark, soft laugh, cutting Gerald off, and we didn't so much as glance his way. "Come now, Winifred. Ms. Sutton had already attempted to ruin lives and reputations of three established members of the town, you were to be next. And while I love and adore the people of Estes Park, they're all human, and they love gossip and scandal as much as anyone else. Ms. Sutton's column wasn't going to end with you. Who can say if there was an end in sight? Perhaps no one she wrote about wanted her dead, but someone she was *going* to write about did, clearly. You and your adorable pooch simply need to find out who."

"I'm nervous..." From the Mini Cooper's passenger seat, Katie issued a giggle that proved her statement. "Although, I can't tell if I'm excited nervous or scared nervous."

I spared her a quick glance as we neared the housing development overlooking Mary's Lake. "There's no reason to be nervous at all. Ethel's a normal woman, just like you and me."

Katie made a face. "I think that's the rudest thing you've ever said to me."

Laughing, I acquiesced. "You raise a valid point. Ethel's nothing like you or me. I hope even on our worst days there are no similarities."

"Exactly." Katie had already turned her attention, gazing up at the cluster of mansions. "Although... I wouldn't mind having a similar bank account. Unfortunately we're nothing like her on that aspect either." Another nervous giggle escaped. "This'll be my first time meeting a butler."

At that moment, Watson shoved his head between the front seats, propped his forelegs on the middle console, and gazed out as if he too was captivated by the mansions. As we pulled off the road and into the development, I scratched his head, ignoring the amount of dog hair it added to my car's interior. "Don't get excited, buddy. I'm not sure where you think we're heading, but you're going to be sorely disappointed." I took my other hand off the wheel for a second to brush away one of his hairs that snagged on my eyelashes, and it made me remember the first and only time I visited Ethel's house. "However, if you shed just like this all over the butler and whatever Ethel's wearing, we'll make sure you get a double amount of T.R.E.A.T.S. tonight. You can prove to her that you would make a lovely pair of earmuffs."

Katie shot me a quizzical glance, but was distracted by the view once more.

After my talk with Angus and Gerald, I decided the next step in figuring this out was to confront Ethel Beaker. She didn't kill Birdie Sutton, why would she? But perhaps there'd be some clue in what she said. If nothing else, surely she'd give me some details about Birdie, however unintentionally, that could help me better understand the woman. And if I'd learned anything, it was that the better you knew the victim, the easier it was to find the killer.

After filling Katie in on what was said at Knit Witt, on a whim, I decided she should go with me, so we waited until closing time and piled into the Mini Cooper. Though I'd told Katie that I wished she'd been there when I visited Ethel before, that I thought she would've gotten a kick out of having a tuxedo-wearing butler answer the door in Estes Park, and that I wanted her input and instinct as we spoke to the woman—

all true enough—I also hoped Katie's presence would help me have a different reaction to Ethel. Despite my best efforts, I had yet to control my reactions around Ethel. While I wasn't intimidated by her money, her self-perceived upper echelon worth, or her butler, she managed to get under my skin. *She* triggered all those old feelings of worthlessness and insecurity imparted by cruel comments by belittling teachers. Maybe... with Katie at my side... I could remember I was Winifred Page, strong, capable, determined, *not* a little fourth-grader humiliated by her teacher, even if that little girl still whispered in my ear at times.

After pulling to a stop at the cobblestone driveway, I slid the car into Park, and looked toward Katie once more. "Like we discussed, I think Gerald's right, the answer to who killed Birdie is probably somewhere on that list of upcoming subjects of her column. But we need to be careful as we talk to Ethel. We can't let her know we're aware such a list even exists."

Katie offered a scowl. "I know that. This is hardly my first rodeo with you, Fred. And I love Athena. The last thing I want to do is alert Ethel to the fact that Athena is spying on her at the paper, more or less."

"Exactly." I'd started to open the door, then paused. "Athena was right."

Katie's expression turned quizzical. "What?"

"Athena. She should have been on that list. Ethel hates her. One of the few things Gerald ever did right was help Athena keep her job at the paper when the Beakers were angling for her." Even as I said it out loud, I realized the error of that thought. "Or maybe Athena shouldn't be on the list. I don't think Ethel would see her as important enough for that. And why would she bother? Now that Ethel has majority ownership of *The Chipmunk*

Chronicles, she could just fire Athena and be done with it."

Katie didn't miss a beat. "Don't forget who you're talking about. That quarrel with Athena was forever ago. I bet you anything, Athena doesn't cross Ethel's mind anymore. She's not worth the thought or the effort. Just a little fly Ethel could smash at any moment when she takes her attention off more exciting prey."

Though I laughed, I agreed. "A little dramatic, maybe. But I bet you're right." Once more, I was glad Katie was by my side. As the three of us got out of the car and walked toward the sweeping limestone steps that led to the front door, I reminded myself we needed to keep it that way. We couldn't slip up and draw attention to Athena.

We'd barely arrived at the landing before Katie pushed the doorbell. If it had been me, I would've paused for a few seconds to take some deep breaths, to prepare myself. But maybe this way was better.

Watson plopped down between us, cocking his head in that adorable corgi way. Perhaps he was able to hear the ringing of the doorbell inside or possibly the footsteps of the butler headed our way.

Sure enough, just as a rumble began to build from Watson's chest, there was the sound of locks being unbolted and the door opened to reveal a tall, lanky elderly man, clad in a crisp black tuxedo and shiny black shoes. Mason—I managed to remember the butler's name—peered down his long nose at Watson as his upper lip curled in disgust. From his expression, I almost expected him to issue a growl as well. After a moment, nostrils flaring, his tired blue gaze looked from Katie to me. "Unannounced and with an entourage." Another flare of his nostrils, this time accompanied by a sniff. "Unless you're selling Girl Scout cookies, which the lady wouldn't touch with a ten-foot pole, an appointment is a minimum expectation. *Even* for the uncouth."

I started to offer a retort, but Katie giggled. Both Mason and I turned toward her. She lifted a hand to her lips, but seemed unable to hold in another giggle, this one sounding almost on the edge of a snort. "Get you. You're the real thing, aren't you?"

Those blue eyes went so large, they looked in danger of popping straight out of Mason's skull. "I can honestly say that I have no idea to what you refer."

"Oh stop!" Katie swatted at the air between them as she giggled again. "Please tell me your name is Jeeves."

Nope, I'd been wrong. *Now* it looked like his

eyes were going to pop out. "Jeeves was a *valet*, not a butler, you uncivilized—" Mason stopped himself with another flare of his nostrils and turned to me. "Ms. Beaker is not accepting visitors at this time. You'd best be on your way. Though, feel free to call and inquire if the lady can fit you into her schedule."

Katie giggled again when Mason pronounced schedule with a *shh* sound, earning herself another glare. I rushed ahead before Mason physically removed us from the porch. "We both know Ethel wouldn't find a moment to spare if I called. Part of why I arrived unannounced. I would appreciate if you checked with her." As I spoke, I flitted through the options and chose the one I thought would best get her to show up, and then bent the truth a little. "There have been accusations that Birdie Sutton was under Ethel's employ. Officer Green figured Ms. Beaker would not appreciate the police showing up on her doorstep to follow through with this accusation. But if she was mistaken, I can let Susan know that—"

"Now there's a choice between Scylla and Charybdis." Mason began closing the door even as he spoke. "I'll check which poison the lady desires."

Katie giggled again, though that time it was more

of a laugh. "Scylla and Charybdis! That man is priceless."

I was torn between laughing along with her and giving her a glare of my own. I chose the latter. "I didn't think you'd actually laugh at the man to his face. And Scylla and Chary—"

"Oh stop. Don't forget who you're talking to. Like I wouldn't know that little tidbit from Greek mythology. Just a snobby way of saying between a rock and a hard place." Though irritation was in her tone, it shifted quickly enough. "And I'm sorry, I truly wasn't trying to laugh. And I know it wasn't helpful, but come on, people really live and act like this?"

Despite myself, I finally laughed along. Hadn't I had the very same instinct the first time Mason opened the door to me and Watson? Wasn't that part of why I brought Katie along? I knew she'd get a kick out of it. "No, I can't blame you, but please, don't laugh in Ethel's face."

Katie sobered instantly. "Don't worry. I'll be lucky to get two words out face-to-face with that woman. She makes me feel about two inches tall."

"You're not the only one." Thank goodness I'd brought her along. Uncomfortable interactions or not, the ice was broken, and things were easier. Plus, knowing she felt similar to me bolstered my confidence, for some reason.

Minutes ticked by as we stood stupidly at the door, waiting. Growing impatient, Watson let out an annoyed huff and wandered off, sniffing all over the huge wraparound porch, pausing here and there at some of the more tantalizing scents. I started to redirect him, instruct him to come sit at my feet again, worried it would only close Ethel off more than she'd already be if she arrived and found him leaving a trail of dog hair. Then I didn't. Watson had been patient enough, and even I was struggling to stand still.

Apparently, Katie was experiencing the same. She looked at her watch. "It's nearly been five minutes. Do you think they're just going to leave us out here?"

I shrugged. "Maybe, but I don't think so. Knowing Ethel, it's some sort of power play, just reminding us who's in charge."

"Well, I'll remind her who—"

I snatched Katie's hand right before her finger made contact with the doorbell. "Don't you dare. *If* this is a power play, we give away ours if we show we're impatient."

After another three minutes passed, I was

tempted to push the doorbell myself, though instead I followed Watson's lead. Well... not really. I didn't start sniffing the porch, but I decided to no longer stand at attention as we waited. With a motion to Katie, I led her over to the seating area where I'd spoken to Ethel before. "Let's make ourselves at home."

Another five minutes passed, and then another. Katie and I didn't speak, just watched as Watson continued to explore and then get captivated by a beetle making its way across the planks. If it had been anywhere else but Ethel Beaker's front porch, the experience would've been enjoyable. The early evening air was warm with a pleasant breeze, bringing the scent of pine and the sound of quaking aspen leaves, as the horizon, barely visible from under the eaves of the porch, began to glow a light pink over the edge of the mountains. As the sunset transitioned to a deep purple, Watson lost interest in the beetle, trudged over to us, curled up under the hem of my broomstick skirt, propped his head on the toe of my boot, and napped.

When we passed the half-hour mark, I wondered if Katie had the right idea. Maybe we should ring the doorbell again. Just as I was debating the merits of doing so, or simply getting in the car and driving away, Ethel emerged and headed our way, Mason a few feet behind her.

Ethel wasn't a beautiful woman—at least, I didn't think so. I supposed she might've been the most beautiful woman in town, but I'd be unable to see it because of her horrid personality. But she took my breath away as she walked toward us. Beautiful or not, the older woman had a look only money could buy. She was clad in a slinky, floor-length gown that left her shoulders bare, and with every step, the dangling thin silver chains—I was certain chains *weren't* what she'd call them—that covered every inch of the dress, glistened and sparkled in the sunset. She waited until she sat on the edge of the chair opposite us before she spoke, and when she did, it was to her butler, not to Katie or me. "Just set them on the table between us, Mason. Thank you."

"Yes, ma'am." Mason lowered a large tray to the table, lifted a champagne bottle, popped it, and filled three crystal flutes before turning and walking back into the mansion.

Finally, Ethel addressed us. "I'm attending an event this evening, so I only have around five minutes." She gestured toward the spread. "And though you didn't offer the courtesy of letting me know you wanted to speak to me, far be it from me to not be a gracious hostess. Help yourselves."

Katie didn't giggle, and I could practically feel her nerves buzzing beside me as she took in the tray filled with clearly expensive cheeses and meats.

Ethel reached out and took one of the flutes of champagne, started to say something, then gave the smallest of flinches as her gaze fixed at my feet.

Looking down, I saw Watson's head pop out from under my skirt as he sniffed the air. He emerged, not bothering to glance at any of us, tilted his head so his nose was even with the edge of the tray, took a few more deep sniffs, whimpered, and then finally peered up at me beseechingly.

"You have some nerve."

At Ethel's whisper, I looked back up, expecting her to be grimacing at Watson, though why she'd be surprised at his presence, I had no idea. I quickly realized the notion was wrong. Ethel's attention wasn't on Watson, but near the hem of my skirt. When I noticed the embroidery over the dusty teal-blue fabric, I inwardly groaned. The day had been halfway over before I'd taken the time to notice the image Katie had designed for one of my birthday skirts. And I'd promptly forgotten about it, but now wished I'd taken the time to change before we came to Ethel's. No doubt, it appeared intentional.

She glared at the embroidery for another second or two before meeting my gaze. "It's no secret what I think of my daughter-in-law, but Carla is a member of the family and the mother to the next generation of Beakers. While I expected more than a barista for a daughter-in-law, I don't appreciate you making digs at her with your coffee-dueling-a-scone fashion, though I hate to use that label for such a choice in clothing."

"It's not a coffee." Katie sat a little straighter. "It's a dirty chai latte, Fred's favorite. It was one of my birthday presents to her. And it has nothing—" She switched directions, clearly unable to tell the lie. "Fred also loves scones." Though the embroidered pictures weren't something I'd ever choose for myself, I'd had a good laugh when I noticed this particular option when I'd unboxed the gift. It was clearly a reference to the cardboard scones from Carla's first coffee shop. I couldn't believe I'd worn it to Ethel's, of all places.

Watson whimpered louder, shifting his back legs as he stared up at me pleadingly. A trail of drool made its way down to the floor of Ethel's porch.

"For crying out loud, feed the mongrel." Ethel

snagged the unsliced half of one of the salamis and tossed it over the railing of the porch. "He's going to ruin the finish."

Watson let out a wild, pleasure-filled bark and tore off like he was a greyhound chasing a rabbit. In his excitement, his hind paws skated over the boards for a few seconds, one of them finally making contact with the table, helping him to launch toward the steps.

The hit caused the tray to shake and one of the champagne flutes to topple. I lunged forward, but only managed to hit the base, causing it to spin, spraying champagne through the air as the crystal shattered on the porch. Like the world had shattered right along with it, I sat stunned, feeling trails of champagne make their way down my face. Horror-stricken, I glanced at Katie, finding her white as a sheet and droplets of champagne dripping from her brown spirals. Dreading what I'd find, I finally looked toward Ethel.

She wiped a droplet from her cheek, flicking it to the ground, but that was all. Katie and I had gotten the worst of it.

"I'm so sorry. Watson was just so excited that... I'll pay for the glass and—"

"Do you think I can't handle the cost of a broken

champagne flute? That I need or *want* your spare change?" Ethel's voice was ice and daggers. "I should've known better than to offer pearls to swine."

I nearly choked. Ethel Beaker had done it again, made me feel like a clumsy, bumbling, classless schoolgirl who was below her pity and only deserved her contempt.

Beside me, Katie barked out a laugh, surprising me and pulling my attention to her once more. Though only a moment before her face had been pale, it was now flushed a bright pink. "Come off it. Don't act like you're not enjoying the show. You're the one who picked up half a sausage and tossed it like you were a vendor at a baseball game."

Ethel fumed. "How dare you? How dare...?" She practically sputtered with rage.

At the combination of Ethel's indignation and the fury in Katie's eyes, I fell a little more in love with my best friend and felt Winifred Page, the un-fourth-grade version, snap back into place. Straightening, I looked toward Ethel once more and was surprised at just how calm and collected my voice managed to be. "If I'm judging time correctly, we only have four minutes left, so let's not waste it."

"You think I'm going to speak to you now?" Ethel

started to stand. "And there are not four minutes left. I need to go fix my makeup before—"

"Where did you find Birdie Sutton? Clearly she was doing your bidding." I was pleased to see Ethel halt as I interrupted. "From what I found out about her, she'd done a slew of small-time gossip columns here and there but nothing investigatory. I'm assuming you provided her the information as well?"

"Oh yes. Mason mentioned your little theory." Her pretense of time forgotten, Ethel lifted her chin. The superior motion made me want to stand, to not sit in her presence, from Katie's vibrations beside me, I felt she was having the same struggle. Ethel straightened further, thrusting her chest out, causing the silver chains to ripple over her small breasts and send fractals of light over the space. "Let me make it easy for you. Yes, Birdie was here at my request. And yes, as majority holder at the paper, she was one of my employees. That's not a secret, nor would it have taken a leap to figure out, so don't be so proud of yourself. I made no attempt to hide the connection."

I wasn't overly surprised at her admission. Ethel was smarter than to claim ignorance.

She flicked her wrist toward the back end of the porch. "I set her up in a fully furnished home at the end of this neighborhood, which you know, as you were the one snooping around her house." That part surprised me, but I was unable to figure out how to respond before she sneered again. "I assume you're going to accuse me of being the murderer for some reason? Due to what? She didn't write the articles to my liking? She discovered some dirt on me perhaps? I'd like to say I expect more from you, Winifred Page, but unfortunately, I don't. That sounds like the sort of drivel you'd come up with. But *please*, don't take my word for it. Dig into my life, see what you can find out. Better than you have tried."

Katie snorted, and though I didn't look at her, I recognized the sound that was accompanied with one of her exaggerated eye rolls.

Though I was tempted to inflect my voice with the derision I heard from Katie, I lowered it to barely a whisper and still remained seated. "I don't think you had anything to do with Birdie's death. As you said, why would you? She clearly was only doing your will, obviously." I decided to push a little further than I had planned. "I am curious, who was after me? Doubtless other members of my family... Barry? Percival?" At the faintest flinch I pushed on even more. "Simone? Angus?" The second her eyes narrowed, I realized I'd push too far and attempted to backpedal as to not look like I had inside information. "Who else was on the hit list, Ethel? The Pacheco twins? My mother? Leo? Knowing you, probably even Watson."

As if answering to his name, Watson hurried up the steps once more and headed toward us. I knew it was only a matter of timing, if he hadn't been finished with the salami, there was no way he'd answer my call. Proving the point, he waddled over and began sniffing at the tray again. On a whim, I snagged another of the unsliced portions, a thicker one this time, and handed it to him. Watson hopped and looked at me like he'd never dreamed I'd give him a second Christmas in July so quickly and then snagged it and scurried away like I might change my mind.

Ethel trembled in rage, her gaze following Watson as he disappeared to the other side of the wraparound porch, and then she glared at me. "You always think everything is about you, don't you, little Miss Nancy Drew." Her gaze flicked to Katie, and she gave an eye roll of her own, one that was clearly meant to be mocking. "Of course you'd come to the conclusion that your airhead of a mother, scrub of a boyfriend, and mutt of a dog would be the center of my world. I can *assure* you, not a one of them are worth a second of my attention."

Some relief cut through me. From her reaction, Ethel wasn't going to think of Athena. She'd just assume a couple of the names were lucky guesses.

"But Fred is worth your attention, isn't she?" Katie finally stood, matching Ethel's raised chin, sounding triumphant. "You can't quit thinking about *Fred*, can you? She's so important to you that you were going to have a whole column about her."

For the first time ever, Ethel Beaker was speechless as she gaped at Katie. A flush rose to her cheeks, like she'd been caught.

Maybe if I used the moment correctly, I could take advantage of her being taken off guard. "So who do you suspect, Ethel? You didn't kill Birdie, so who did? I know I didn't. I didn't even get the chance to read whatever she was going to say about me. Delilah couldn't care less what's said about her, and Carl and Gerald aren't capable of—"

She laughed, loud and sharp. "And there's where you're wrong. You think you have everyone's number, that you've got us all figured out. Do you believe I fed Birdie lies? I can promise you, I didn't. Every word was true."

I sat, considering her meaning.

"Surely there's a few brain cells behind that mop of a red mess you call hair." Ethel gave me a pitiful look. "But maybe not. That would be expecting too much for you to add two and two together. How could you *ever* imagine that a man who has illegal ties to the drug trade and has financial deals with the kind of organizations that operate in secret and shadow would be capable of murder? Even *if* you discovered physical proof of his presence on the very night of the murder." She smiled, a wicked thing. "I'm almost disappointed." With another kaleidoscope of colors, Ethel whirled and headed toward the door. She was nearly there when Watson pranced happily back from the other side of the porch. I moved to rush toward them, thinking she might attempt a kick, but Ethel merely flung open the front door, stepped in, and slammed it behind her.

My heart racing, I sat back down in relief and patted my thigh, calling Watson to me. He practically ran, probably thinking I had another sausage roll or something for him. Instead, disappointment filled his eyes as I offered him nothing more than a caress.

"Wow." Katie breathed out a shaky sigh and collapsed in the chair beside me once more. "Wow... that was like a *Real Housewives* episode."

I couldn't hold back a laugh, and I grinned over at her. "That's exactly how Percival refers to her."

Then I frowned, growing serious again, and looked back at the closed door. "Granted, I'm not the best at reading Ethel, but I think she truly believes Gerald killed Birdie."

Katie was quiet for a second, then whispered, "Or... she arranged Birdie's death to frame Gerald."

I whipped back toward Katie and considered. Ethel had been adamant about it being Gerald. *Too* adamant? Too convenient? "I don't see why she would. It's one thing to take Gerald down in public, and another to set him up for murder. But... maybe there's more to Gerald and Ethel's past than we know." It looked like I'd be talking to Gerald again sooner than I expected. I was about to expound on the theory, then gaped as Katie started stuffing what remained of the untouched charcuterie tray in her purse. "What in the world are you doing?"

"I guarantee you that spread cost more than the bakery brings in over two days. I'm also willing to bet she'll just throw it away." She shrugged and continued to shove things into her purse. "So, one salami for me... one salami for Watson..."

TEN

Speaking to Gerald had to wait until the next day. Actually, it had to wait until the following day was nearly half over, thanks to the Cozy Corgi Bookshop and Bakery being so busy. Maybe my memory was faulty, but I could've sworn after the Fourth the year before, the tourist population dropped significantly, but this year they just kept coming. I had to remind myself that I was glad for it; it was a good thing. Though I typically would've had a breakthrough pondering while my hands were busy with other things, no fresh ideas came as I helped customers with books. I just kept turning over the same theories and possibilities.

I didn't think Gerald killed Birdie, but I could be wrong. Katie's instinct that Ethel had set Gerald up seemed far-fetched, but if she had the right amount of motivation, then maybe. Most likely it was someone on the list of upcoming column features, but if so, which one? Maybe it made me a horrible super sleuth, but I'd already mentally checked off Percival as a suspect. My uncle wasn't a murderer. The same was true for several others on the list. I couldn't see Myrtle Bantam killing anyone at all for any reason other than protecting birds—although maybe that was exactly what Birdie had found out. Perhaps Myrtle had *already* killed someone to protect birds and now needed to protect herself. I could see Mark Green killing someone. It wouldn't be the first time I'd considered the possibility, but that in and of itself almost erased him as a possibility from my mind. And Susan? I figured I'd just ask her directly; no way she killed Birdie. But if I kept striking people off the list, then what good did the list do? Then I'd be back to no suspects at all. Although, that was a possibility as well, wasn't it? Maybe there was no suspect. The whole thing could've just been an accident.

When the tourists slowed down around two in the afternoon and I didn't feel guilty for leaving Ben once more, Watson and I headed to Gerald's office, which was located in a tiny strip mall that sat close to the rainbow slides at the base of Chipmunk Mountain—both were still heavy with tourists. I decided coming in unannounced was my best bet to get a genuine reaction from Gerald. This time he wouldn't have Angus to moderate for him.

With a roll of my eyes at the title of Gerald's law firm painted in golden script on the glass, I pushed open the door and walked in. A thin woman, probably in her late sixties or early seventies, peered around a huge desktop computer that I guessed hadn't been cutting-edge since the turn of the century. "Welcome to G & J Associates. How may I help you?"

It took all my effort not to roll my eyes again at the name. There were no other associates. Only Gerald. He'd simply stuck an ampersand between his initials to make his business sound more grandiose. "I'd like to speak with Mr. Jackson, if I could."

The woman's gaze flicked toward the computer but didn't linger long enough to truly check. "I'm sorry, I don't think you have an appointment. However, I can check Mr. Jackson's schedule and..." Her prim voice died away as she glanced down at Watson beside my feet, clearly noticing him for the first time. For a moment, I thought she was going to say the law office wasn't a dog-friendly establishment, but then she looked up at me again, eyes narrowed. "I know who you are. You're Winifred Page."

"I am." I gestured downward. "And this is Watson."

She didn't respond to that. "I know why you're here. I'm aware of your reputation." She slid over, clearly in a rolling chair, so she was no longer hidden behind the massive computer. "And I think you're awful. Coming here to accuse Mr. Jackson of killing that reporter woman. He would *never* do such a thing. Mr. Jackson is a good, kind man. *You* should focus on selling books. That's what you do, isn't it? He doesn't deserve to have you trying to ruin his life."

I was speechless for a few seconds. I'd known I had made a bad impression on the woman the one time we'd spoken on the phone, due to laughing when I realized what Gerald had done with the name of his firm. She hadn't appreciated that, but I hadn't expected the hatred I saw burning behind her eyes. Her defense of him was so strong I nearly asked her if she was his mother.

Her chin quivered, as if in her fury she was near

tears. "You can turn right around and go, ma'am. Mr. Jackson isn't here anyway, and you *don't* have an appointment, nor will I be making you one."

After debating for an uncomfortably long time, I opted to sit in one of the three cushioned chairs arranged against the wall. "I'm sorry you feel that way, but I'll wait until he returns." I wanted to catch Gerald off guard, and there'd be no way to do so if I left the woman. No doubt she'd get right on the phone to warn him.

She bristled. "He's not... Mr. Jackson is... out for the rest of the day."

The woman was such a bad liar I nearly felt sorry for her. "That's okay. I'll wait."

The quiver in her chin strengthened to the point her lips shook. She clenched her teeth so tightly I could see the muscle twitch in her jaw, and then, with another roll, she disappeared behind the computer.

Part of me was tempted to stand once more and reposition so I could see behind her desk, check to see if she was texting Gerald, but I couldn't bring up the nerve. Instead I strained my ears, listening for the tapping of keys or the click of a cell phone. I couldn't hear anything. Then, I did. Sniffling. Was she crying? To my surprise, a wave of guilt washed over me at that, unexpected and unwanted. And, I thought, undeserved. I wasn't trying to hurt her. I wasn't even trying to prove Gerald was guilty of murder. I nearly called out to tell her so, because for some reason, despite the hate in her eyes, she inspired a protective instinct.

Instead I stayed where I was and bent down to unhook Watson's leash. He gave a dramatic shake, eliciting a cloud of dog hair, carrying on like the leash had been wrapped around his entire body. The little grump even peered up at me to make sure I noticed.

If I hadn't been afraid of disturbing the secretary, I would've reminded him he wasn't on a Broadway stage.

After the shake, Watson gave a long catlike stretch, and then padded over to the chair farthest from me and began to turn in circles, clearly getting ready to curl up underneath. But then at another sniff from behind the computer and the intake of a ragged breath, he looked up. Though I shouldn't have been surprised, knowing that despite his grumpy disposition Watson had an instinct for those who needed comforting, I gaped as he stopped in the preparation of his nap, plodded over to the desk, then hesitantly peered around the edge. Another sniff sounded, and Watson disappeared.

The room was silent for nearly a minute and then the soft squeak of wheels drifted to my ears and I had no doubt what had just happened. Watson had worked his magic, and the secretary was probably on her knees, either stroking him or her arms wrapped around him.

The woman's reaction was... over the top and intense. Maybe she really was Gerald's mother, but I didn't think she looked nearly old enough. But to be so overcome by my presence that she was moved to—

Another possibility entered. Why was I instantly assuming mother? Perhaps... lover? That made more sense, given her perceived age, but the idea of Gerald with someone just felt... wrong somehow. I didn't think it was my own repulsion toward the man; he just seemed the type to be alone. The fallout from the article about Gerald was clearly tearing her apart.

After a bit, I stood and quietly walked over to peer behind the computer. What I found was what I'd pictured. The woman was seated on the floor and stroking Watson's fur, not seeming to mind the mess of hair she elicited.

Even with tear streaks on her cheeks, the woman was very well put together. Clean, neat, tidy, every hair in place, the makeup soft and nearly unnoticeable, her faded dress ironed so crisply that even in the middle of the day, there were still sharp creases in the fabric. She was just as put together as Ethel, but the comparison only highlighted the difference between the two women. Everything about Ethel screamed that she practically dripped in wealth. I had the opposite impression of Gerald's secretary. I was willing to bet she had little money and few things but that she took pride in both her possessions and appearance. Maybe too much to assume in such a brief time, but it felt right.

Feeling me staring at her, she looked up, flinched, and with a final pat on Watson's head, stood, using the edge of the desk to help her do so.

His job done, Watson spun, trotted quickly back around the desk, and returned to his chosen napping spot.

"You have a sweet dog." She smiled in his direction, but it faded when she focused back at me. "Gerald is a good, good man. And you're wrong to try to pin this on him."

"I'm not." Maybe I said it because she inspired

that protective instinct, or maybe, *hopefully*, it was more to let her know I hadn't narrowed down my list so much as to not include her if need be. "I *don't* think Gerald killed Birdie."

She flinched again and blinked. "You don't?"

I shook my head. "No, I don't." Why bother elaborating that my list of reasons for thinking that were all rather negative reflections of Gerald?

After studying me for a few seconds, she seemed satisfied and sat back in her rolling chair. "Good. Then maybe you'll help clear his name. I've heard you're smart." She didn't give me a chance to respond before continuing. "I don't know what I would do without Mr. Jackson. When my husband died, he stepped in and practically rescued me. I would've been homeless. Mr. Jackson helped me find a tiny little house that's affordable, paid the first month's rent, and even gave me this job. He may not be perfect, but the things that horrible Birdie woman said were a pack of lies. He wouldn't do such things." She gestured toward the computer. "I would know. I do all his appointments and recordkeeping." She leveled her gaze at me, revealing a flash of strength, before she repeated, "I would know."

"Paulette, will you get—" The door burst open

startling all three of us, and Gerald Jackson hurried in but stopped short when he saw me. His eyes narrowed instantly, and he shifted his glare from me, to Watson, then back to his secretary—Paulette, apparently. "Surely Ms. Page doesn't have an appointment, does she?"

"No, sir." Shame filtered over Paulette's features, but she brightened instantly. "But she's here to help clear your name."

He scoffed. "Yes, you're not the first person to try to tell me that." Gerald's glare returned to me. "Time will tell, but I'm not going to hold my breath." His internal debate was clear, but he surprised me by finally motioning toward the door I assumed led into his office. Or... possibly a drop off over a cliff. "Well, come on, then. Let's get this over with." Gerald motioned and led the way.

With what I hoped was a friendly smile over my shoulder to Paulette, I followed.

Gerald's office was the stereotypical layout for a lawyer. A large mahogany desk was placed two thirds of the way into the small room, in front of a large picture window overlooking the river that ran beside the rainbow slides. Bookcases lined the parallel walls, and there wasn't a blank space on any shelf. With the dark rich colors, stained glass lamp, and large oriental rug, it was easy to forget that G & J Associates was located in a small strip mall.

Gerald plopped down in the large leather chair behind his paper-strewn desk, tossed his briefcase on the corner, and motioned once more, this time toward the two smaller, yet still impressive, leather armchairs in front. "Take a seat, but I'd prefer if the dog stayed on the floor."

Maybe I was being overly sensitive, but I couldn't help but feel the insult of him referring to Watson as simply "the dog." Yes, I knew Watson was a dog, but the locals, especially those who were on friendly terms with my family, all simply referred to him as Watson. Then again, it had been a long time since Gerald and I had been on friendly terms. Not that we'd ever been on good terms exactly, but neutral at one point.

I chose the armchair to the right. Without instruction, Watson sat beside me at attention.

Gerald launched in before I had the chance. "I know Angus thinks you can help, and now clearly you've worked your magic on my secretary, but I'm under no delusions. I'd like to deny that you have any skill in this, but you've proven you can figure things out from time to time. However, you've made your feelings about me very clear, so I can't see why you'd be invested in clearing my name. Other than simply wanting another feather in your hat."

I opened my mouth, getting ready to talk about how I valued honesty and justice over personal squabbles with someone, but discovered I didn't have the energy, or the patience. Instead, I leaned forward slightly. "I won't go in circles with you on how we might feel about each other. It would be pointless and a waste of time. Instead I have some questions, about things in the article and about some new theories that have been raised. You can be honest, or you can lie. Or not answer them at all, I suppose. Whether you trust me to help or not, however, I'm more likely to be able to help if you're honest."

His next internal debate was just as obvious as the first. "Fine, let's—" As he spoke, he reached toward his briefcase, his hand closing around air. He looked over, confused, then sighed. With a shake of his head, he swiveled toward the other corner of his desk, picked up his phone, and punched a button. "Paulette?"

"Yes, Mr. Jackson." Though I couldn't hear her on the other end of the phone, Paulette's voice drifted in through the open door of the office.

Gerald noticed as well and scowled behind me,

then slammed down the phone and raised his voice. "I left my kombucha in my car. Get it, please."

"Yes, Mr. Jackson." Unlike Gerald, Paulette's voice didn't raise, and a few seconds later, I could hear the clack of her shoes and the opening and closing of the front door.

I almost marveled at him. There he was, under scrutiny, partly for his use of cannabis-infused kombucha, and Gerald didn't seem to let it faze him. Some of Birdie's article came back, where she'd hinted that the local lawyer might have an addiction. I'd say that was more of the truth behind it than any bravado on Gerald's part.

He refocused on me. "So, what are these new theories?"

I'd ask about the kombucha later, if our time together didn't go south before then. "Just different scenarios, involving the possibility of it being a setup. If Birdie Sutton was truly murdered, could it have been made to look like you were the killer? Granted, that's a little far-fetched, as you admitted yourself you were there that evening, and you brought the jars of kombucha to soften her up. It's not like they were planted there by someone else."

"Sounds like you've already made up your mind that me being set up isn't really a theory at all."

Gerald pushed up his glasses and wiped the sweat off his shiny brow as he leaned back into the chair and folded his arms. "So why bother?"

He surprised me; maybe I surprised myself. Gerald was right. Though I hadn't realized it, some part of me *had* discarded that theory. It was clear Ethel hated him enough to do so, but something about it just didn't click. And as far as setups went, what had anyone actually set up at all? Gerald had admitted he was there.

Regrouping, I twisted the question. "Even so, let's play with it for a second. Let's say you were set up to look guilty. Who hates you enough to frame you for murder?"

"Ethel Beaker, of course." Gerald didn't hesitate. "And the feeling is mutual, clearly."

Before I could respond, the outer office door opened and closed, and Paulette's steps filled the space. She entered Gerald's office, holding a large thermos in each hand, and walked around his desk to place them beside him, all the while casting a gentle expression toward Watson. "Here you go, sir."

"Thank you, Paulette." It was more of a dismissal than an actual thank-you, and he called after her as she walked away. "Please remember to shut the door."

She did so without another word.

"Who else besides Ethel?" I pushed, trying to get us back on track. "She's the obvious choice."

Gerald didn't answer, instead unscrewing the top of one of the thermoses and then taking a long drink, followed by a sigh that would have better accompanied a man lost in the desert finally discovering water. No doubt Birdie's addiction accusation had been accurate. After a few moments, Gerald blinked, seemingly remembering he wasn't alone. Clearing his throat, he looked at me again. "I'm sorry, what was that?"

"Who else might try to set you up besides Ethel? What other enemies have you made? Who's angry at you?"

"Ms. Page, I'm a renowned lawyer. Since your father was a detective, I'm certain you know how this goes. In any legal case, there are winners and losers. One side always leaves the courtroom angry. If you want to know how many enemies I have, simply count the cases I've represented, and then look at the opposite sides. You'll find quite a list." He took another sip, a quick one. "But I'm more inclined to think along the lines of Angus. Maybe you should do what he told you to do. Not focus on me but on

Birdie. *She's* the one who's dead. Figure out who *her* enemies were, not mine."

I had to bite my tongue at his reference of Angus telling me what to do. I'd learned how fruitless it was to expect any enlightenment from Gerald. Instead I let my anger at him guide my next question. "Well, then, let's start at suspect number one. You."

Gerald had been midsip, and as he straightened in offense, kombucha splashed out of the thermos and over the front of his shirt and tie. When he spoke, there was a dangerous edge to his voice, one I wasn't sure I'd heard before. "I knew it. Angus, Paulette, and the rest of the town can think whatever they want about you. You've gotten it into your craw that you don't like me, that you think you're better than me, more enlightened. You're ready to hang me from the gallows without a shred of proof. You won't mind making something up to get me there."

I started to defend myself at his accusation, but it had been less than ten seconds before that I had thought that very thing, how Gerald was unenlightened. "If you really feel that way, then take away any ammunition I might have. Birdie laid out the case against you in her column. So refute it." As my voice rose, I noticed Watson stand, as if preparing to come to my defense. I flung a hand toward the thermoses.

"What about those? Clearly you have a substance abuse issue. Who's your supplier?"

"Let me refresh you on law, Fred. Marijuana can't be sold in Estes Park, but it's entirely legal to have it in your possession and to consume it." He leaned forward slightly, and again there was that dangerous quality to his tone. "And as far as my supplier? The same place *your* stepfather used to get his stock of edibles he enjoyed."

Score one for Gerald. Not to be outdone, I leaned forward as well. "Barry no longer goes to the Green Munchies. And if you recall, it ended up having ties to the Irons family, or at least some of its employees did." Though I'd intended it as an accusation at Gerald, a chill ran down my spine, all of it way too close to home.

"I have no ties to the Irons family." Gerald's eyes went suddenly cold. "*I* didn't kill your daddy, Winifred."

I flinched, reeling back like I'd been slapped.

Gerald gave a similar motion, as if surprised at himself. "I'm sorry. That was—"

I didn't give him the chance. I didn't care, just went on the attack. "Maybe you do, maybe you don't. And while I wouldn't be willing to invest a cent in one of your ridiculous schemes, I'd bet every dime I have that Birdie was right, that you have ties to underground organizations, the mob, a gang, *something*. I'd even be willing to bet you didn't know what you were getting into when it started." The look that crossed his face, mingled with the memory of Angus's words the day before, made me confident in what I threw at him, despite the anger that motivated my words. "Even your best friend tried to warn you off some of the investments—he said so himself. How deep were you when you realized who you were dealing with and that you couldn't get out? How close to the truth was Birdie? Were you tangling other people up in these *investments* so you could get rich, or because you were afraid for your life?"

He took another sip, his hand and thermos trembling so much that more dribbled over his shirt. "You don't know what you're talking about."

The phone rang, causing Gerald to flinch again and spill more kombucha.

I kept going. "How deep are you, Gerald? I don't think you killed Birdie, but what about the organization that has their claws in you? Did they take her out because of the article?" The phone rang again, but I ignored it. "Are you worried you're next on their list?"

Gerald didn't respond, only gave a painful-looking swallow.

He was afraid. Clearly. And it confirmed everything in Birdie's smear piece. When the phone rang again and he reached for it, a wave of nausea washed over me. If it was true, then in some way, shape, or form, even if Gerald didn't realize it, he was tied to the Irons family.

He lifted the phone and opened his lips but couldn't seem to make any words come out.

There was a basic awareness of Paulette's voice saying Gerald's name on the other end of the line, but I barely noticed. "Are they connected to you throwing cases? Is the Irons family forcing you to intentionally lose, or is it your own scheme to get rich from insurance companies at the cost of your clients?"

Watson whimpered, clearly uncomfortable hearing me so upset.

Gerald shook his head. His voice barely a whisper. "No, those aren't connected. My investments have nothing to do with my agreements with insurance companies. That was long before—" His eyes went wide, realizing what he'd admitted. "It's not how it sounds. I—" Gerald started to rush ahead, then remembered the receiver in his hand, looking at it as if he wasn't sure what it was. "Hello? Who is this?"

I couldn't make out a sound on the other end.

Gerald raised his voice, panicking. "Hello?"

Though I still couldn't hear a response, Gerald relaxed. "Oh, Paulette. Yes. What is it?" He paled at her response and nodded. He shook his head again, clearly realizing Paulette couldn't see his response. "Sorry. Yes, put him through."

I wanted to keep pushing, punch away at what he'd just admitted, but feared he'd demand that I leave. Though I suddenly realized I'd been completely forgotten anyway.

Gerald took a deep, shaky breath, as if trying to calm himself, and when he spoke, he almost sounded like himself. "Marlon. What can I do for you?"

It took a second for the name to register. Chief Dunmore. And Gerald was nervous.

Though that had been true, a smile broke across his face, and the nerves seemed to disappear. As they did, he also seemed to remember I was there, and he turned a victorious gaze on me. He hit a button on the phone console and then twisted fully toward me, a defiant lift to his chin as he spoke into the air. "Sorry, Marlon, I'm not sure I caught that. Could you please repeat what you said?"

"Of course." Chief Dunmore's voice filled the room. Even from those two words, I could tell he was on the job. "Ms. Sutton's autopsy came back, at least enough of it. It's been ruled an accidental death. Possibly suicide, but more than likely, accidental."

Gerald's triumphant beaming increased, and though he spoke to Chief Dunmore, his gaze locked on mine. "So, *no one* killed Birdie. Least of all me."

When there was a hesitation on the other end, Gerald glanced back toward the phone.

"Well... mostly." Though Dunmore's voice remained professional, an apologetic quality seeped in, the kind used when breaking bad news to a friend. "The toxicology report on Sutton's blood was part of the autopsy, of course. The levels of THC in her system were outrageously high. Maybe not if she was an avid user, but from all indications, she wasn't. It was the equivalent to being poisoned. So... considering you provided the cannabis-laced kombucha—"

In a panic, Gerald hit the button he'd pressed before, and cut me off from whatever else Chief Dunmore said. As he smashed the receiver against the side of his face, Gerald swiveled around in his chair toward the window and lowered his voice. Even so, I could still hear him. "Yes, I've increased the potency of my recipe, but I guarantee you it's still safe, even for the nonconsumer, taken in the right dosage."

There was a pause.

"I didn't *force* the idiot woman to drink them all at once. She hadn't even tried a sip when I left."

Another pause.

"Are you planning on taking me in? Do I need to call my—"

Dunmore must've cut Gerald off.

After a few moments, Gerald nodded. "Okay, thank you. I appreciate you letting me know." He swiveled back around as he spoke. "I'll contact my lawyer so he's prepared to—" His words cut off as he noticed me and Watson again. His face reddened. "Sorry, Marlon. I need to call you back." Without waiting, he hung up the phone and looked at me. "You heard him yourself. Birdie wasn't murdered."

I gaped at him, almost laughing. "Yeah. I also heard what did kill her."

"I need you to leave, Ms. Page. I've a long list of things to do today."

"Starting with calling your lawyer." I couldn't help myself.

Instead of responding, Gerald picked up the phone once more and punched a button. "Paulette, can you get the police chief back on the phone. It looks like we may need to have Ms. Page and her dog escorted from the premises."

I stood, offering Gerald a cold smile. "You needn't bother. From the way it sounds, you have much bigger problems to deal with than the local bookseller and her dog." Spinning, I tapped my thigh. "Come on, Watson. Let's leave Mr. Jackson to enjoy the fruits of his harvest."

ELEVEN

The soft pink of the sunrise glistened in the dew coating the aspen leaves and making its way down the pine needles. Actually, I wasn't sure if they were dewdrops or remnants of an early morning rain, but either way, the mountainside surrounding my cabin was even more magical than normal. As if the beauty wasn't enough, several yards away a mother elk and her calf stood grazing at the opening of a small clearing, taking space from the rest of the herd that remained in the trees. White spots speckling the baby's tan hide seemed to echo the dewdrops.

My hand rose of its own accord, resting at the base of my throat, causing the end of Watson's leash to brush against my chin. I started to speak, to whisper to Leo how I couldn't imagine ever getting used to this—even though by this point I'd literally seen thousands and thousands of elk, it never got old. But I couldn't bear to break the silence, so I simply stood, my other hand linked with his, warmth cutting through what remained of the morning chill from where our shoulders pressed together, and stared. It was rare that more than a couple of days would go by without me being hit with a wave of gratitude for the life I was living. I hoped I never took it for granted.

A low rumble issued from Watson, and I hissed at him, not taking my eyes away from the elk. "Be still, buddy."

Leo chuckled. "You're not going to want to take on a mama elk, Watson. She'd make a herd of stampeding elephants look like a parade of poodles." He squeezed my hand. "I never get tired of this. I wondered if I would. It's my job after all, I'm surrounded day after day. But it only seems to get better. How could anyone—"

That time, Watson's rumble was accompanied by him darting away, catching me off guard. His leash whipped free, and I made a desperate grab at it, missing.

"Watson! Don't!" A lick of fear washed through me as I yelled. A corgi was a strong herding dog, but no match for the angry, protective hooves of a mother elk.

In unison, Leo and I both darted after him, the peace of the morning shattered.

Watson made it about three feet before darting left, doing a zigzag around the bush. He came to an abrupt stop at a large pile of rocks and stuffed his nose into a crevice, then reared back with a disgruntled huff.

Confused, I looked back and forth from the rock pile to the mother and baby elk speeding away toward the protection of the herd.

Leo caught on before I did, laughing as he caught up with Watson and snagging the end of his leash. "What are you going to do with the chipmunk if you caught it? Bring it home and use it like your stuffed lion and duck to be a new bedtime buddy?"

A chipmunk. With a final glance toward the herd, I attempted to slow my adrenaline. "I swear, I can't figure him out. Nine times out of ten, he just stares at the chipmunks like they're putting on a mildly entertaining skit for his enjoyment, and then, when I least expect it, Watson proves he can do more than eat and sleep."

He stuffed his muzzle back into the crevice, huffed once more, and looked back at me with a pitiful whimper.

"I know, buddy. You just wanted a friend." I bent slightly, stroking the side of his face with the back of my fingers. "You scared me to death. I thought we were going to have a trampled-corgi situation."

"Me too." Leo let out a shudder, shaking off his nerves and glancing toward the rising sun. "I suppose we should get back. You need to get down to the Cozy Corgi soon."

"Probably so." Letting him guide Watson, I slipped my hand back into Leo's again, and we headed back the way we'd come on the makeshift trail. While I didn't think I'd ever grow tired of the Colorado majesty, as it typically did, it faded from my mind as other thoughts tumbled and started to swirl. "I think the theory you came up with last night was probably spot-on. With as much as Gerald drinks his kombucha, he'd have to steadily increase the amount of marijuana in it, or... THC—" I shrugged, not knowing how brewing kombucha worked or the finer details of drug use. "—whatever would make it more potent."

"No doubt." Leo continued the conversation we'd had the night before as if no time had passed. "That's how it works. He would have to steadily keep building it up in order to have a steady effect. That's true with all drug use, of the legal and illegal variety. It's part of the reason there are so many over-doses when a person relapses. They go back to whatever level they were at when they stopped, but now they're clean and not used to it, it's too much for their system, and they can't handle it."

There was a darker tone to Leo's words that indicated personal experience rather than textbook knowledge, and I slowed slightly, looking at him in concern.

He didn't need an explanation and just shrugged one of his shoulders. "Family... old... *friends*, I guess you could say. You know."

I didn't know, not really. I was aware of Leo's past in broad, sweeping generalities. Knew there was hurt and darkness there. And while I didn't feel like he was hiding anything, or lying, when Leo spoke about his past, it often reminded me of what people said about soldiers returning from a war. It was a different world, one they experienced alone... well, with their fellow soldiers... but with outsiders, they might as well have experienced that alone. As before, though tempted, I didn't push for details. Leo would tell me when he was ready.

Even so, I started to ask him if he was okay, but before I could, he pushed on. "Actually, I've considered that since we spoke last night. I think that's what was happening to Carl on July Fourth. If we're right, which it sounds like we are, and Gerald's been increasing the potency of his kombucha, I'm willing to bet Carl was reacting to the stronger batch. And though there's a lot of assumption here, I'd say it's probably a safe bet that Carl doesn't indulge nearly to Gerald's level but enough that the kombucha isn't dangerous to him, so it has a more drug-like effect on him."

Leo's theory caused Carl's strange behavior the other night to push aside my concerns about Leo's past. "That makes complete sense. And if we follow that train of thought, and Chief Dunmore was correct and Birdie was either an infrequent or a first-time user, it could prove extremely dangerous for her."

"Exactly." Leo did a little dance as Watson darted forward, threatening to tangle his leash around Leo's legs when we rounded the corner, bringing my cabin into view. Managing to stay upright, Leo cast an indulgent smile to where Watson strained at the end of the leash and continued. "From the impression you got from Gerald's end of the conversation, it sounds like Birdie had more than one jar of the stuff." His brows knitted. "Although, that seems kind of strangely intentional. If she wasn't an avid user, why would she decide to go from zero to sixty?"

I considered for a moment as we crossed the clearing near the porch. "I think that was just her personality, or at least the way she drank... in general. Katie mentioned that she'd never seen anyone drink so much coffee so quickly. It sounded like Birdie just sat there, pounding away on her computer, and literally drank coffee after coffee as if it was water... or air." I pulled out the keys and started to unlock the door, Watson prancing at my feet, ready to be inside. "If she sat down and started to write her next article or make final edits... whatever... after Gerald left and started to drink the kombucha like she would coffee, then I can see her going through several. And from what I understand, ingesting marijuana in different ways causes the effect to alter. Maybe it took longer for her to feel high. I suppose it could have felt like she truly was just drinking water or some form of lemonade or whatever and had already consumed two or three of them before she felt anything strange." I paused once more when we were inside, something not adding up. "Although... it seemed as if Dunmore is considering either an accident or suicide. Why suicide? I'll call Susan on the way into town, see if I can get any details out of her."

"I bet he thinks she jumped over the balcony... or

fell over." Leo sounded as if that was obvious. "If she was high and accidentally tripped over the railing somehow then that's an accident. If she jumped, thinking she could fly or..." His eyes narrowed and he shook his head. "I was going to say that would be suicide, and maybe that's what he's thinking, but really, that's still an accident."

Watson disappeared into the bedroom, then returned and trotted to the fireplace with his stuffed duck clamped in his mouth. The fire wasn't lit, but he settled in on the hearth, rested his head on the fuzzy yellow stuffed animal, and fell instantly to sleep.

"Looks like you were right. Watson did want the chipmunk to join his stuffed-animal collection." I smiled at him and then to Leo, though my thoughts returned to Birdie. Had she been finishing up the article about me as she'd downed jar after jar of kombucha? Was Dunmore right? It was no longer a murder but simply an accident? Her accusations from the day before her death flitted through my mind. Tying Gerald to drugs, investment schemes, insurance fraud, gangs, the mob... possibly the Irons family. Unaware I'd even crossed the room, I plopped down in the overstuffed armchair beside the fire, where I typically sat to read before bed. Still thinking, I let my gaze travel over the Watson memorabilia gathered on the mantle. The photo of him and his Cozy Corgi sweatshirt, the various likenesses of him—the whittled in wood figure given by Duncan Diamond, the knitted version given by Angus Witt. The tintype photo of Watson and me dressed in 1920s garb.

"What if...?" I hesitated, for some reason afraid to say it out loud. "Birdie made some pretty big accusations against Gerald." I tore my gaze from all the Watsons on the mantle and looked at Leo. "And not just about Gerald, but about the Irons family too. Maybe she got a little closer to the truth than they liked."

"*They* being the Irons family, not Gerald?" Leo sat on the sofa, his arms resting on his knees as he stared over at me.

"Maybe..." Again, I returned to the mantle, letting all the little Watsons fade in and out of focus as I considered, drifting back through all that had occurred since moving to Estes Park. All the seemingly random events that had turned out to be connected. Maybe this one was as well. But where to start? Where to turn? Then it hit me. "The Green Munchies."

"What?"

I turned back to Leo again, and as I answered his confusion, my clarity solidified. "The Green Munchies, the pot shop in Lyons. I'm not saying it's involved, but it's the only connection we have to the Irons family, at least the only one that is present and accounted for. Maybe there are some answers there."

"Fred..." Leo grimaced and hesitated, almost sounding apologetic when he spoke next. "If that place is still connected to the Irons family, which I don't know how likely that is, given all the reporting that happened after Branson and Chief Briggs were revealed to be who they were, I can't imagine the Irons family would still involved there once it was made public that they had ties to the place where the murder occurred. The FBI has got to have them under surveillance, right?"

I considered, then nodded. "Yeah. I bet you're right." I started to let it go but couldn't. "It's probably going to be a complete waste of time. But I think I'm going to go down there once I close the bookshop today. Just talk to whoever's working, see if anything triggers or something feels off."

"Fred..." Leo repeated my name, the apology still in his voice. "If they are involved, then you're putting yourself in..."

When he hesitated, I knew where he was going.

Getting ready to ask me not to go, to stay away from it. Unlike Branson, from what felt like a lifetime ago already, I knew Leo wouldn't demand or insist. And his request would make it all that much harder to deny him.

His eyes narrowed once more, and he cocked his head, clearly changing directions. When he spoke, his voice was a bit brighter. "How about this? And I know I'm asking a favor, but how about you either take the morning off from the Cozy Corgi and I go with you—I'd offer to call off at the park tonight, but I can't. Or we could go tomorrow evening when we're both off." He raised his hands, as if in surrender. "I know you can handle yourself. I'm not saying that. I'll just be a nervous wreck—"

I'd already stood and crossed the room, and I cut him off by placing both hands on his cheeks and kissing him. Then I pulled back slightly. "I love you."

A baffled smirk played over his lips. "I love you too, but what'd I do to bring that on?"

"You're just you." I gave him another quick kiss and sat beside him on the couch. "And you let me be me, even if me being me causes you worry." I pulled out my cell phone. "I know they won't mind, but let me call Katie. If she and Ben are okay with it, I'll go in later."

. . .

If I'd hoped the half hour drive from Estes Park to Lyons would provide any inspiration on where to begin other than the hope something would be triggered or feel off, I was sorely disappointed. As I pulled the Mini Cooper into a parking spot in front of the Green Munchies, I didn't have the hint of a plan. I'd even lost some of the initial fire behind the impulse.

Watson, however, was on cloud nine, and very atypically ungrumpy. Perhaps he'd been excited to postpone his mascot duties at the Cozy Corgi or, more likely, was reveling at spending the morning with Leo. It never ceased to amaze me that even with all the time Leo spent with us, every occasion with Leo was like the corgi version of catnip. Of course, I couldn't quite blame Watson for his reaction. Turned out, Leo was the Fred version of catnip as well.

Leo paused at the front door and glanced over his shoulder to where I still stood by the car. "You okay? You've got a strange look. What are you thinking?"

I felt my cheeks burn, and I waved him off. "Oh, nothing. Just... trying to come up with a plan." Putting a little get-up in my step, I quickly joined

Leo and Watson on the porch and gestured for him to open the door. "Let's wing it."

Though things had been rearranged since I'd been in before, which seemed like a lifetime ago, the Green Munchies still felt like the combination of an Apple computer store and a fancy bakery. Everything was sleek, modern, and expensive. One side of the store was artfully arranged with endless marijuana paraphernalia, tools, and equipment, all of them as foreign to me as if I'd been dropped into a chemist's lab. On the other, the section was divided in half, with one wall taken up by a brightly lit glass display case, showing endless types of dried cannabis in various forms. Some of them looked like ground-up oregano, others like dried balls of seaweed. The mirroring case offered a selection of baked goods that would've made Katie proud. Fancy bars of chocolate, thick brownies, assortments of candy, beautifully decorated cupcakes, and cookies—all containing an ingredient Katie left out of her creations at the Cozy Corgi.

When I noticed the tall woman standing behind the bakery portion, I realized the shop had one more comparison that hadn't been present before when the late Eddie had worked there. Not only was it one part Apple store, one part bakery, but with the beautiful, voluptuous blond, it was one part Victoria's Secret. Her sapphire-blue gaze slid over me as if I was a ghost and landed on my park ranger.

Leo was winding Watson's leash around his hand, making it shorter. "For sure don't want you getting into anything in here. That could spell disaster."

"Actually, we do have a very small collection of dog treats with minuscule traces of CBD oil in them. All the benefit"—her voice, as sultry as her appearance, dipped when Leo faced her—"none of the fun."

He flinched—maybe at her beauty, maybe at her directness, or both—then stood. "I wasn't aware they made that for animals. But Watson's good. He gets enough tr... er... *snacks* as it is." When he glanced my way, holding his hand out to me, there was no blush in his cheeks as had been in mine only moments before, and not even a hint of being self-conscious. "I think we'll pass on giving Watson that experience."

"I agree." I stepped closer, slipping my hand into his, then met the woman's eyes, and *I* was the one who faltered. "Sorry. I'm a little nervous. We're from out of state, and... people don't really do things like this where we're from."

Leo's hand twitched in mine, but he didn't try to correct my mistake.

Why had I said that? Talk about foot-in-mouth disease. If the Green Munchies was part of the Irons family, there was no doubt anyone working here would know about me. Even if it wasn't, plenty of people in Lyons visited Estes Park all the time. The woman could've come into the Cozy Corgi or read about us in the paper. It wasn't like Watson and I didn't stick out in a crowd.

"We get a lot of that. Trust me, I won't steer you wrong." The woman chuckled, and as she spoke, her gaze slid past me one more time, finding Leo. "I'm Danielle, and I'll be your budtender. Where would you like to start?"

Still kicking myself, I remained silent, hoping Leo would take the lead, figure out how to navigate around my mistake. Though no plan had been in place, I would've defaulted to my normal direct approach. But now there was no way I could inquire about Gerald or how cannabis could be used in kombucha.

Rising to the task, Leo gestured toward the bakery case. "Definitely something like this. Neither of us smoke anything at all, so the idea of inhaling doesn't sound appealing. But dessert... that we can do. Is that a good starting point?"

"Absolutely. A lot of people feel that way."

Danielle slid open the case, pulled out the plate of perfectly arranged, elaborately decorated, chocolate-covered strawberries, and once more only had eyes for Leo. "You do have to be careful. Take these, for example. If they were the boring chocolate-covered strawberries, you could eat as many as you want, but for someone who hasn't partaken before, no more than one, at least for a few hours, to judge your reaction. In edibles, it can take a while for the effects to arrive." She leaned forward on the counter, not trying to hide the fact she was highlighting her cleavage. "For a man as well-built as you, for instance, it will go through your system differently because of your metabolism and muscle mass than it would for —" She flicked her wrist my way. "—her, and her slower metabolism, or—" She gestured down her body. "—little old me." Given that she was barely two inches shorter than I was, there was no doubt as to her implication.

For the first time, Leo bristled and almost broke character.

Before he could come to my defense, I finally jumped in. "Would that be true if you put it in liquid form... adding it to..." I shrugged as if struggling to come up with an example. "Hot tea, wine, or an energy drink?"

She finally leveled a stare at me but didn't answer my question. "Unfortunately, we don't sell any cannabis-infused drinks. But I do have a chocolate cake that looks like it would be something you would enjoy. There's also some candy that's easily—"

"Danielle!" a voice called from the back, and as it continued, grew louder. "That shipment is supposed to be here in about half an hour or so. Do you want me to..." A young man stepped through the door that led to the storeroom. I'd been through that particular door before, and as he stared at us, I couldn't help but wonder if he knew there'd been a dead body back there at one point. Unlike Danielle, the man barely looked at Leo, instead focusing on me, glancing down at Watson, then back up at me. "Oh... you. That Estes Park bookshop lady. You're here."

"Tommy!" Danielle bit out the man's name, all sultriness evaporating and those blue eyes turning to ice. "You're mistaken. This couple is visiting from out of state. Go back and wait—"

"No, she's—" He broke off at Danielle's glare.

"Actually..." Making a quick decision, I kept my attention trained on Danielle's face. "He's right. I am the bookshop lady from Estes. I wasn't honest with you before."

"Oh, really?" Danielle didn't meet my eyes.

"Well... that's okay. We..." She darted a disgust-filled glance at Tommy and back once more. "We have quite a few customers from Estes Park, more than a few of them want to keep things discreet." Finally her gaze lifted to mine, and she smiled, one that almost seemed relieved. "I'm sure that's your situation. Don't give it a second thought."

Beside me, I could feel Leo start to speak, and I squeezed his hand, stopping him, wanting to have another heartbeat or so to judge what I thought I sensed.

The corner of Danielle's smile faltered, and she moved from side to side for a second before addressing Tommy. "Go wait for the shipment."

She'd known I was lying the entire time. No doubt. I could feel it, which could only mean one thing. But unfortunately, it also meant I wouldn't get any clearer answers than if I'd stayed with the tourist-from-out-of-state angle. Even so, since my cover was blown, might as well push and see what other reaction I got.

"That's not why either. I'll be direct." I released Leo's hand and moved toward the counter, though I wasn't tempted to offer a cleavage-highlighting move. Behind me, I heard Watson's nails click on the floor as he joined me. "Tommy was right. I do own a bookshop, but I also look into murders. I know that probably sounds strange."

She blinked, unsure what to say, and solidified my earlier suspicion further.

"I'm investigating, I suppose you could say, a death that involves cannabis-laced kombucha." I debated which direction to go, even though I knew I wouldn't get a straight answer. As typical, I went with the most direct route possible. "Does Gerald Jackson get any of his supply through you?"

She straightened, and with a lift of her chin returned to her normal self. "As I told you when I thought you were here for genuine purposes, our clients' privacy is of the utmost importance. I will neither confirm nor deny anyone who shops here."

I pushed again... just to see. "Okay then, do you or the Green Munchies have any connection to the Irons family?"

The infinitesimal flinch was barely noticeable, but it was there. Danielle started to shake her head, and then maybe realized I'd noticed and changed directions. "It does not. I know of the store's past and of the... questionable activities that went on here. I can promise you, neither I, nor the Green Munchies has any connection, in any way, shape, or form, to any crime syndicates." I started to speak, but she cut me off. "Since you're not here for product, and even though you may look into deaths occasionally, and you are not the police, I'm afraid I'm going to have to ask you all to leave."

Some of my frustration with her, and if I was honest, at myself for my reaction to her at the beginning, took over. "If you know what happened here before, then you're also aware there were people who paid the ultimate price for their involvement with the Irons family."

Her perfect chin pointed just a little higher as her sapphire-blue eyes looked down her scoped nose. "You and your dog are barking up the wrong tree, I'm afraid. Surely you realize with all that went down here before, if there was even a hint of something illegal occurring, the FBI would crash down on us like lightning."

At her mention of the FBI, I couldn't hold back a flinch of my own. Though I tried not to, I darted a glance toward Leo. Hadn't he said that very thing less than an hour before?

"Now, again, I'm afraid I'll have to ask you to leave." She looked from me, to Watson, and then to Leo, and for once, there was no flirtation in her gaze. "All of you."

. . .

The three of us piled into the car and were headed back to Estes within moments before I turned to Leo, whose lap Watson occupied, as he'd refused to get into the backseat. "Well, we don't have any confirmation on Gerald, or Birdie for that matter, but it's clear Danielle knew who we were the entire time and played along."

Leo, proving he'd been on the same page, didn't need any explanation. "And from Tommy's reaction, they'd obviously been warned you and Watson might make an appearance."

"Which means..." I felt a chill pass through me, despite the warm July sun coming in through the windshield. "They *are* connected with the Irons family. I'm not sure if I find being aware of that helpful or terrifying."

"I know what you mean." Leo focused outside on the road, his voice distant as he stroked Watson, adding to the ever-present layer of dog hair inside the Mini Cooper. "What we don't know is if this indicates the FBI isn't watching, if they're waiting to gather more evidence, or if the Irons family has FBI connections as well."

Watson and I were nearly to the door of the Cozy Corgi when loud cat-calling across the street caught my attention. Two twentysomething women had just emerged from Cabin and Hearth and were waving frantically in my direction. Thrown off, I halted where I stood, nearly causing a man staring at his phone to collide with me as he walked from the other direction. Sidestepping him, I glanced back at the women and finally understood as I caught the words *cute, fuzzy butt* drift across the street while the woman on the right squeezed her hands together in excitement like a five-year-old at a birthday party. I grinned down at Watson.

"You appear to have been discovered by more members of corgi fandom."

Not bothering to look up at me, he merely glowered at the commotion across the street, and then trotted the other way, pulling at the end of the leash when he was stopped just shy of the front door.

There was more *cooing* and *ahhing* from the women, probably at getting a perfect view of the *cute, fuzzy butt* in question.

Deciding to meet him halfway, I pointed from Watson to the Cozy Corgi sign and gestured into the bookshop before giving a friendly wave and following Watson's lead. If the women were truly corgi fans, they'd be over in a matter of moments. If so, Ben or I would probably be able to sell them a book or two from the corgi section—cultivated for just such occasions—and would owe Watson a bucketload of treats for the flourish of attention he'd have to endure. I couldn't even blame Watson's grumpy disposition for not enjoying such adoration. The true corgi fans were rather intense, and even I found the obsession of fuzzy butts a little awkward. Sure, a fluffy corgi bottom was cute enough, I supposed, but I was much more drawn to the pointy ears, the judgmental chocolate eyes, and the stubborn, food-obsessed personality. Or maybe I'd simply found myself in dog form.

Sure enough, before Watson had settled into his sunshiny napping spot and I'd barely begun to thank Ben for covering yet again, the women burst through the door in a whirlwind of giggles. After a quick scan of the bookshop, they made a beeline toward Watson. I started to head that way, then noticed Carl Hanson over their shoulders, staring out the window of Cabin and Hearth. His depression was palpable from across the street. I changed directions on a whim, and abandoned Watson to his fate. Luckily, I was certain Ben would intervene for him before the women attempted to snap selfies with Watson's fuzzy butt.

Deciding not to question if my impulse to visit the Hansons was more in an effort to ease the dark cloud over the shop, or to take advantage of the situation for more insight, I simply gave in to the plan and hurried up to the bakery.

Katie and Nick were in the rhythm of things, and I marveled at the easy team the two of them made. The bakery was still busy, considering the breakfast rush was over by so late in the morning, but the easy flow of baking and customer service was a seamless dance between them.

I only allowed a couple of seconds to admire before stepping to the counter and catching Katie's attention. Her brown eyes widened, and she hurried over. "What did you find out? Fill me in."

"Nothing specific and nothing definite." I

glanced behind, checking for ears, and sure enough one of the tourists stood from his table and headed our way with a coffee mug. "I'll fill you in later. There's too much to say at the moment, but this whole thing may be bigger and deeper connected than we figured."

"Deeper connected?" The line between her brows had barely begun to form before it smoothed again and she breathed out a whisper, "The Irons family?"

"Maybe. You're a quick one, Katie Pizzolato." I couldn't help but smile as I shrugged. "But like I said, I'll fill you in soon. In the meantime, could I get an assortment of your empanadas to go?"

That time, her eyes narrowed. "Bribery?"

"See? You're quick, like I said." I smirked. "In this case, I prefer to think of it as a combination of a friendly gesture and a loosening of lips through the perfection of the world's most wonderful baker."

"The flattery wasn't needed." Katie winked even as she started selecting the glossy, golden empanadas. "But since it's true, I'll take it and let it pacify me until I can get the details."

. . .

"One minute!" Carl's voice rang out from somewhere in the back as Watson and I walked into Cabin and Hearth.

I crossed through the path formed by a high-end log buffet set and a collection of log lamps with tawny leather shades and placed the saran-wrapped tray of empanadas on the counter. A quick scan of the shop revealed no tourists and neither of the Hansons. Giving in to another impulse, and with a little tickle of guilt, I hurried back down the trail and slid the deadbolt as quietly as I could. The empanada endeavor would have a higher chance of being productive if we weren't interrupted.

Watson glared at me as I returned, still furious over being abandoned to the administrations of the corgi fan club. Before I could attempt reparations again, Carl emerged from the back and halted as soon as he saw us. He swallowed and shook his head as if warding off a bad dream, and then his gaze landed on the tray of empanadas and his headshake transitioned to a sigh of defeat. "You're an evil woman, Winifred Page. You know my weakness and you take full advantage."

I didn't try to deny it. "Katie sent over two kinds. Mincemeat and cherry."

Carl groaned as he peeled back the plastic and

took a deep sniff. "You're evil, but thank God for you. Or at least for Katie." Without trying to determine which was which, he snagged the nearest one, took a bite, sending a shower of golden pastry crumbs over the counter, and groaned again. "Heaven."

Watson whimpered from where he sat with his back toward me, trying to peer up over the counter at Carl and then craning to see toward the back, clearly expecting to find Anna rushing toward him, laden with his favorite all-natural dog bone treat.

"Oh, Watson, I'm sorry." Carl spoke through another spray of crumbs. "How rude of me. Anna would skin me alive if she was here. I'll be right back." Still clutching the empanada, he started to return the way he'd come.

"It's okay." I reached over, touching Carl's arm, stopping him. "I brought some, Katie just finished baking them." I pulled two of the large treats from the pocket of my brown broomstick skirt and offered them to Watson.

His grumpy eyes went wide, and it was a testament to how irritated he'd been that he hadn't caught the scent as we crossed the street. Opening his mouth wide, he managed to grab them both at the same time. The top one nearly slipped free, but like the fuzzy shark Watson was, he lunged and secured it determinably. Whirling, he practically pranced across the shop and wriggled beneath the log bed he frequently chose as his private snack location.

I watched him disappear without a flicker of guilt at the double portion of treats. He'd more than earned it by fulfilling his morning roles of both puppy detective and mascot.

When I turned back to Carl, he was on his second empanada. "I can't decide which kind I like better. One is like a main course and the other dessert."

"Luckily, with six of each, you don't have to. Although I suppose you will have to share." Before I finished the thought, I caught my own mistake. There'd never been a time when Watson was present that Anna hadn't rushed to greet him. "You indicated Anna isn't here, didn't you?"

He nodded, and even as he took another bite, the brightness that had sparked in him at the sight of the empanadas dimmed, and he seemed to deflate over the counter. "Left for Florida this morning. She's going to spend a day or two with Betsy and little Timothy." As always, Carl didn't mention their youngest daughter's husband and father of their grandchild. "She said she... needed some space."

Despite their bickering and Anna's controlling,

often cutting, mannerisms with her husband, the two of them were peas in a pod and inseparable. It surprised me that she left without him, especially after asking me to look into things. "Did… something else happen between the two of you?" I didn't have to adjust my tone or anything. The Hansons were friends, and I cared more about their marriage than gathering any clues. "Are you okay?"

"We…" Carl had started to pick up a third empanada but placed it back on the tray and met my gaze, clearly knowing I was asking as a friend. "We had a… disagreement last night, I suppose you could say. She wants me to cut off all contact with Gerald, and not just the investments and the kombucha, but… everything."

Once more I stretched out my hand and placed it on his arm, offering support, not really knowing what to say.

Apparently, it was enough, as Carl continued, "He's my friend. Has been for decades." He shook his head and stared off into the shop, though I got the sense he was seeing the years pass by and not any of the furniture. "But… I can't deny Anna has a point. I don't want to believe it, but… maybe Gerald's not exactly the man I always thought he was."

It was exactly the reason I'd come over, and I

took a second to remind myself to balance snooping and friendship. Then realized that because of that friendship, and Anna's request, the two were really one and the same. "You think some of the things Birdie wrote about Gerald were true?"

Again, Carl started to shake his head and paused. "I don't know. I don't want to believe it, but things just don't add up. Although, maybe they do and I'm just letting Birdie's accusations, *everyone's* accusations, cloud my judgment of my friend."

"That could be true." I squeezed his arm and let him go. "Or maybe your kind heart and years of friendship have clouded your judgment of who Gerald really is."

That time, he didn't start to shake his head in denial but simply nodded. "I'm afraid that may be true. Even if I couldn't bring myself to say that much to Anna."

A loud crunching sounded in the moment of silence, and I figured Watson had started in on the second bone.

"If you don't mind me asking, what aspects are you beginning to think might be true about Gerald?"

A little sad smile played over Carl's lips. "I know Anna asked you to look into things. She didn't say so, but I know her."

"Do you mind?"

"Nah." The smile became a little more bitter-sweet. "It's out of love, and I can't blame her after the investments. A couple of them are for sure not going to work out, but maybe some of the others will. Either way..." He finally picked up a third empanada.

"Do you know anything about those investments, Carl? Any idea of where Gerald got his leads or his information? Why he chose the specific investments he did?"

"Anna asked me the very same things, although hers were more of an accusation of me being an idiot than really asking." He winced as he chewed, and a blush rose to his cheeks. "Can't blame her on that either. I didn't ask for details. Gerald just presented things to me, and I took his word on it."

"Don't beat yourself up about that." To my surprise, I meant what I was saying. "He was... er... *is* your friend. Friends trust each other."

He cocked an eyebrow. "*You* tried to warn me."

True enough, but there was no need to rub salt in the wounds. "Carl, if I'm direct, can I trust you not to mention my theories to Gerald? Or anyone else for that matter, besides Anna of course."

To his credit, Carl hesitated, considering. We

both knew the only thing he and Anna loved more than pastries was gossip. "I think so."

It would have to do. "It goes back to one of Birdie's accusations. Have you ever seen anything that would make you think Gerald has dealings with the darker elements of society? For investments or... other things?"

"I don't think so." He didn't have to think about it. "Granted, I've never met the people he did investment dealings with, but nothing's ever felt sinister."

It was the answer I suspected. "Do you know if he was close to Chief Briggs back in the day? Did they have any dealings?" I knew I was showing too much of my hand but couldn't stop myself. "Did he ever have any interactions with Branson?"

Carl straightened, surprisingly catching on instantly. "No way. Gerald wouldn't have been involved with them. Not in that way. He's not part of the Irons family."

"I don't think he is." Maybe it was spin, trying to give Carl an out and not feel like he was betraying his friend, but it was also a real possibility. "But I do wonder if maybe he accidentally got involved with them, unknowingly, and they sort of trapped Gerald into doing their bidding."

Once more, Carl focused on something or

nothing over my shoulder. "Maybe. I hate to even consider it, but... maybe."

"Have you spoken to Gerald yesterday or today?" When he shook his head, I decided to truly take Carl at his word. "Then you probably haven't heard the results of Birdie's autopsy?"

His eyes widened behind his glasses, and he shook his head again. Before I could answer, he made a move to leave the counter. "Let me make sure no one interrupts us."

I stopped him with a hand on his arm again and felt my cheeks flush. "I already locked the door. Sorry."

He actually chuckled and waved me on.

"I was with Gerald when Chief Dunmore called. Birdie's death was ruled an accident or suicide, not a murder."

"That's wonderful! So Gerald's not a sus—"

"Gerald *is* still a suspect, but not in the way we imagined." I rushed ahead, trying to rip off the Band-Aid. "The toxicology report indicated a harmful level of THC in her blood, provided by the kombucha Gerald gave her, which could make him culpable in her death."

Carl just stared at me.

I pushed a little further. "Have you noticed a

difference in the kombucha, Carl? Did it feel stronger to you lately? Is that why it affected you so much on the Fourth of July?"

The nod he gave was so guilt-ridden, it was clear Carl thought he might as well be crucifying his friend. "Yeah, he told me he'd increased the recipe, that it was better. But... neither of us thought it would affect me that much. I'm still not sure that's what was going on that night."

I could tell he didn't believe that last part. "Does Anna know that detail?"

A solitary nod. "Yeah. That was part of the drama yesterday."

None of this was news, not really, and it didn't do more than confirm that even one of Gerald's dearest friends was having doubts, even if he was adamant Gerald wouldn't be involved with the Irons family and the like.

Watson emerged, catching our attention as he trotted lazily back across the store, paused at my feet, showing all was forgiven as he demanded a scratch between the ears, and then curled up under my skirt.

"I do wonder about what Birdie said regarding —" Carl sounded like he was speaking to himself and broke off abruptly.

I refocused on him, feeling like he'd been about

to say something important. "What, Carl? Don't hold back. You're aware I'm not fond of Gerald, but you know I'm not going to do anything to set him up or make him look guilty for things he didn't do."

"The stuff she said about what Gerald did to some of his clients." He sighed, closed his eyes, and began to rub his left temple.

After a moment of silence, I decided he needed a prompt. "Intentionally losing their cases to get money from insurance companies and such?"

Still keeping his eyes closed, Carl nodded yet again. "Yeah. I never would've thought of it, not once, but with Birdie putting that thought in my head, and thinking back, I..." He sighed, heavier and more guilt-ridden than ever.

"What, Carl? What is it?"

"I'm not saying it proves anything. I'm probably looking for ghosts where there aren't any." He finally met my gaze again. "I never even noticed before, but when I recall all the cases he lost... well..." He gave a weak shrug. "Gerald was never really upset about them, you know? I just chalked it up to Gerald being Gerald—cheerful, easygoing. Admired it, actually. He lost a lot of cases, but he never let it get to him. He was always light and hopeful. He'd simply say he'd do better next time, practice makes perfect, or

there's always a silver lining, something like that."
Carl blinked, and I waited, wanting him to finish on
his own. He did. "But if he was getting paid off every
time he lost a case, then... in reality... he was still
winning, kinda. If he was making money under the
table every time he lost, then no wonder he was
always okay with it."

With the revelation of Birdie's toxicology report,
and how it implicated Gerald, I'd forgotten that line
of Birdie's accusations. Even Gerald's admission that
such a thing happened had been overshadowed by
his possible connections to gangs, drug dealers, and
the Irons family.

And even if it was true... I mentally shook
myself. There was no *if* about it. It was true. Gerald
had admitted as much, though not to what extent.
So... even though it was true, was it important? It
didn't have anything to do with Birdie's death. It
didn't even have much to do with clearing Carl's
association with the man as Anna asked me to do.
But it was huge, and important, so it had to connect
somehow. Everything was such a jumble of Gerald's
secrets and misdeeds that every turn provided more
questions and confusion than anything else.

Though I was physically present at the Cozy Corgi for the rest of the day, I was completely useless. I often thought best while occupied with other things, but helping customers wasn't always conducive to trying to force puzzle pieces together. Such was the case for the hours following my conversation with Carl. So while Watson napped, I shrugged off bookselling duties to Ben and occupied myself by unboxing the new shipment of books and reorganizing shelves in the new release, mystery, and wildlife sections.

While the mundane task allowed my brain to roam free, it didn't solve anything—only clarifying more and more of the puzzle pieces, and not two of them came close to clicking together. If only I could see the image on the metaphorical box, the puzzle pieces were supposed to make. Unlike so many times before, I wasn't trying to solve a murder, at least not directly. I supposed if Birdie had died due to Gerald's kombucha, then he truly was negligently responsible, but that wasn't the type of murder I was used to. I chuckled inwardly at that thought. What did it say that I'd gotten used to murder? Although, as a detective's daughter, I supposed some part of me had always been used to murder. But again, that wasn't the particular puzzle I was trying to put together.

Was the image supposed to solidify into an assortment of Gerald's misdeeds? Or was that missing the forest for the trees—perhaps the Gerald aspect was only one small puzzle piece in the image that would ultimately be of the Irons family? *Or* maybe I was in the entirely wrong puzzle box altogether. Perhaps Birdie's autopsy was wrong, or at least a red herring of sorts. If so, then I needed to return to the names that made up the hit list Ethel had provided to Birdie.

As the store hours drew to a close, out of sheer desperation, I called G & J Associates. Gerald had to be rattled after Chief Dunmore's revelation the day before. Chances were high if I pressed hard enough, I could get some sort of reaction from him— more about his finagling the insurance systems or play up the connections Leo and I had assumed between Gerald, the Green Munchies, and the Irons family.

I was so caught up in trying to decide which direction to attempt, the receptionist's sharp voice brought me back to the moment and made it clear I'd missed her first greetings. "Hello? I can hear you breathing. It's not a smart thing to prank call a lawyer's office."

"Oh, Paulette, I'm sorry. I dialed and then got lost in my thoughts."

There was a pause on the other end. "I'm sorry. Who is this?"

"Sorry again." I forced out a laugh, trying to sound lighthearted. "This is Fred... er... Winifred Page." I started to pause there but remembered who Paulette had responded positively toward. "My corgi, Watson, and I came in yesterday."

There was another hesitation but only for a moment. "Yes. I recall. I... uh... don't believe Mr. Jackson cares to speak to you."

Another laugh, less forced this time. "I imagine not, and honestly, I can't blame him. However, I'm not going to take no for an answer."

At her intake of breath, I could practically see her bristle in the way she had when we'd arrived the day before. "I'm afraid that's not how Mr. Jackson does business. And... while I don't intend to be rude, you're not the police. You can't force him to speak to you."

I wasn't playing it smart. I needed to be direct with Gerald, not his receptionist. I tried to think of another way to worm Watson back into the conversation, but failed. I'd already gone too far down the path. "Maybe not, but as you may have noticed, I'm rather determined. If he won't speak to me, I'm afraid I'll have to drop by and wait, just like I did yesterday. I'll bring Watson with me, though." I said the last bit in a rush and instantly wished I hadn't. Paulette might've connected to Watson, but she wasn't a child who could be persuaded to ignore her job duties for the promise of a puppy visit.

"I'm afraid, Ms. Page, you'd be wasting your time." Her voice was prim, as the first time I'd called months ago. "Mr. Jackson isn't available."

"You've given me that line before, Paulette. I know it's part of your duties to say that, but that won't keep me from trying." Maybe there was another way to soften her up. "Can I bring you anything? Since I'll be at your office in a few minutes, I'll happily bring you anything from the bakery. Katie has these marvelous mincemeat empanadas. Or if you prefer something sweeter, maybe a lemon bar or chocolate espresso torte. Perhaps a chai tea latte?"

When she spoke again, Paulette's voice was a little softer. "Thank you, but no. And I'm afraid I'm not making it up. I'm the only one here. Mr. Jackson hasn't been in the office today. He truly isn't available."

The way she said it made me believe her. And really, it didn't surprise me. With everything going on, Gerald had a lot more important things than showing up to work. "Have you heard from him? Has he... left town?" It was the nicest way I could think of asking if he'd fled.

To my surprise, she answered. "I've not heard from Mr. Jackson since he left the office yesterday, shortly after you and Watson, in fact." Before I could speak again into the pause, Paulette continued, and this time her voice had a slight tremor in it. "I've... tried to call him several times today."

She was worried. That didn't surprise me either. She'd been fiercely defensive of him on the phone and then again in person. It made sense, given she felt indebted to him. "Do you..." I paused, wondering how to ask if she was concerned that he'd hurt himself with all the stress. "Are you concerned about his safety?"

"No. Of course not. Mr. Jackson would never..." She sniffed, and again I heard a tremble in her voice. "It's just that, there's so much going on. He's extremely stressed. And all the things people are saying about him. He's gotten letters from..." She cleared her throat, and some of the steel returned to her tone. "Never mind. I'm sure it's nothing. It's not the first time Mr. Jackson hasn't come into work and not informed me. Part of the privilege of owning his own business."

I wasn't surprised at that either. Gerald was for sure the type to slack off and not bother to let his own secretary know. Either way, I'd gotten as much as I could from Paulette, but I felt sorry for her. She was worried, no matter what she claimed. "Well, I won't stake out the office, but I'd be happy to bring you something if you'd like, make you feel a little better. Trust me, a dirty chai and one of Katie's empanadas will perk you right up."

Another sniff and Paulette's voice softened once more. "That's very kind of you, Winifred, and thank you, but no. I have about another hour of paperwork to do here, and I'll be headed home myself, but I appreciate the offer. Pat your sweet Watson for me." She hung up without waiting for me to say goodbye.

I only considered for a few seconds, and I had

snagged Watson's leash before I realized I'd decided. In less than five minutes, Watson and I hopped back into the Mini Cooper and were headed out of town once more, that time to Glen Haven.

Though the drive was half the time it took to get to Lyons, the road was much curvier, full of switchbacks, and more wooded. As always, by the time I pulled off the paved road onto the gravel-and-dirt lane that led to my sisters' houses, my cell reception was long gone. Of course, it was only then I had the thought of texting Leo and letting him know where I'd gone. I considered backtracking to where I'd get a few bars but shrugged the notion away. Katie and the twins knew where I'd gone, and while I had a feeling Gerald was going to be furious at me, I wasn't genuinely concerned he'd do me any bodily harm.

I drove past my sisters' houses and continued several more yards before turning onto a little bridge that crossed the river, and then I headed back down the other side. Gerald lived directly across from Zelda and Verona. The lane and river were so narrow between them that their yards practically touched, so close they could carry on conversations from their front porches. As I pulled into his driveway, I looked for signs of life and found none. His car wasn't parked in front of the garage as it had been on a few other occasions, and he wasn't lounging on his porch drinking kombucha, which was where part of me had expected to find him... *if* he hadn't skipped town.

Shifting the car into Park, I killed the engine, then stepped out and started to leave Watson behind, certain Gerald wouldn't be home. But on the off chance he was, I didn't want to risk having to return to save Watson from sitting in a hot car. I reached back in, attached his leash, and held the door open for him to jump out.

"Okay, one of us needs to turn on the charm, and I'm afraid I don't have it in me. So, it's up to you. Try to work a miracle like you did with Paulette yesterday."

Unconcerned, Watson didn't even spare me a glance, instead eyeing a chipmunk scurrying along the riverbank.

"Good grief! Those things are everywhere, and don't you even think about it." With a gentle tug on his leash, that prompted an annoyed grunt, I directed, and Watson followed.

My hopes of catching Gerald at home dwindled as we stepped onto the porch. Every window I could see had the curtains drawn. I supposed he might be stressed or depressed enough to want to block out the beautiful day, but still. Knowing I'd get no answer, I rang the doorbell, waited, then rang it again.

Clearly exasperated, Watson plopped down at my feet, making a show of arranging his head just so on his paws.

I resorted to knocking—still nothing. Without meaning to, I let out a huff, one that reminded me of Watson. Snorting a laugh, I looked down to find him staring up at me. "Dear Lord, I think I'm turning into you."

Either not caring, or figuring there were a lot worse lots in life, Watson answered with a huff of his own and plopped his head back onto his paws.

Hating to give up, even though I knew it was pointless, I stared across the stream to the twins' houses. I could pop over there, see if they'd noticed him coming or going throughout the day. Although, Zelda and Verona were probably both at Chakras, and their husbands at Ark & Whale, finishing up with the day's tourists. But maybe my nephews and nieces were home and they'd seen something.

While I tried to make up my mind, a sound reached my ears—barely audible from the river water tumbling over rocks.

When I realized what it was, I felt stupid. A car engine. Obviously I'd left mine on. It wouldn't be the first time. The Mini Cooper didn't have an ignition; it simply started when the key fob was inside, but it didn't turn off automatically when you walked away from it with the fob in the pocket of your skirt.

"All right, I give up." I left the porch, Watson trailing intentionally slow behind me, and returned to my car. Only I hadn't left it running. Cocking my head, I realized I could still hear it, that it was close, and... behind me. I walked to the garage door, and the sound was louder, so I pressed my ear to it. Strange, it was definitely coming from inside.

Why in the world would— The internal question hadn't even finished forming before the answer arrived and brought with it a spike of adrenaline. I began to pound on the garage door, which did nothing, of course. Then I knelt, attempting to slide my fingers beneath the garage door and the concrete driveway. I couldn't, not that I'd be able to lift the garage door even if I had managed to get my fingers beneath it.

Watson whimpered, feeding off my energy, and began to sniff around the seam, then sneezed. I was willing to bet he smelled what I couldn't.

Dropping his leash, I hurried around the garage, hoping there'd be a side entrance. There wasn't. However, there was a window. Using my hands as a shield, I pressed my face to it, trying to see in. A few rays of the early evening sun hanging over the mountains cut through the window, making it where I could barely form an image through the dark haze of the interior. Sure enough, there was a car inside, and I could just make out a silhouetted mound behind the steering wheel. Though I couldn't see any details, my heart sank, certain I'd located Gerald Jackson.

It wasn't until Watson shoved his weight against my leg that I was moved into action. Something about the sad slump of Gerald's body had frozen me in place, making the options of what I should do swirl in my mind. Finally tearing my gaze away, I glanced down at Watson with a smile of thanks as I dug my cell phone out of my pocket. Instead of dialing 911, I tapped Susan's name, which I'd added to my favorites a couple of months ago when she started including me on some cases. As long as she answered, she'd require less explanation than dispatch.

I stood there several seconds staring at the window with the cell pressed to my ear before I realized it wasn't ringing through. Thinking I must've missed when I tapped her name, I looked at the screen, only to remember I was in Glen Haven and there was no cell service whatsoever.

Another moment passed as I debated hopping the stream and running to Zelda's or Verona's house to use their landline, but I discarded it instantly. Though I couldn't see Gerald clearly, I believed he was dead. Maybe in the way his body seemed to be angled or just a gut feeling, I wasn't sure. Either way didn't provide enough certainty to leave him to make a call. If there was even a chance there was life left, I should be dragging him to fresh air, not leaving him where he was.

But how to get in?

Leo had taught me how to pick a lock, I could probably break into the front door, but I wasn't sure how quick I'd be. If there was a chance, Gerald needed fresh air as soon as possible. I could crash my car through the garage door. As I turned to head back to the Mini Cooper, a large rock caught my attention and I hurried over. It was heavier than I thought, but with a groan, I managed to tear it out from of the ground.

"Get out of the way, buddy," I made a shooing gesture with my chin at Watson, for all the good it did.

He continued rushing around at my feet in a panic, barking.

Making it back to the window, with another loud

groan and a sharp pinch in my lower back that nearly took my breath away, I forced the rock over my head, preparing to throw it at the window with as much strength as I could muster.

"What in blazes are you doing, woman?"

The gruff voice from out of nowhere startled me, and I let out a yell, both of surprise and pain as I twisted the trajectory with a flinch and dropped the rock, barely missing my foot.

Watson let out a howl and danced out of the way —unhurt, thankfully—then turned toward the voice and began growling in earnest.

"Oh shut up, you fat rat. You're the one breaking and entering, not me."

I stared at the huge man, so thrown off I was unable to place him for a few seconds until the bushy bright red hair that covered his head and face caught the sunlight, and then it clicked. Rocky Castle, the owner of Rocky Road Tours and hunter of Bigfoot. Instead of the repulsion and irritation I typically experienced at the sight of the man, I only felt relief.

"Rocky, thank goodness. I—"

"I noticed the tiny yellow thing you call a car drive past my house a little bit ago, figured you were going to your sisters' or something. Then remembered you like to stick your nose in people's business, so thought I'd come check to see if you were harassing Gerald." Rocky stomped toward me, anger flashing in his sky-blue eyes. "Sure enough, here you are, trying to break in. This time *I'll* be the one turning *you* in to the cops. Don't think I haven't been waiting to pay you back for ratting me out to that cop woman. I wasn't allowed to run tours for *over a month*. You know how much income I lost? And what business of yours was it if I was having a drink on the job? I wasn't even close to being unfit to drive."

"Rocky!" I yelled his name, trying to break through his diatribe.

He kept right on going. "If you think for one second—" He glared down at Watson, whose growl had gone dangerous enough even Rocky couldn't ignore he was about to be attacked. "If you don't call off your rabid rodent, I'll smash that little—"

I hit him. I couldn't remember the last time I'd hit anyone, if ever. And I honestly wasn't sure if I did to get his attention or because he threatened Watson. Either way, as my punch bounced off his chest, we both froze and stared at each other in shock.

Rocky didn't lift a hand to me—as I would've expected him to do if this situation had been presented in advance—and he didn't retaliate at

Watson. Instead a smirk began to form. "I knew you were fiery. Told you before, we'd make a good pair. I like a woman—"

When I hit him that time, I didn't care why. "Shut up! Gerald is in the garage, he needs our help. I think he might be dead."

His smirk faltered, though there was a laugh of unbelief in his voice. "What?"

I gestured toward the window. "Gerald is in his car, in the garage. It's running. I think he's dead."

Rocky looked from me, to the window, and then shoved me to the side as he darted toward it.

Though it hadn't been done out of maliciousness, the impact caught me off guard, and Rocky was strong. I stumbled sideways, trying to get my footing, but tripped over Watson, who yelped and then howled as I crashed to the ground.

Watson's commotion was drowned out as Rocky let out a howl of his own and cursed before pulling back his fist and slamming it through the window. With blood dripping from his hand, he leaned toward the hole and yelled inside, "Hold on, Gerald! I'm coming!" Rocky didn't so much as glance our way as he rushed past and disappeared around the other side of the garage.

Still growling, Watson made an attempt to rush after him.

With another twinge in my back, I lurched forward and grabbed Watson, pulling him to me. "It's okay, buddy. It's okay."

Rocky continued to yell Gerald's name, and there was a loud thump, then another, accompanied by a crash. I didn't need to see to realize Rocky had just kicked open the front door.

By the time I got to my feet and had a hold of Watson's leash so he wouldn't go after Rocky again, I heard the garage door opening. I hurried around to see Rocky struggling to open the driver's side door of Gerald's car.

"It's locked!" Rocky's yell got louder, more panicked. Releasing the door handle, he slid his large fingers into the crack of the partially rolled-down window and tried to pull and yank. Despite his strength, the window didn't give.

"Hold on, Rocky. Let's try—" I'd started to enter the small garage but stepped back as Rocky hurried around the car, grabbed a shovel hanging on the wall, hopped on the hood of the ancient car, and began to smash at the windshield.

He was so wild, so huge and frantic, that for a second all thoughts of Gerald and the situation vanished. Rocky looked like the fabled Bigfoot that he tracked. I was further shocked to realize his cries had turned to sobs and tears streamed down his face and into his mess of a beard. I'd forgotten he was friends with Gerald. The two of them had a frequent game night with Angus and Susan Green's brother. When the windshield shattered, Rocky leaned in, unlocked the door, slid over the side of the hood and threw the door open. He started to pull Gerald out from the car but had to pause again to undo Gerald's seat belt, and then he dragged Gerald out of the garage and laid him in the driveway beside the Mini Cooper. He was yelling at Gerald the entire time, though his words were so garbled with emotion, I couldn't make them out.

Whatever Rocky's words, they were useless. My instinct had been right. Gerald was dressed in a suit and tie, and he looked ready for the office or the courtroom, save for the bright red patches over his face.

"Rocky..." Trying to keep my voice soothing, I touched the back of his shoulder. "He's gone. He's—"

"No!" Rocky flung a large arm wildly behind him and collided with my thigh, causing me to stumble once more.

That time, I didn't fall. Instead of trying to stop

him, I simply turned around and led Watson through the broken front door and into the house, where I used Gerald's phone to call the police.

It took Susan Green and Brent Jackson to pull Rocky away from Gerald. Even when they did, he shoved Brent away and lunged toward his friend again. When they had to resort to cuffing Rocky, I turned away from where I'd been watching at the living room window. There were a million reasons to despise Rocky Castle and Gerald Jackson, but it hurt to see both the death and the genuine grieving of a friend.

I sat on Gerald's worn-out sofa and stroked Watson as he curled up beside me and placed his head on my lap. I didn't even comment about how affectionate and clingy he was suddenly being. But after several minutes, his presence, his warmth, and the soothing feel of his fur through my fingers worked their magic and my brain was able to let go of the trauma outside and return to the moment.

A glance around Gerald's living room and into the small kitchen made me wonder. Just like Gerald's car, everything was small, rundown, and out of date. If the accusations, and my theories about him for that matter, were accurate, something didn't add up. Gerald wasn't living like a man making a fortune at the cost of his clients or from investment schemes and frauds with underground dealings.

With Susan, Brent, and Rocky's voices drifting in from outside, I only took a couple of seconds to consider. Perhaps I should've felt guilty about what I chose, but... I didn't. Who knew if I'd get this chance again?

Even though there was no way they would hear me through the commotion, I still lowered my voice to whisper to Watson. "Come on, let's see what we can find out, and be quiet."

Doubting I had all that much time, especially now Rocky was subdued, I decided to make a quick trip through the house. I only had a few minutes. I wanted to make the most of it, and I figured there were better places to do that than a living room or kitchen.

There was only one hallway, with three doors leading off it. The first one was a bathroom, the second Gerald's bedroom... which tempted me to stop there. However, the third was Gerald's office. Perfect.

With a glance over my shoulder to reveal no shadowy silhouettes making their way into the house,

I entered the room, waited for Watson to follow, and then quietly shut the door behind us.

When I dropped Watson's leash as the door clicked, he gave me an appraising look, and then apparently decided I was fine as he trotted across the room, lowered his nose to the floor, and began his own sniffing and snorting-filled exploration.

I went straight to the desk, sat in Gerald's chair, and punched a button on the desktop's keyboard, bringing the screen to life. A rectangle came up on the screen requesting a password. For some reason, that surprised me, Gerald didn't seem the type to worry about such things, especially in his own home. And while I wasn't about to waste time trying to figure out the password of a man I barely knew, it seemed to confirm that Gerald had things to hide.

Angling away from the computer, I started to pull out the bottom drawer of the desk. Before I could discover whether it was locked, the letters strewn across his desk caught my attention. Their envelopes were ripped, crumpled, and littered the desk and the floor nearby. A couple of the letters were crumpled as well. I picked up one of the smoother ones and began to read. Then the next and the next.

I don't know how much time passed, enough to

get through about ten of the letters, before the office door opened and Susan stepped in. After folding her arms, she cast a glare at Watson—who growled at her from across the room—and then cocked her eyebrow in my direction.

"You have nerve, I'll give you that. Officer Jackson and I practically lost our lives trying to wrestle down that redheaded gorilla out there, not to mention the *dead body*, and you waltz in here and start to snoop. Did you even consider turning off Gerald's car?"

The thought hadn't crossed my mind. "Susan, I just—"

"Whatever." She waved me off before I could finish the excuse neither of us would buy. "Besides, I told you I welcome your help on this whole mess anyway." She stepped inside and closed the door behind her. "Find anything good?"

I almost smiled at her. I never would've guessed the two of us would've gotten to such a place. Instead, I held up one of the papers. "I'll say. Letter after letter of—"

Watson snorted, pulling both of our attention to him. I got the distinct impression he wasn't as impressed by Susan's and my teamwork, but wasn't overly concerned about it either, as he turned and began sniffing at the base of a closet door.

Refocusing on Susan, I gestured over the sprawl of papers. "Gerald was in danger of getting disbarred. From the way it sounds, it was a pretty sure thing. He was also having charges brought against him for insurance fraud and embezzlement. Some of these are over a week old. So, many of these weren't triggered by Birdie's article."

Susan crossed to the desk and started to pick up one of the letters but paused, giving me a surprised expression. "Really? That's unexpected."

I'd thought the same, but already had a theory rolling around. "I'm wondering if whoever got the dirt for Birdie to use had already shared it through back alley means with these people. Maybe the article was just the cherry on top, simply reveling in the public shaming."

"And by *whoever got the dirt for Birdie*, I assume you mean Ethel?" Susan didn't bother to wait for a response before scanning the letter in her hand, letting out a low whistle. "Wow. Add these to the likelihood he was going to have charges for the drugs in Birdie's system, no wonder Gerald took matters into his own hands. His life was basically over anyway."

I flinched. "Matters into his own hands?"

"Struggling with euphemisms today, Fred?" Susan scowled. "Suicide."

A little of my typical irritation with Susan drifted into my tone. "No, I understood that. But you think Gerald killed himself?"

"Well, let's see..." That time she propped a hand on her hip and let her own annoyance show again. "He was in a locked car, in a locked garage, in a locked house. Not to mention, if what the Jolly Red Giant out there claimed is accurate—after he stopped the wailing and fighting—Gerald only had on a seat belt. It wasn't like he couldn't get away if he wanted to. And..." She lifted a finger as if I'd been about to interrupt. "The splotches over his skin seem to indicate that he died of carbon monoxide poisoning, asphyxiation, or a combination thereof instead of being killed somewhere else and then had the scene set up to resemble a suicide. Of course, the coroner will have to confirm that." Sirens sounded in the distance. "Speaking of, it sounds like the cavalry has arrived."

I started to respond but was distracted by Watson scratching at the closet. I had to lean in the office chair to peer around Susan to get a better view. "What is it, buddy?"

He didn't look over or respond, just continued scratching.

Susan turned to inspect as well. "Oh good Lord, is this the part of your routine where the dog discovers a body stuffed in the closet or the stashed murder weapon?" She bent down a little, directing her voice toward Watson. "Hate to break it to you, fleabag, there's no murder weapon. The lawyer did it himself."

Before I could stand, despite her words, Susan trudged over, twisted the closet door handle, and threw it open.

Watson darted inside.

"See?" Susan peered in after him. "No dead body. No murder weapon."

I joined them, and when Susan straightened, I poked my head in to see what had captured Watson's attention. Reaching down, I grabbed the handle of a suitcase and lifted it up. As I brought it into the office, Watson followed, hopping frantically at my feet.

Susan groaned. "Here we go." Though she might've been trying to sound annoyed, she'd failed to sap the curiosity from her tone.

After a couple of clicks, I opened the suitcase. Before I could take stock of what was there, Watson darted his head in, snagged something between his teeth, and then scurried across the room.

"Watson, don't—" I started to get up to take it away, but stopped when I recognized the yellow bag he was ripping open. "It's beef jerky."

"Of course it is." Susan rolled her eyes but sounded a little impressed. "How in the world did the fat hamster smell *that*?"

"It probably had a rip in the bag." I'd already refocused on the suitcase and couldn't believe my eyes. "Susan... check these out."

As I held up a passport and bundles of cash, Susan knelt beside me and began to rifle through the contents. "What in the world?"

In addition to the first two items, there was another bag of beef jerky, along with a couple of packages of trail mix, a few changes of clothes, and some hygiene supplies.

Susan looked from the passport to the contents and back again. "A fake name and all this. Seems like Gerald was ready for a quick getaway."

"A fake name?" I snagged the passport back from Susan. *Robert Fulsome.* "Maybe it's more than just a getaway bag. Maybe this is his real identity or the name he uses when he does work for the Irons family."

"The Irons fam…" Susan had been unzipping the pocket in the top half of the suitcase but gaped over at me. "Good grief, Fred. Branson *really* did a number on you, didn't he? You're obsessed."

As I tried to think of a good defense, Susan finished unzipping the pocket and pulled out a couple of notebooks and began to flip through. After several moments, she let out another long whistle when she reached the midway point of the first one and then angled it toward me. "What does this look like?"

I scanned it, but it wasn't until I reached my own name that it clicked. "People who did investments with Gerald. Or, in my case, had investments taken out in their name." I scanned the list again: Rocky Castle, Mark Green, Petra Yun, Carl Hanson, Etta Squire, Opal Garble, Pete Miller, me, Simone Pryce, Marcus Gonzalez, on and on and on, full of names I knew and others I didn't. On the far side of each page was a number and differing hand-drawn symbols that resembled a blend of hieroglyphics and Chinese letters.

"Looks like a suspect list to me." Susan scrunched up her nose. "On the off chance Gerald didn't kill himself." She glared at the list, and I knew she was focusing on her brother's name, and she gave a small shake of her head. "This is like a who's who list of the most gullible in Estes Park, and it goes back years, clearly. There are people on here that have been dead or gone for quite a while."

Something Susan said triggered a thought, and I stared at her. "Susan, if Gerald was ready with a getaway bag to be snagged spur of the moment, then why would he kill himself? Even if he was worried about his career, reputation, or one of these names on the list, why not just grab his bag and go? He'd be gone before anyone would think to look for him. Suicide doesn't make any sense."

She rolled her eyes. "Did Gerald Jackson *ever* make any sense?"

Katie and Leo had spread an assortment of food over the coffee table in my living room. It had been the birthday of one of the park rangers, and they'd thrown a potluck for his celebration, so Leo had brought over some leftovers. Combined with a few leftovers from the bakery and a freshly baked batch of empanadas, our late-evening gathering had turned into quite the smorgasbord.

Though he spent most of his time sitting at Leo's feet, getting crumbs and small morsels passed down to him, Watson frequently made the rounds—sniffing around where Katie sat on the floor and then doing the same to me on the couch, snagging any crumbs we were responsible for.

Katie eyed him from over the screen of her laptop while she nibbled on a piece of fried chicken from Leo's offerings. "Tell you what, Watson's worth his weight in gold. Either way you look at it, he's either saving you money from hiring a maid or helping you avoid sweat equity by cleaning yourself. He's a regular Hoover." At his name, Watson trotted back to Katie, hope filling his expression. All he got for his trouble was a gentle bop on the nose. "I take it back. There's nothing regular about you."

"That might be true for cleaning up anything edible..." I pointed to the spot beside Katie that Watson had just vacated. "Except for the trail of hair he leaves behind."

"Don't you listen to her." Leo leaned over, scratching Watson aggressively enough it seemed he was intentionally stirring up the hair. "What you leave behind isn't tempting like all the food crumbs would be to rodents and insects. You're only making sure your mama doesn't have to hire an exterminator, aren't you?"

Watson beamed up at Leo with his typical adoration. He whimpered and received a corner of empanada for his effort.

"You're a pushover." Pressing the point, I too leaned over and playfully shoved Leo's shoulder.

He merely shrugged. "Maybe, but from the way it sounds, Watson more than earned his keep today."

"Can't argue with you there." I refocused on Katie. "Any luck?"

She shook her head but didn't look up from the screen as she responded with her mouth full. "I'm not finding any sort of footprint left by Gerald's alias. Nothing connecting him to the Green Munchies or even to his investments. It's like none of his extracurricular activities existed."

After leaving Glen Haven, I'd called Katie to fill her in, and before I knew it, we were deep into speculation mode and decided we'd have one of our brainstorming nights. Working things through with Katie and Leo often helped me figure out where to train my spotlight next. Plus... snacks!

For several minutes, the room was filled with the sound of Katie's clicking computer keys, the crunching of pastries, and the alternating clacking of Watson's nails against the hardwood and his impatient sighs as he waited for his next morsel.

Leo had moved on to one of Katie's lemon bars when he spoke again. "I'm not overly surprised there's not much about Gerald online. The Irons family would be too careful to let that happen if he is tied to them in some way, plus, Gerald would have the connections to them we all share, and those aren't atypical. Practically everyone in town had dealings with Branson or Chief Briggs. Even finding out that Etta Squire was involved in his investments doesn't say that much. She was a park ranger here for decades. Chances are, I had just as much involvement with her as Gerald." He glanced my way. "Not to mention Gerald goes way back. He grew up with your family. It's not like Branson, who showed up to town with the fake identity one day." His thick eyebrows knitted. "Why are you grinning like that?"

Chuckling, I leaned forward once more and wiped my thumb over the stubble of his upper lip. "You're covered in powdered sugar."

He grinned. "Nah. I'm just naturally sweet."

Katie made exaggerated vomiting noises, prompting Watson to sit up straighter and cock his head quizzically in her direction. "Good grief, you two. Remember that this isn't a honeymoon suite and there's a single lady in the room."

Leo snagged my hand before I could pull it away, pressed the back of it to his lips, and made ridiculous squeaky kissing noises. He leered at Katie as he ended the kiss with a loud smack.

"You're gross." She tossed the remainder of the empanada she'd been eating at him, causing Leo to duck. The wedge of crust sailed over the back of the couch and landed out of sight.

Watson sprang into action, taking his cleaning duties very seriously, not to mention happily.

Sitting back up straight, Leo cast a meaningful stare toward Katie. "Don't complain about being a third wheel. I've tried doing my part. How many times have I attempted to set you up with—"

"Shut up, Smokey Bear." Katie started to reach for another morsel of food from the makeshift smorgasbord and thought better of it. "I don't want setups, blind dates, or *anything* at all. I'm content on my own, more than, actually. I simply don't require nauseating displays of physical affection over dinner." She cast him a playful scowl, then refocused on me. "I'm coming up empty as well. Even with the list of people Gerald roped into his investment schemes, I'm not finding anything online about it. Either they were so small-time they didn't measure up or were big enough they're well hidden."

"I'm voting for the latter option. Especially if the investments were schemes run through the Irons family." I sighed in frustration. "Maybe Susan is having better luck going through old court cases Gerald lost, whether intentionally or not. *We're* just going in circles. How do you uncover secret investment schemes when you have no idea what you're looking for? Even Carl couldn't give me specifics on what exactly he was forking money over to Gerald for. The way it sounds, it was just generalities and talks of percentages and promises of high returns with limited risks. I'm tempted to speak to Angus. He seemed a little more informed on what Gerald was doing, and mostly disapproving of it. But... I can't, not tonight. Probably not tomorrow either. He's going to be devastated about Gerald."

"That's part of what I can't understand." Leo reached for one of the lists. "Gerald involved both Mark Green and Rocky Castle in his investments. It's bad enough he did it to several other members of the town who he was friends with, but those two... It's hard to imagine him trying to screw them over. Including Angus, their little group was like the four amigos. Goes back to what I was saying before. Gerald didn't just show up here one day. He's had connections going back his entire life. Even if he truly had some secret identity, I can't believe *none* of his relationships were real or heartfelt."

Though Gerald hadn't garnered much respect in my book, I was struggling with that as well. "I don't know. Maybe he just got in too deep, too caught up." I snagged the other paper, the list of Birdie's features, of which Gerald was on. "He was hooked on the rush of it, like an addiction. Or... pressured in such a way by the Irons family he didn't have a choice."

"I'm still not convinced about the Irons family." Katie rushed ahead, probably sensing me getting ready to reiterate my preferred theory. "These schemes can be pretty all-encompassing, not only for the victims, but even for the people who came up with them, and there's some crazy ones out there." With a hand occupied by the remains of a raspberry-and-white-chocolate brownie, she nodded toward her computer. "For about fifty years, at the turn of the century—the previous turn of the century, not this last one—there was this group of well-to-do British women who went around to all the shops while wearing specially made clothes with hidden pockets and practically stole the London merchants blind. They called themselves the Forty Elephants, or that's what others named them, I can't tell."

"The Forty Elephants?" Leo cocked an eyebrow.

"Yep." Katie nodded enthusiastically before I could get us back on track. "Apparently animal names are a thing. There's a group in Venezuela called the Piranhas, present-day, not over a century ago. *They* roam around and cut off women's long ponytails and braids, right out in broad daylight, and then rush off. They sell them to high-end salons for up to a thousand dollars apiece. Some of the women have started to be proactive. Cutting off their own hair and donating it to charities to use for cancer patients."

Leo caught my exasperated expression and chuckled.

I shot him a glare and turned back to Katie. "Well, no wonder you're not finding any connections between Gerald and the Irons family if you're in midbinge on the weirdest gangs you can google up."

Katie didn't bat an eye. "I can multitask. It's how I do my best thinking."

Watson reemerged from his hunt for the thrown morsel and began making his rounds once more.

I passed him what remained of my empanada and patted his head. "Okay, that's more than enough human food for you tonight."

Either not understanding or choosing to ignore the edict, Watson swallowed the bite whole and looked back up expectantly.

I patted his head again and then returned to the list. I scanned through the names, then with a jolt, repositioned, scooting to sit closer to Leo.

"If you two start kissing, I'm outta here, and I'm taking the food with me." Katie narrowed her eyes at me. "I might also take your hair, Fred. It's long, red, and beautiful. And if it's worth a thousand dollars—"

I merely rolled my eyes at her and held my list up to Leo's. "Maybe the answer is right in front of us. We've got the list of suspects we were going to look at when we thought Birdie was murdered, and the list of Gerald's... victims, I guess you could say. And there are some that are on both. And, then once we get those, there might be a chance they'll correspond with the research Susan's doing into the court cases."

"You still don't think it's a suicide?" The teasing left Katie's tone. "Maybe that's exactly what we have —an accident and a suicide. Maybe that's why there's nothing to find."

"I don't think so. I might have, if Watson hadn't found that suitcase. From the way it looks, Gerald was ready to leave and start a whole new life at a moment's notice. If he had that option, why would he kill himself?" Instead of waiting for an answer, I continued to compare the lists. Birdie's was short enough that it was easy to scan through. "There're four people who are on both. Mark Green, Carl Hanson, Simone Pryce, and... me."

Leo peered around the paper so he could make eye contact with Watson. "Use your sniffer, buddy.

Is it your mom who's leading the double life? Is this the proof we've all been looking for?"

"Hopefully we can all agree to take *me* off the suspect list." I elbowed his arm with a chuckle.

Katie and Leo both made noncommittal noises, making me laugh again.

Still chuckling, I compared the names and grew serious. "Considering how much Gerald was keeping hidden, maybe I shouldn't say this, but I think we can take Mark Green off the list. Leo's right, Gerald, Angus, Rocky, and Mark were close. I believe their friendship was real. You should have seen Rocky today. I never would have dreamed he had such emotion or could care about someone so much. Maybe that's horrible to say, but... it's true. If the same is true for Mark, I don't think he would hurt Gerald."

"I agree with you." Leo was serious as well. "I'm sure the four of them had arguments and fights every once in a while, and though they were kind of a strange combination, they felt like a makeshift family of sorts."

"Maybe so," Katie chimed in, "but I'd also take Carl off the list. I know people can do horrible things in the heat of the moment that they would never consider any other time, but I can't believe Carl would hurt anyone. Ever."

"Neither can I." I felt that almost as certainly as I did about myself. "So all that leaves is Simone Pryce."

The three of us shared knowing glances as Watson managed to make an ungraceful, seal-like leap, twist his head, snag a pastry that sat too close to the edge, and scurry away. I was too caught up to either laugh or to hurry after him to fruitlessly attempt to wrestle it out of his mouth. "Now that I think about it, that's not the only connection. I've never gotten the sense that Simone and Ethel were particularly fond of each other, but we can't overlook it. Simone is Ethel's daughter-in-law's business partner, so the two of them have plenty of interactions. And Ethel hated Gerald with a vengeance."

Leo considered for second, but sounded unconvinced when he spoke. "So... you're suggesting Simone might be doing Ethel's dirty work?"

"Maybe." I nodded.

Katie sounded less convinced. "But don't forget the reason Simone was on the first list was because she was slated to be the topic of one of Birdie's smear jobs. We've already determined that list for sure came from Ethel. That would mean Ethel's using her for her dirty work *and* getting ready to take her down." She grimaced. "I hate to say it, but I think I like the Irons family theory better."

"Me too." I nodded. "But Ethel is just complicated and devious enough that I don't think we should overlook it. And at least it's a trail to wander down. Even if it's not the right one, it might lead us somewhere."

The following morning, I went directly to the Koffee Kiln. I'd like to say I was brave, nonchalant, or daring, and simply waltzed right in. I wasn't; that would be stupid. Instead I asked Leo to call from his cell, just in case my number had been saved in their system, and ask to speak to Carla. He was told she wouldn't be in until that afternoon, but he could leave a message or a call-back number if he wanted. He declined.

After that, I waltzed right in.

Though the breakfast crowd at the Cozy Corgi bakery was just that, *a crowd*, every single morning, the Koffee Kiln wasn't doing too shabbily in their number of patrons either. Most weren't taking advantage of the pottery making and painting aspect of the shop during that time of day, but the drug the Koffee Kiln offered—caffeine, in liquid and pastry form—clearly kept people coming in.

Unlike Carla, a genuine smile crossed Simone's face when she saw Watson and me heading to where she was stationed at the espresso machine. She waved but waited until I was close to whisper with a chuckle, "I thought you'd be in any moment."

I flinched, lost for words for a second. *She'd thought I'd be in?* Because Gerald died the day before? Was she going to confess? I shook the notion away instantly. "You did?"

She smirked. "With Leo calling to check to see if Carla was in? I know you're direct, but that was even less subtle than normal for you. Not that I can blame you after the other day." She laughed. "Or all the other times before."

"You... Leo..." My words failed at being caught, but from the heat flooding over my cheeks, my blush didn't.

Simone pointed to the large telephone system at the end of the counter. "Carla's got the phone numbers for everyone in town *and* their dogs." She laughed again, eyeing Watson. "She doesn't like to be caught unaware."

I wanted to ask how in the world she had Leo's number—it wasn't like cell phone numbers were listed—but decided it wasn't important. At least not compared to why I was really there.

"Dirty chai, right?" Simone didn't wait for a response and moved back behind the espresso machine. "Care to make it a double?"

I hadn't planned on getting anything, but who was I to reject a gift from the caffeine gods? "You bet, thanks. Might as well go all the way and get one of your chocolate espresso scones as well."

"Care to make *that* one a double as well?" She grinned.

"Sure, might as—" I shook my head, changing my mind. I knew, even if I had two scones then and there, that within an hour of returning to the Cozy Corgi, I'd wander upstairs and get something from Katie. The madness had to stop somewhere. "No, thank you. I should probably spread my gluttony at even intervals throughout the day."

In less than a minute, Simone slid both the dirty chai and the chocolate espresso scone my way, then pulled a dog treat—of the store-bought variety—from under the counter. "Carla forbade me from ever giving our favorite little corgi treats, but I'm an equal partner in this business, so I'll do what I want." She winked at me. "As long as you don't tell her and get me in trouble, in any case."

When she leaned over the counter to offer it to Watson, the metal spirals in her long dreads clinked together as they so often did. The sound always seemed to rub Watson the wrong way, but even though he cringed, he powered through and gave a little hop to reach the offered treat.

Simone didn't wait for a response before motioning to someone behind me. "Tiffany," she addressed the teenaged employee as she approached. "Do you mind manning the shop on your own for a little bit? I'm going to take a break."

"Sure. No problem." Tiffany gave me the once-over and returned to her duties.

Simone pointed toward the back. "Do you want to meet in the kiln room for privacy?"

"Am I that obvious?" I shouldn't have been surprised, Simone always struck me as quick, and she was just as direct as I tended to be.

"It's not about being obvious. It's just about me not being an idiot. You're either here because of Birdie, Gerald, or both." Simone didn't wait for me to respond and led the way down the hall.

The last time I'd been in the kiln room, I'd found a dead body, or Watson had, rather. Despite myself I glanced to where the woman had sat, covered in clay, almost expecting to see her there. It seemed Watson was of the same mind as he padded over and sniffed the floor in that very area.

"He's quite the dog, that one." Simone studied Watson, then turned to me as she sat at the nearest chair. "You want to start, or is it okay if I just cut to the chase and tell you I didn't kill Birdie or Gerald?"

I sat across from her, studying her as she had Watson. "The official word is that Birdie's death was an accident and Gerald's a suicide, so why would you assume—"

She rolled her eyes as she chuckled, though her voice wasn't unfriendly. "Because you're here, Fred. Again, you know I'm not an idiot, so don't treat me like one."

"Point taken." At times her directness rubbed me the wrong way, but I liked her, at least I thought I did. "What connections did you have with Gerald?"

"Not much." She shrugged. "As you know, I've taken some knitting lessons from Angus, so I ran into Gerald a couple of times there, but other than that, as you also know, he was even less likely to darken the door of the Koffee Kiln than you. I'm not sure which of the two of you Carla's mother-in-law detests more, but Gerald seemed better able to keep his distance."

Sipping the dirty chai, which was almost as good as Katie's, I studied her more as I tried to figure out which direction to go. Simone had delivered the lie flawlessly. Not a twitch, not a glance to the side, not even a hint of nerves or tremor in her voice. If I hadn't seen the proof, I would've believed her completely. I tried again. "So... you didn't have much connection to Gerald, but... some?"

"That would be a fair assessment, I suppose." Still she sounded relaxed. "And as far as Birdie, there was no connection at all. I knew who she was, but she never came into the Koffee Kiln."

Having left the spot where he'd found the body and already having his fill of sniffing the room, Watson padded over, did a couple of circles on the floor a few feet away, and curled up.

I increased my directness. "Did you have any personal... or business... dealings with Gerald, no matter how small?"

For the first time, Simone's eyes narrowed, but if I'd blinked, I would've missed it. "I believe I've already answered that."

"Yes, I suppose you did." Instead of pushing, I switched angles. "What about with the Green Munchies? Are you a customer of theirs?"

"I..." She was thrown off, but only for a moment, the question clearly hitting her from left field. "I'm not sure what business that is of yours? If I am, there's nothing illegal about it, but I'm not saying that I am. Why? Did overdosing on his kombucha play a factor in Gerald's *suicide?*"

"The way you say that, makes it sound like you're certain it wasn't a suicide."

"We've already crossed that bridge, Fred. You're here. I'm not an idiot." Though Simone still smiled, her eyes had become cold and her voice a touch flat.

"As far as I know, no, it didn't play a factor in Gerald's death, at least not directly." I hesitated, hearing Susan's growling voice in my ear as I considered sharing information that wasn't public knowledge, but it would be soon enough, and I was curious about Simone's reaction. "Overdosing on kombucha *did* play a factor in Birdie's death, in a manner of speaking."

"Really? I'd not heard that." Simone crossed her arms, then uncrossed them before reaching between us to break off a piece of the scone from my plate. "That is curious."

She almost nailed it, almost. But if I was right, something about the way Simone delivered the sentiment made me think she'd already known. Hoping to throw her off, I jumped right back to Gerald. "Did Gerald ever talk you into investing money with him?"

She blinked, I could see the lie rise to her lips,

then saw it go. She leaned back once more and took her time to finish chewing the bite of scone she'd snagged. "Yes, he did." It sounded like the admission cost her. "Obviously, you already knew that."

"If so, then why did you tell me you had no further connections with Gerald?"

She bristled. "Because it's none of your business, Fred. And because I didn't have anything to do with Gerald's death, or his suicide, or Birdie's, for that matter, *and* you're not actually the police or the FBI. I don't owe you any explanation."

I flinched—for the second time in two days, the FBI had been brought up. That felt significant somehow.

Simone kept going. "Strange that you're sitting across from me casting stones when I know for a fact you also had investment dealings with Gerald."

"No, I didn't. Or... I didn't choose to..." I shook my head. Why in the world was I explaining that Carl had invested in my name? "How did you know that?"

She shrugged, the motion causing the coils in her hair to clink together again, and her voice returned to friendly neutrality once more. "How did you know that *I* did?"

Though I used drinking the dirty chai as an

excuse to study her, I knew Simone wasn't fooled. I decided it didn't matter. Simone was aware she was being interrogated, in a matter of speaking. She'd agreed to it. And... she'd lied, and then been intentionally and obviously vague. Not to mention that she was much more informed than made sense.

Or maybe it did make sense. Carl had been the one to make the investment in my name, and he was one of the most adept at gossip in the entire town. He could've mentioned it to Simone himself or to someone else and it had made its way through the chain of ears to Simone. But... Carl had been trying to keep his dealing with Gerald a secret from Anna, so that didn't flow either. So... *how would Simone—* Another option flitted in before I'd even finished the mental question. "You arrived in town out of the blue and managed to immerse yourself in it almost instantly. How did you do that?"

Simone laughed and patted my hand, and for the first time in any of our interactions, I felt belittled by her. "It's called moving to a new place, Fred. People do it all the time. And if I'm not mistaken, *you* did it here not all that long before me."

It suddenly occurred to me this wasn't the first time Simone had been well-informed. She'd known all about the Irons family and my history with

Branson before the two of us had even met. She'd chalked it up to local news and town gossip, which was believable, but maybe it was deeper than that. "True enough, you moved here not too long after everything went down with Branson, the chief of police, and other members of the Irons family, and you've been central, or at least closely attached, to more than one murder."

She leaned forward, resting her elbows on her knees, her long dreads falling forward with a cacophony of clanking—causing Watson to lift his head with a gurgling grumble—and narrowed her dark eyes at me. "That's true in one case. There was a murder in my business. It's not true with Gerald or Birdie. I was not involved with either of them, at least no more than you were."

"Yes, but I'm not lying about my involvement with Gerald, and I'm not being coy about any dealings with the Green Munchies." I tilted my chin defiantly. "And I'm sure you remember that particular establishment had direct ties to—"

She laughed, loudly, and somehow possessed the quality of sarcasm, though not cruelty. "Are you kidding me? The Irons family?" That time she tilted her chin. "I'm almost flattered."

"You're *flattered* that I might wonder about you

being involved with a dark, murderous, poisonous, invasive criminal mafia?"

If my accusation stung her at all, Simone didn't let on. "Come on, now. Between the two of us, which one is more likely to be involved with the Irons family?"

I flinched and felt my temper spike. "*Me?* Are you serious? The Irons family killed my—"

"Think about it." Simone's tone was conversational again. "Everything you're flinging at me is doubly true about you, much more than that, actually. How many deaths have you been involved in since you moved to town? And you're the one who dated a member of the Irons family. And isn't it convenient, when you were captured by that very organization, held at gunpoint, that somehow you survived, not only survived, but the head honcho of the Irons family, at least the head honcho of the Estes Park connection, as far as I've heard, got shot instead. For all anyone knows, it was a power play from you and your gang-member boyfriend's part to rise up the ranks."

I laughed, and even I couldn't deny the insane quality to the sound.

Apparently Watson picked up on it as well as he

stood and came to sit at my feet, looking at me in concern.

"I thought you said you weren't an idiot." I was speaking louder than I meant to. "Even if a fraction of what you said is true, that would be absolute suicide. For Branson and me to kill someone above us in the Irons family? In case you haven't noticed, he's gone, and I'm still here. That's the most ridiculous—" I stopped myself with a shake of my head, hearing my own words. Why in the world was I even humoring this at all?

"Rather brilliant, I'd say." Her eyes were cold and steady as she studied me. "One step in your plan to gain power. You could stay, looking like a victim who'd barely escaped death, and can still call the shots here in Estes. All the while your boyfriend is acting on whatever the other portion of the plan is. So again, I say, between the two of us, who's more likely to be responsible for Birdie's accident and Gerald's suicide?"

My cell rang in my pocket. I'd forgotten to turn it to mute.

I stared at Simone, completely floored.

The phone rang again, which was fine as I had no idea what to say, was so thrown off that I'd almost forgotten why I'd come in the first place. When it showed Susan's name on the display, I stood, walked away, and answered with a whisper, "Hey."

Susan didn't bother with pleasantries. "Gerald's autopsy isn't finished yet, but we've already got enough to know it wasn't a suicide. There were bruises over his chest and arms that were revealed under his suit, which would indicate he was restrained in the car."

"Restrained in the..." I couldn't hold back a gasp and glanced over to see Simone studying me. I'd ask Susan questions later.

"So, you are right. We officially have a murder," she continued as if I hadn't spoken anyway. "Where are you? I'm going over to his office. Thought you might want to... that it might be helpful to..." She growled. "Where are you?"

"The Koffee Kiln."

That gave her pause, but she didn't ask. "Fine. I'm already in the car. I'll pick you up in less than five minutes."

"Okay." I started to hang up and then heard Susan's voice continue on the other end.

"Oh, and Fred... bring the fat hamster."

SEVENTEEN

"I have no idea what I was thinking. Clearly I just hadn't had enough coffee." Susan shot me a glare as she brought the police cruiser to a stop in the strip mall parking lot outside of G & J Associates. "Why didn't you tell me I was being stupid and remind me you're capable of driving yourself?" She groaned and wiped at a haze of corgi hair that had been drifting across the dash. "Oh, good grief, since I drove you here, that means I'll also have to drive you back."

"Well, I didn't have a second to—"

"Granted, it's as much my fault as it is yours." Susan kept going, clearly unable to ebb the flow of her rant. "I had the two of you in here before, after that wreck in your other Mini Cooper. I *just* stopped finding dog hair in here less than a month ago." She twisted around to glare at Watson in the back seat. "Actually, it's your fault. What's wrong with you anyway? If you don't need that much hair to stay warm, then why grow it in the first place?"

Watson beamed at her, an expression I'd never seen him give Susan.

She gestured toward him as she turned her glare back to me. "The fat hamster's proud of it. He does it on purpose, to be obnoxious, just like you."

I couldn't disagree with her. Watson did look proud of it. I also couldn't resist egging her on. "What do you mean 'just like me'? I don't shed *that* much?"

"Shed? I was talking about you being obnoxious on purpose. Just to..." Her blue eyes narrowed. "You just did it again. How can someone so frustrating turn out to be helpful at times like these?" Without waiting for a response, she whirled around and flung open the driver's side door, got out, and kept muttering. "I'm cursed, I tell you. First a lifetime sentence cleaning up my idiot brother's messes, then a whole slew of superior officers thinking they know more than me just because they're men, and now a glorified librarian and her fleabag just happen to not be complete morons whenever someone dies." Susan leaned back down to peer through the door, a fall of short hair hanging loose around her face—so different than the typical tight ponytail she normally wore. "Well, get out. I didn't bring you here to relax. Every second you stand there is another layer of dog filth I'll have to try to clean."

Though I couldn't see my own face, I figured my expression matched Watson's from a moment before. "I'm just enjoying the production, Susan. It's like you're auditioning for a one-woman show on Broadway."

"Get out." She barely got the words through her gritted teeth before she slammed the door.

I grinned at Watson. "We should probably do as she says—she is armed and definitely dangerous."

Watson and I exited the police cruiser, and sure enough, the whirlwind of hair that followed caught the morning sunshine, making it look like golden confetti exploding from the car.

Susan groaned again, but refrained from comment, then stepped toward the front door of the law office. "I've got a warrant, so we're legally allowed to break—" She stopped talking when she gripped the handle and the door swung open. "Well, that's odd."

When Watson and I approached, Susan held out her hand to slow us down, then placed it on the holster of her gun as she peered in. She flinched, and surprise lit her voice again. "Paulette? You're here."

We followed Susan in without any more hesitation. Paulette was behind her desk just like she had been before, but she looked tired and strained.

"Of course I'm here. I always arrive at least half an hour before opening time to get everything ready for the day, brew Mr. Jackson's coffee, and..." Her voice seemed to catch, and only then did I realize her eyes were bloodshot as she turned them beseechingly to Susan. "I'm glad you're here. I've been worried."

Susan and I exchanged glances. We hadn't expected Paulette to show up to work the day after her boss died.

We didn't have to inquire before Paulette continued. "I've not heard from Mr. Jackson for *two* days." She started to stand, but her trembling arms didn't appear capable of supporting her on the desk, and she sank back down into her chair. "That's happened before, of course. Mr. Jackson doesn't owe me any explanation where he goes, but with everything going on..."

"Paulette." I headed toward the desk, jumping in before Susan could, fearing she'd be too abrupt. "Haven't you heard about..." Of course she hadn't, clearly. I changed directions. "I'm sorry, but we have some hard news to share with you."

A hand rose instantly to the base of her throat,

fingers closing to form a loose fist, and tears began to stream instantly. "Oh no. No, no."

I took a quick breath. "Gerald—"

"I'm sorry to inform you, Ms. Gibbons—" Susan shot me a glare that clearly communicated for me to let her do her job. "—we discovered Mr. Jackson's body yesterday evening. We were too late to save him."

Paulette covered her face with both hands as she wailed. After an uncomfortable moment, she began to sob and collapsed over the papers strewn across the desk.

I gave Susan a glare of my own, wishing she'd let me handle it a little more gently. I walked behind Paulette's desk and laid a hand on her thin, shaking shoulders. "I'm sorry, Paulette. I can't imagine what a shock this must be." Even as I said it, that part baffled me. News of Gerald's death had spread like wildfire through the town, as every bit of salacious gossip always did.

Watson had followed and wedged himself between me and Paulette, leaning slightly against her leg.

Watson's contact, more than my own, seemed to rally Paulette somewhat. Still sniffing, she angled her head to see Watson and laid a hand on him. He looked up, first at me, then at Paulette.

She started to speak, refocusing on me. "Did he...? I've been worried that... Mr. Jackson's been so upset with some of the letters he's been receiving about his license. The article that horrid Birdie woman wrote... He's just not been himself. Did he...?"

Though she was clearly addressing the question to me, I faltered with moving wordlessly before I turned to Susan for assistance. I had no idea how to answer, considering the revelations Susan had revealed in the car on the way over. After discovering the bruises on Gerald's torso, the police had inspected the car, and found corresponding marks on the seat that also indicated ropes, or that some other type of bonds had been used. The car had been old enough that the marks on the material hadn't been noticeable at first, until they realized what they were looking for. There'd not been any evidence of whatever had bound him.

"We found Mr. Jackson in his car, in the garage. The car was running." Though Susan didn't offer a reassuring smile to Paulette, there was a touch of gentleness behind her matter-of-fact tone. "It looks like he took his own life."

"Oh no! I was afraid he'd... I can't believe... Just like my sweet Walter." Paulette let out a wail and slid from her chair, the motion causing it to roll a few feet behind her as she collapsed to the floor and wrapped her arms around Watson.

It took me a second to parse through what she'd said, not only because her words were garbled with tears. The answer came quickly enough and was obvious. Walter must've been her husband. Horrible, to believe two people you were close to died by suicide. Unsure what to do, I caressed her shoulders again, as soothingly as I could. I had to hand it to Susan, she'd managed that well, being completely honest while not giving away any of the new discoveries that hadn't made it into the local gossip chain yet.

Susan shifted uncomfortably from foot to foot, observing Paulette and Watson easily, and then looking toward Gerald's office, clearly wanting to get on with it.

After a few moments, Paulette's sobbing began to ease. Even so, Watson had to give a sharp jerk to yank his head from out of her embrace. He sneezed as if catching his breath and then padded a couple of feet away and sat, clearly feeling he'd met the obligation as a stand-in support animal.

Paulette cast him a tear-stained smile, attempted to stand, but seemed unable. After pulling the chair back over, I bent, steadying her enough so she could return to her seat. "Can I get you anything? Water, coffee?"

"No. Thank you. I just..." She perched her elbows on the desk and rested her head in her hands. "I just need a minute."

"Take all the time you need, Ms. Gibbons." Susan kept her voice formal. "Do you mind if we search Mr. Jackson's office? See if we can find any clues?" I was surprised she didn't simply state that she had a warrant to search the premises.

"Clues?" Paulette sat straight again. "Why do you need clues if he...?" She shook her head as if saying it was too painful, then lifted her chin—prim once again and more like herself. "No, Mr. Jackson doesn't like people in his office without being there. Not even me."

"Ms. Gibbons, I have a—"

"Paulette." Softening my voice, I shot Susan a warning glance. "I know I wasn't Gerald's favorite person, but I think in this case, he'd be okay with it. To make sure he gets justice."

She turned her tired eyes to me, confusion replacing the prim attitude. "Justice? If he—" She squeezed her eyes shut for a heartbeat and took just that long to indulge in a steadying breath before forcing herself onward. "—killed himself, what justice is there?"

Though I wasn't looking at her, I could feel Susan's glare cutting into me, and I switched angles, using the more formal tone Paulette seemed to appreciate. "You said yourself, all the things written about Mr. Jackson, how they were dragging his name through the mud. Perhaps we can get him justice that way. Maybe something Officer Green or I might find in his office could help clear his name."

Anger flashed across her face, and I could see the refusal rise up again. She seemed to catch herself and shook her head. "You're right. Mr. Jackson went through enough humiliation over the last week. There's no need for him to suffer more of it after his death." Paulette turned back to Susan, the overly formal quality returning to her words as well. "You may enter his office."

Susan bristled, just slightly. "Thank you."

Paulette responded with a tight nod. "If I can help, please let me know." She closed her eyes once more but kept speaking. "After Walter died and we lost the case, I would've been destitute without Mr.

Jackson. He gave me a job, secured my housing... I... owe him."

I squeezed her shoulder, unsure what else to say, then followed Susan toward the office.

"You can stay out here with me, little pup," Paulette cooed to Watson as I walked away.

When I heard his nails clicking across the floor, heading to me, I turned, feeling embarrassed. "Sorry, Watson's not big on social graces, and he does like to have his nose in the middle of things." I offered an apologetic smile. "Literally."

Though she looked a little disappointed, or hurt, Paulette only nodded and began shuffling the papers on her desk into a folder.

Susan bugged her eyes out at me as we walked into Gerald's office, then lowered her voice. "How in the green blazes did that woman not hear about her boss being dead? If I'd known we'd have to do that, I would've brought Officer Jackson along, put him on babysitting duty."

"Ever the softy, aren't you?" I received a judgmental eyebrow arch for my comment. "I get the impression she lives a pretty solitary, maybe even lonely, life. I doubt she's spoken to anyone since she left the office yesterday. Who knows, since Gerald wasn't here, maybe she didn't even speak to another human since the day before that."

Susan considered, then seemed mollified. "When you put it that way, I have to admit, she's figured out the right way to live life if she's able to avoid human contact for so long." Without waiting for more small talk, she motioned to Gerald's desk. "You take that. I'll start with the file cabinet. And *you*—" With her hands on her hips, she leaned forward slightly, addressing Watson. "—sniff around and see if you can find a snack covering up some clues. And try to keep your shedding to a minimum."

Paying her absolutely no attention at all, Watson trotted across the room—for once not bothering to sniff the thing—and disappeared into the shadowy footwell of Gerald's desk. Within a minute or two, I had no doubt we would be treated to corgi snores.

"Useless," Susan muttered, but I thought I detected a grin at the corner of her lips as she turned and opened the top drawer of the file cabinet. "Surprise, surprise. Lawyer boy wasn't diligent with paperwork. Or maybe he simply didn't have that many cases."

I went to work at the desk. Like the one at his house, papers were a complete mess over the surface, but none of them were crumpled and wadded up like the ones the day before. The only thing of interest was his large leather-bound planner. Not expecting to find much, I flipped through and stopped short within a couple of flicks of the page. Unlike the list at his house the day before, all meetings were listed with first initial and last names. There were no notes or details, though the symbols were present, one or two by each name. "Susan, look at this. Gerald used symbols for his appointments like he did with his investors."

She hurried over to inspect, then gave a satisfied nod. "Great. It's *something*. They look a little different than the ones we saw yesterday, but I could be wrong." She tapped my shoulder, hard enough to make me need to regain my balance, as she strode back to the file cabinet. "Good work. Keep going."

Sure enough, within a few more minutes, Watson's snores filled the office, accompanying the shuffling of papers. Every once in a while, a sniff or sigh would filter up from behind the desk, but other than that, there was no noise. Susan and I didn't toss around theories or suspects; we just worked.

As so often when my hands were occupied, my brain began to sift through all the other information. I landed on Simone almost instantly. While I was both surprised and glad Susan had contacted me and wanted me to join her in the search, I would've preferred if her summons had occurred half an hour later and given me a chance to finish up with Simone. Things had felt like they were heading downhill, but sometimes that was when the most answers were uncovered. Simone had already slipped once, though she confessed to lying to me quickly enough. But there was more to her, much more. I could feel it. If anything, her defensiveness proved it. How she'd gone on the attack, having the audacity to accuse me of being with the Irons family.

Not that brilliant a ploy, really. Though bullying wasn't a huge problem with college students as it was with elementary and high schoolers, there were a few occasions when I'd had to deal with it in my classroom. And more than one of them turned the accusation back onto their victims, just as Simone had attempted.

I moved on to the second drawer of the desk, letting out a mental, self-accusing snort as I did so. Why had I gone to my time as a college professor for examples of that, when most of the days of my marriage were nothing but that? There was no argument, no difficult moment, no negative issue that wasn't turned around and placed at my feet, even if it had been Garrett who'd been at fault. A cruel word or comment from his lips was often accompanied by an accusation of me causing him to say such things, and in turn making him feel bad about himself. There were a million examples of those. What Simone had done felt similar.

Although, when I thought about it objectively and from a third party's perspective, her accusation almost made a sick sort of sense. I was the one constantly involved in murder since moving to Estes Park. I had been dating someone with a secret life, someone who turned out to be a murderer. And I had survived meeting members of the Irons family face-to-face by outrageous means. I had to admit, if I was looking into it, I'd suspect myself as well.

Still, I knew I hadn't killed Gerald. Simone... not so much... She'd had secret dealings with Gerald— maybe just the investments, but maybe some connection to the Green Munchies as well. Had the relationship gone south and Simone took vengeance? Was she working with the Irons family and was the one slated to carry out his execution?

At the thought, Katie and Leo's objections returned to me. Why would the Irons family kill Gerald? Why would he work with them to begin with? I'd initially thought money would be the motivator, but after being in his home, I didn't think so.

Although that didn't add up either. The man was on the verge of losing his license for taking insurance companies' money under the table for screwing over his clients. That money had to be somewhere.

"I wish we could find a list of all the clients Gerald betrayed."

I hadn't realized I'd spoken out loud until Susan looked up from where she was kneeling beside the file cabinet. "What?"

"Oh, just..." Still finding nothing, I shut the desk drawer and opened up the final one. "Just wishing we had a list of who Gerald lost cases for, like the list of the future victims of Birdie's column. It would be extremely helpful to have the names of all the clients Gerald betrayed for insurance payouts. Surely that would give some answers. Maybe someone who's connected on all three lists?"

"Be patient. I'm going through the cases and I've got Brent shuffling through them as well. It's not like there's only one thing on our plates. And, no—" She lifted her finger at me as I started to speak. "—I can't give you the list, it's more than my job is worth. You'll have to go through Gerald's decades of cases the old-fashioned way to see who corresponds with the lists you—" She froze, all except for her eyes, which narrowed dangerously. Her voice matched.

"Wait a minute... there's a list of Birdie's future victims?"

"Of course there is. It's—" I stopped, realizing my mistake. "Oh, did I not show you that?"

Her furious glare was all the answer I needed.

Crud! The thought hadn't even crossed my mind. Although if it had, I wasn't sure if I'd show her, as I didn't want to get Athena into trouble. "Sorry... there... is one. I'll show you when we're done here."

"Yeah." She nodded, sharp and furious. "You sure will."

I started to apologize, but then couldn't come up with a good reason that would do anything other than stoke the fires of Susan's anger, so I finished searching the desk and found nothing. When a few minutes passed, I spoke cautiously. "It's strange that we found things at Gerald's house but nothing here. Nothing at all. Not even a record of won and lost cases."

"It's not that weird. If Gerald was worried about getting caught with his investment schemes and his backroom deals with insurance companies, he'd hardly keep them here. This would be the first place people would check. Although, I had my hopes—Gerald never struck me as overly intelligent." She closed the file cabinet door and then reached for the final one before she peered over at me. "Athena?"

"Excuse me?" I looked up, confused, but it cleared instantly and was accompanied by a shot of guilt. "Yes. Athena. But please don't mention it if you don't have to. I don't want it to come back and hurt her job."

Susan didn't bother to answer one way or another and pulled open the bottom drawer. She started to reach in, then paused. "Fred..." Her voice was a whisper. "Here's another one."

When she pulled out a small suitcase matching the style of the one we'd found in his home closet, I stood and headed her way.

Susan didn't wait, and unlike the one I'd opened, the clasps on this one were already released. "No food in this one, no wonder the mutt wasn't helpful." She pulled out neatly folded clothes, some hygiene products, and a passport. After looking at it, she passed it my way.

Peter Rice. "Different alias than yesterday."

She nodded and moved to the zipper in the top portion of the suitcase. "Maybe you'll get your wish. Makes sense we'd find a list of all his investors at home, and a list of insurance companies he had deals with here in the office. At least as much sense as anything Gerald did." She slipped her hand inside and felt around, but the frustration that crossed her face answered even before she spoke. "Nothing."

Disappointment cut through me, but I wasn't surprised. Like Susan had said only moments before, Gerald would've been stupid to leave proof in his place of business. It was unbelievable enough that he'd left his getaway pack in an unlocked file cabinet. Surprise mingled with the disappointment when I looked over her shoulder to see inside and found the suitcase empty. "Snacks aren't the only thing Gerald forgot to pack. There's no money in this one either."

"Huh!" Susan returned to the clothes, unfolding each of them roughly by giving them a shake. Nothing fell out of them. "You're right."

We searched for another unfruitful hour. Even so, we boxed up nearly everything that wasn't nailed down. Susan called Officer Jackson to come babysit, as she put it, Paulette and gently escort her home. By the time Susan had driven Watson and me back to the Mini Cooper, I'd given her the list of names of Birdie's intended targets, and though she scoffed, I filled her in on my suspicions of Simone Pryce, the Green Munchies, and the possible connection to the Irons family.

EIGHTEEN

I managed a quick wave and smile to Ben when I finally arrived at the Cozy Corgi, before making a beeline to the stairs. I should've taken Simone up on her offer of a double scone. It was nearly lunchtime, and I was ravenous. Watson more than made up for my rudeness by bounding over like a newborn fawn and nearly knocking Ben into the customer he was helping. I was halfway to the bakery when the front door of the bookshop opened again, and for some ridiculous reason, I looked over to see who it was.

Angus Witt walked in and barely scanned the shop before he found me and strode my way.

So close! I could practically hear the empanadas calling my name. It wasn't an exaggeration that I could also make out the sweet assortment of Katie's pastries join in the empanadas' lure by singing a siren song of sugar, butter, and cinnamon.

I made it back to the base of the steps as Angus

reached me, and I offered him a gentle smile as my stomach rumbled.

He didn't seem to notice and grasped my hands. "I need you to solve this."

There was no clarification needed. The desperation in his eyes said it all. At the speed with which he crossed the shop, several of the tourists turned our way and studied us with open curiosity. I peered into the mystery room, found it empty, and motioned with my head. "Come on, step in there."

Angus followed and joined me on the antique sofa. It was warm enough that no one had lit the river rock fireplace. "I need you to figure out who murdered Gerald." Even as we sat, Angus didn't let go of my hand. "I need you to figure it out quickly so I can kill them."

There was such fury in his typically kind green eyes that it transformed his grandfatherly appearance to something shockingly intimidating. And in that moment, I didn't think he spoke of murder in hyperbole. He meant it.

"The thought that someone would go into his own home, murder him, and then have the audacity... the gall... the disrespect to try to make it look like he..." Angus trembled and squeezed my hand so tight I sucked in a breath. He pulled back instantly. "Sorry. I need to get a hold of myself."

"It's okay. Gerald was your friend. It only makes sense that you'd be upset." After leaving Paulette, who hadn't even known Gerald was dead, I was thrown off by Angus's proclamation that Gerald had been murdered. Maybe it had gotten out that the police suspected foul play, but I wasn't sure how. I decided to tread lightly, both to not give too much away and to hopefully avoid insulting Angus. "You think it was murder? What have you heard?"

"Of course it was murder." He snorted the words out and seemed to backtrack. "Gerald wouldn't kill himself. I know... knew him nearly as well as I know myself. He wasn't a perfect man, and he had a host of flaws, but he wouldn't kill himself, no matter what was going on."

"You also believed that Birdie was murdered— that was why you came to me in the first place. To help clear Gerald of that accusation. But it turns out she wasn't murdered, as I'm sure you've heard, it was an accident. One that Gerald was potentially responsible for."

"*This* was murder. *Actual* murder, intentional." Angus grabbed my hand again. "I'll help you. Whatever we need to do to figure it out, I'm behind you a hundred percent. I'm going to rip apart whoever did this limb by limb, piece by piece."

I never would have dreamed the elderly knitter could be so scary. "Let's say Gerald was murdered." I hurried on before Angus could continue his diatribe. "Can you think of anyone who'd have cause to want him dead?"

"If I could narrow it down that quickly, I'd go after them myself instead of being here with you." Angus released my hand once more, just in time, as his grip was beginning to tighten again. "Like I said, Gerald had his faults, and there are plenty of people who had legitimate reasons to hate him. Unfortunately, too many to narrow down. And again, that's why you're one of the ones I'm turning to for help figuring this out. I trust you and your intelligence the most."

"*One* of the ones you're turning to?" What did that mean? Before he had the chance to reply, the implications of what Angus had said clicked, and I was genuinely surprised. "Angus... you knew the accusations Birdie made against Gerald were true, didn't you?"

He didn't hesitate, didn't blink, didn't look away. "Yes, I did."

I was nearly speechless but not quite. "Then why did you ask me to—"

"I asked you to help us figure out who was setting Gerald up for murder. Like I've already said, Fred, I knew Gerald's faults. The ability to kill someone wasn't one of them." Angus's tone was matter-of-fact, neither cold nor defensive.

"So it's forgivable that Gerald had no problem ruining people's lives by intentionally losing their cases to get money from insurance companies as long as he didn't kill anyone?" I didn't attempt to keep the judgment out of my voice.

"I believe I was fairly direct about that with you as well when we met at my shop the other day. Gerald and I were friends, and he respected me greatly, but unfortunately he didn't always heed my advice."

I stared at him, blown away.

Angus smiled at me. A gentle thing, one that he'd bestowed on me several times before. "I can see I've disappointed you, that you think less of me now."

"I'm sor—" I shook my head, cutting myself off. I wouldn't apologize for the truth of what he said. Besides, he was already aware of it. "I expected more of you, that's true. I always wondered how you were so close with..." I started to say Gerald, but then realized it went further than that. Leo had been right. Gerald, Mark, Rocky, and Angus had been like the four musketeers. Angus always seemed the odd man out, the one with class, the one who was trying to keep his friends on the straight and narrow. I struggled to superimpose this new reality of Angus over the appearance of the man who sat in front of me. Maybe it shouldn't have been that hard. What was that saying? *You'll know a man by the company he keeps*, something like that. The truth had been in front of me all the time. The only way Angus was an exception to his friends was that he simply had more shine and polish. "Yes. I did expect more of you. Although now I realize how intentionally obtuse that was."

"That saddens me, as I hold your respect in high regard, but I don't judge you for it." Genuine disappointment crossed his features, altering his small smile. "Nevertheless, part of why I have that high regard for you is that I know you put your personal feelings to the side so justice is served."

He'd said that very thing to me the other day, but now I felt foolish and couldn't keep the bitterness out of my tone. "That's not true for you, though, is it? You set justice aside because of your personal feelings."

"That's true." Again, Angus made no attempt to deny or sugarcoat. "So, will you help me figure out who murdered my friend?"

Maybe I should have gone back to pretending I wasn't sure if this was murder or not, but I didn't bother. "No, I won't help *you*, but I will try to find out who murdered Gerald. And I'll accept any information or leads or instincts you have. But I won't be doing it *with* you. And when I figure it out, I won't report it back to you so you, Mark, and Rocky can take matters into your own hands. I'll go directly to the police."

The smile changed again to the one I'd come to expect, the one that had fooled me into not seeing the full measure of the man—or had flattered me into not seeing it. Even though I'd just insulted him, he looked at me with respect and admiration. "You are something, Winifred Page. Utterly spectacular."

Annoyed that I still possessed the ability to be flattered at his praise, I pushed on. "But you knew about his investments? I remember you saying he went against your advice regarding those. Do you know who he was involved with? There's been some strange connections to the Irons family, and they'd for sure have the ability to—"

"Now who's letting their personal feelings affect

how they perceive reality?" The admiration left his expression, and his tone sounded as if he was addressing a student who'd suddenly become a disappointment. "Don't let your own obsession cloud your intelligence, Winifred. It's always been one of your strengths, to be able to see things as they are, not how you want them to be."

I flinched, and anger rose, as did embarrassment, which only made the anger spike hotter. It was bad enough to have other people insinuate I was obsessed with the Irons family, seeing them behind every shadow. It was even worse from someone who'd just shown their own lack of integrity. "Why is that so far-fetched? Murdering someone and making it look like a suicide isn't exactly beyond their capabilities."

"It wasn't the Irons family, Fred." He sounded bored. "Why would they waste their time on someone like Gerald? I loved him like a brother, but he was small potatoes and easily pushed about and manipulated. If he was having problems with the Irons family, they wouldn't go through the bother of setting up his death like they did. They'd simply kill him and be done with it."

It angered me further that Angus's argument against the Irons family was the first one that made sense to me, caused me to question. "But, if he owed them money, if they wanted to make him an example —" Even before I finished, I knew that was wrong. Once more, Angus was right. Just killing him would've been more of an example than trying to make it look like suicide.

"This was personal, not business." The kindness returned to his eyes, and the disappointment left his voice. He still sounded like he was speaking to a student, but this time instructing, not belittling. "Surely you can see that. It's not just covering tracks. It's a way to humiliate him. Make him seem like a coward—that he couldn't take it, that he couldn't face all that he had done, so he offed himself."

"Suicide doesn't indicate someone was a coward. It just—"

With a sigh he stood. "You can be as politically correct as you need to, Fred, and I'm not going to argue the realities around why a person might kill themselves, but what you need to be looking at is how such an act is perceived and why someone would do that to Gerald." The coldness returned, as did that flash behind his eyes that made him scary. "Just in case you need some motivation to leave your obsession behind and stay in reality, you'll want to figure this out before I do, because as I've already demonstrated, I *will* put my personal feelings before justice."

I sat there, stunned, and watched him walk away. It was like I'd never met the man before. And again, I was nearly as disturbed at myself as I was at Angus. I considered myself an exemplary judge of character, but I never would've seen that coming.

I was utterly useless for the rest of the day, which was starting to be a very unhelpful pattern. Maybe it was defiance or maybe I just needed the comfort, but I lit the fire, despite the heat of the July day, gathered my half of the paperwork Susan and I had taken from Gerald's office, curled up on the sofa, and began to go through it again, piece by piece. I knew I wasn't playing it smart going through them out in the open. Susan had made it clear she was breaking protocol by letting me take some of them, but her dismissive shrug had communicated that she trusted my judgment and my eye more than the others at the station. Out of respect for that, I only did one piece at a time, and put another book on top of it anytime someone else came into the room. If it didn't lead anywhere, I'd pull out the computer and start researching Gerald's court cases, even if it would take a hundred times longer that way without Susan's resources.

Watson was more than happy to be useless as I went over paper after paper. He played the part of a snoring round puffball in the center of his oversized ottoman.

When Katie and the twins closed up the Cozy Corgi and left, the two of us hadn't moved an inch. Katie had offered to break her plans with Paulie so she could stay and help, but after the interaction with Angus, I was still in a terrible mood and felt like I had something to prove. Atypically, I wanted to do it on my own.

Unwilling to break the dinner plans I had with my family, I was just getting ready to put everything away—after the doors were locked, I'd spread scores of papers over the sofa—when a name caught my attention from my photocopies of Gerald's planner. With a gasp that caused Watson to interrupt his snoring with an annoyed snort, I pulled the papers closer to me, hardly believing what I was seeing.

Beaker.

It was the only name written on that date, and since it was scheduled for two days from today, it was a meeting that would never occur. *P. Beaker.* 2:00 *PM.* There were two of the scribbled drawings—

hieroglyphics, codes... whatever they were—beside the appointment.

It took me several moments to figure out who the P was. Clearly not Ethel or Carla. Then it hit. Jonathan. Jonathan Beaker. Carla's husband, Ethel's son.

What in the world was Ethel's son meeting Gerald Jackson about? No doubt he knew how much his mother hated the man. I'd not had much interaction with Jonathan, but he'd always struck me as rather passive and... though it sounded judgmental... more of a sponge than anything with a backbone. Clearly I'd been wrong about him too, if he'd been willing to meet one of his mother's enemies behind her back. Unless... unless there was some ploy between mother and son to take Gerald Jackson down.

Excitement coursing through me for the first time in hours, I flicked back through the pages of the planner, and there it was, complete with the same symbols as the other one. How had I missed it the other times? It didn't matter. It didn't change the fact that P. Beaker had met with Gerald one other time. I double-checked the date to make sure my figuring was correct. It was. They'd met on July 1, before Birdie's column had premiered in *The Chipmunk*

Chronicles. Three days before the tell-all about Gerald was published.

It took everything in me to continue putting the papers away and head to meet my family. If the Beakers were involved, I needed to proceed with caution. To go slowly. To be smart.

NINETEEN

"Oh, Fred! And Watson!" Hester Gonzales called to us in greeting as she hurried from behind the hostess stand. Though her smile was bright, her tone indicated more apology then greeting. "Marcus is going to be so sad to have missed you and your little darling." She must've seen the truth across my face as she pulled back from her warm hug. "Don't worry, I won't take his place and snap photos of you or pry into any murders."

Habaneros was a frequent hangout spot for Katie, Leo, and me, occasionally joined by Paulie and Athena as well—not to mention for my entire family. No matter how many times we ate there, Hester's husband embarked on the same routine every single time. He was desperate to have a murder in his restaurant so Watson and I could solve it.

"Dinner won't be the same without a photo shoot, but I'll eat enough queso to cover the loss." I smiled at Hester as she stood from petting Watson, who'd only slightly cringed out of the way. "I'm meeting my family here. Mom just texted and said they're on the patio. I feel less guilty bringing Watson when we can eat outside."

She waved me off as she grabbed a menu. "Don't think twice about it. Watson's a celebrity." She indicated the vast assortment of framed photographs of Marcus and famous people of various importance before she led us through the brightly painted restaurant. "You know we have a weakness for those." She dropped me off at the table and promised to send the server over promptly.

I did a double take at the small table. I sat between Mom and Percival. "Where are the twins and the kids?"

Watson and Barry entered into a raucous and joyous greeting, cutting off Mom's answer and earning a few glares from a table of tourists nearby.

"Good thing the appetizers haven't been delivered yet." Percival pulled a sour face that was more for show than anything, at the hair rising from where Barry greeted Watson. "Or they'd be wearing a fur coat."

Gary simply rolled his eyes and leaned around his husband to press a kiss to my cheek in greeting.

Watson finally settled to a quiet happy whining, and with a slightly guilt-ridden glance my way, curled up under Barry's chair.

"That dog has good taste." Mom grinned, patted Barry's hand, and finally answered me. "They were planning on it, as you know, but some old friends came into town spur of the moment and are only spending the night, so they had to cancel. I told them they could bring their friends along, it's not like it's a private party."

"Then I would've taken a pass." Percival issued a dramatic sigh. "Twins. More twins." He lifted his eyebrows as he gave me a bug-eyed stare. "*Apparently*, these are friends they met back in the day at one of those twin conventions. They are also a situation of twin brothers marrying twin sisters. It's like a sick cult or something. Why, if it weren't for those sweet Pacheco boys who work for you and Katie, I'd think all twins are looney tunes."

"Percival, really." As normal, Mom attempted to chide her older brother, for all the good it would do.

"I hardly think you're in any place to call someone else looney tunes." Though he addressed Percival, Gary focused on me and made a show of pointing toward Percival's wrist. "Check out your uncle's new purchase."

"Rude!" Percival let out a little screech, shoved Gary's shoulder, and then swiveled back around toward me, excitement replacing his offense. "But really, he's right, you must see it. Isn't it perfect?" He stretched out his long thin arm so his wrist was mere inches from my nose.

I had to lean back slightly to keep it from being blurry and took a few moments before I responded to make sure none of the laughter I felt would be heard. "I don't think I've ever seen a watchband covered in fur before. Purple fur at that."

"Oh, Fred." Barry shook his head like I just made an egregious error as Percival yanked his arm back.

"Purple! It's *boysenberry*, clearly. It matches my fur coat." He shimmied his shoulders. "I'm going to be the talk of the town."

"You already are, dear." Gary patted Percival's thin shoulders. "And not just because you're wearing a fur watch, in July of all times."

"It's perfectly acceptable to wear a fur watch in July." Percival pointed toward the river that wound its way along the sidewalk. "There's a mist in the air. I could catch a chill."

"I don't know what Phyllis and I are going to do without you all to entertain us for three weeks."

Barry chuckled. "Fur watches. Here I thought I'd seen everything."

"Actually, it's faux fur, of course." Percival stretched out his arm again and waggled a finger, encompassing Barry's torso. "And a grown man who doesn't own anything in his closet without some garish version of tie-dye shouldn't cast aspersions."

Some small part of me had considered canceling dinner after all, but I was glad I hadn't. I'd needed my family's ridiculous brightness. "You all are more absurd than a sitcom." I angled toward Mom and grasped her hand. "I'm going to miss you too, but I know how excited you've been for this trip."

"Ever since I opened Barry's present on Christmas, it's been about the only thing I can think of." Mom cast a quick smile at Barry and turned back to me, looking like a little girl in her excitement. "Getting to tour all the healing crystal caves of Scotland, it's a dream."

At that moment, the server came over and delivered three huge ramekins of bubbling queso. I gaped at my family after she'd taken our order and left. "Did you forget the twins weren't coming? There's almost one bowl for each of us."

"We know your fondness for cheese, dear." Mom

pushed one of the bowls toward me. "And you had a stressful week, you deserve it."

"Considering all the pastries I have during the day, I'm not so sure that's true, but I like your logic." I grabbed a chip and scooped a heaping portion. "And I'm sure it says absolutely horrible things about me that I'm rather glad Leo had to work tonight, and I don't have to share."

We got lost to cheese for a while. Or rather, I got lost to cheese while Mom spoke of all the different types of crystals they expected to see on their cave tours, and the hope she'd be able to bring home a large souvenir of unpolished jasper.

When the cheese was gone and our dinners were delivered, Watson wandered back over to sit by my side, making clear his expectation of being slipped pieces of chicken and steak from my sizzling fajita platter. Percival took the disruption in Mom's excitement about the trip to lean in with a lower voice. "Like your mother said, you've had a busy week. Any word about Gerald?"

The light, happy feeling of the dinner vanished instantly. Percival, my mom, and Barry had all grown up with Gerald. In adulthood, he'd been friends with all three men, including Gary. I supposed he'd been friends with my mother too, but she'd experienced some of the same dismissive behavior that I had from Gerald.

I didn't have to consider if I was breaking confidences. Well... I knew I was breaking confidences, but I didn't have to consider if my family was trustworthy. They were. And even though Percival and Gary were the on-again, off-again ruling gossip champions, tied with the Hansons, I had no doubt they wouldn't share anything they shouldn't.

As I slipped Watson a slice of chicken, I glanced around just to make sure no one was listening in. They weren't, and thanks to the pleasant sound of the river tumbling over the rocks, that made the likelihood of anyone accidentally hearing fairly unlikely as well. Even so, I lowered my voice and leaned in at the table. "Definitely wasn't suicide. There were—" I started to explain about the evidence of being secured they found on Gerald's body, and about the phone call I'd gotten from Susan later that afternoon that the contents of his lungs confirmed that he had died by carbon monoxide poisoning and affixation. Maybe that was too much for them to hear about their friend. "The autopsy came back with proof that Gerald didn't kill himself."

Mom sighed in relief, and Barry gave an affirmative nod. "I knew he wouldn't do that." Percival nodded as well, but Barry kept speaking. "It didn't matter—all the lies in the article about him, all the stuff people saying. Gerald wouldn't kill himself just because of a bunch of gossip."

From the looks Mom and Gary both flashed toward Barry, it was clear this had been a subject of discussion, one in which they'd disagreed, though maybe they hadn't said so out loud. I did it for them and tried to do so with as much gentleness as I could. "They weren't lies, Barry. From what I can tell, everything Birdie wrote about Gerald was true."

Barry flinched, then shook his head. "No, kiddo." He shrugged. "Sure, maybe he had some bad investment schemes and didn't lead people in the right way with those, but there wasn't malice in that. And sure, he liked his infused kombucha, but we all know I'm not one to pass judgment on that, but he would never intentionally swindle his clients."

"I agree." Percival spoke up again. "Granted, he could be selfish at times and a little self-absorbed, perhaps, but who isn't from time to time? Gerald wouldn't have ruined people's lives just to make a buck."

For a second, I considered not saying anything, letting them go ahead and believe what they wanted to about their friend, but I couldn't. "It is true. We found evidence that he was on the verge of losing his license because of it and facing some lawsuits. And... I spoke to Angus this afternoon. He was aware Gerald was double-dealing with the insurance companies."

"What?" Mom's eyes widened, and her gasp more than proclaimed that while she might have thought ill of Gerald, she never would've predicted such a thing from Angus. "I can't believe..."

Gary didn't seem surprised, but Barry and Percival both stared at me, and I could see the war raging behind their eyes, but then the two of them exchanged looks and gave twin sighs of defeat.

It was Mom who recovered the quickest, maybe because she hadn't been as fooled regarding Gerald, or maybe because she'd been a detective's wife and trusted her instincts. "So, a client of his killed Gerald in retribution for intentionally losing their case?"

"Maybe." I winced, and when Watson pawed at the toe of my cowboy boot, I slipped him another piece, this time of steak. "That's what Angus thinks. That's why he came to me this afternoon, wanted to make sure I didn't think Gerald killed himself and that I would work to find out who killed him." I glanced around the table but leveled my stare on Mom. "I have to say, I've not had the right measure of Angus. The fact that he knew what Gerald was doing and didn't seem to have a problem with it, and when we were talking, he made it very clear that if he found out who killed Gerald before I did, he'd take matters into his own hands."

Speechless, Mom lifted her hand to cover her mouth with her fingers.

"Don't judge too harshly, Fred." Barry spoke, heavy sadness in his tone. "The two of them were as close as brothers. I'm not saying what Gerald did was right or Angus looking the other way was right either, but when you're close to someone, when they're like family and someone hurts them, it's only natural to want to... take matters into your own hand, as you said."

It was rare that I blatantly disagreed with Barry anymore, but that time I did. "As you're aware, I do know what it's like to lose family, we all do. And I do want justice and closure. I do want to find out who the people are who are responsible for killing Dad." As I spoke, Mom reached over and closed her hand over mine, giving it a supportive squeeze. "But I don't plan on killing whoever it is myself, or having someone else do it for that matter."

Proving I was more important than chicken or steak, Watson propped his head on my knee in that moment and peered up in love and concern. I stroked between his ears, taking comfort. Smiling, Mom did the same.

"No. I suppose you have a point there. And I do know what you've been through." He slipped a tie-dyed arm over Mom's shoulders. "What you've both been through. I'm sorry I spoke so rashly. However, I do hope Angus was just speaking out of the heat of the moment."

"I don't think he was." Though it was only a couple of hours away from the interaction, some part of me was already pushing back against it, whispering that I'd misunderstood or read into his reaction as it was so unexpected from a man I'd seen as nothing but gentle. But I hadn't misunderstood, and from his intensity, I didn't think it was just a matter of being in the heat of the moment.

We ate in silence for a few minutes, Watson returning to his chicken and steak begging, and then Gary spoke again. "It sounded like you think there's another possibility than one of Gerald's clients trying to get revenge?"

Hesitating, I glanced toward Mom, not wanting to cause her pain or put more of a cloud over her departure the next day. But I also wanted her input. "I was wondering about the Irons family."

Sure enough, she winced.

Instantly I regretted bringing it up and though I still thought it was an option, I switched to my newest theory. "But I think I might be wrong about that. I just discovered"—I leveled my gaze on each of them, especially Percival—"that Gerald was meeting with Jonathan Beaker."

From their expressions, no explanation was needed. People all over town knew who the Beakers liked and didn't like.

"Ethel." Percival's whisper had exultation in it, like he'd just solved the murder himself. "I've often wondered about Jonathan, how controlled he must feel with her as his mother. I bet you anything he was meeting with Gerald to plot against her. If she found out, she'd not hesitate before killing Gerald. Of course she'd have someone else do it." His eyes widened, and his voice shot up in excitement. "I bet she had Birdie taken out as well. Probably was afraid she'd be the subject of one of the next 'A Little Bird Told Me' columns."

"Oh goodness. I can't believe I... things have just been so busy." The concerns over Birdie felt like ages ago and old news. I'd forgotten for the rest of the world it had only been a matter of days, and that not everyone had Susan in the police department giving them inside information. "This is also extremely confidential, but Birdie's death was an accident... while she was unbelievably high. However, Gerald was going to probably be on the hook for that as well because he provided her with the cannabis-infused kombucha, and it had levels in it that weren't appropriate for someone who didn't have a built-up tolerance for it."

Mom gave another groan as if it was all too much, though Barry sat a little straighter, like I'd just said something hopeful. "Or maybe this is all a setup from Ethel. She could've provided kombucha with toxic levels of cannabis in it so it looked like Gerald..." His words trailed away, as did the hope in his eyes as I shook my head.

"No, and Gerald confirmed it. Besides that, you're right about one thing. Ethel was behind it, but behind the *column*, not the *murder*. She provided a whole list of people she wanted Birdie to write snuff jobs about."

"Now that sounds like Ethel." Percival snorted out of disgust. "I'm surprised it was just you, Fred, that we weren't all going to be the subject of her little ploy."

I met his gaze. "*You* were on the list."

He flinched. "Really?"

I nodded.

"Huh." He blinked, shared a look with Gary, and then turned back to me. "Did you... happen to see what my column's topic was going to be about?"

"No, I just saw the list." When he brightened at that, I pushed a little bit. "Do we need to be worried? Just because Birdie's dead doesn't mean Ethel can't still use what she knows."

His brightness dimmed a bit, but barely, before he forced out a laugh and waved it off. "Oh, my darling niece, if you get to be my age and you *don't* have enough dirt in your past to fill up a measly gossip column, then you're doing something wrong."

When Gary chuckled at that and didn't seem overly concerned, I was somewhat mollified. I was tired of finding out dark secrets in people's pasts. It was one thing when it was Gerald, or even discovering Angus wasn't quite as harmless as I thought him to be. It was a whole other issue if it was family and friends.

Percival seemed to read my mind and leaned nearer. "Well... maybe I should confess, just so you'll not have to worry."

I couldn't do more than gape at him.

His tone dipped, growing more serious and quieter. "You know my boysenberry coat?"

I nodded, dread filling my gut.

"It belonged to a woman named Charlotte Rockefeller. You know... from the Rockefellers?"

At his cocked eyebrow, I force myself to nod that *yes, I had heard of the Rockefellers.*

"Well, interestingly enough, she was a twin also. And back in the day—" He swallowed, then glanced toward my mother as if breaking the news to her too. "—she wore this coat all over town, New York, obviously. I... well... I killed her for it."

"What?" My voice went higher than I'd intended, causing Watson to jump beside me. Then realizing who I was talking to, I smacked my uncle hard on the shoulder.

He snorted. "Wait! I'm not done. I must make a *full* confession and get it off my conscience. It's been eating me alive." He thrust out his wrist again. "I ran into her twin... er... Scarlet Rockefeller, and she was wearing this spectacular matching watch. Well... needless to say, Scarlett is now back with her twin, Charlotte, and the watch is back with the coat."

I smacked him again. "I hate you."

Percival roared with laughter, causing Watson to growl, which only made Percival laugh even louder. After a moment, Barry and Gary joined in as Mom scowled. "I swear, you nearly gave me a heart attack."

The rest of the meal continued on in a light-hearted manner, Mom and Barry giving further details about their trip, and Gary and Percival talking about a musical they were planning on seeing in Denver the following weekend. But after the bill was paid, we all sat there—the sunset growing pink over the mountains, the rushing river lulling and hypnotizing, while moths flitted dangerously close to the candles on our tables—and began to mull over theories of who might have hurt Gerald. After a while I didn't join in, just listened to their speculations, while my own possibilities percolated in my mind.

Mom leaned closer, accidentally nudging my arm with her shoulder as she did. "What is that?"

"What is—" I followed her gaze to the sketches I'd been absentmindedly drawing on the back of the receipt. "Oh, in Gerald's appointment book and some of his other things, he put these symbols by people's names. They don't seem to be anything known, some type of abbreviation or something. I think he made them up."

"That sounds like him." Mom shifted so she could see the receipt easier. "Gerald always presented like he was an open book, but even in school he'd do things like that, keep secrets, make it look as if he knew things no one else did."

"Maybe that's how he's been doing dastardly deeds all this time without getting caught." I circled the one that had been drawn by Jonathan Beaker's name. "They could be nothing, but also might be the thing that cracks this wide-open. But if he made them up, no way to know. We haven't found the key or anything that defines them."

Mom considered and continued studying the drawings she spoke. "Did you ask Ms. Gibbons about them?"

"No." I gave her a quizzical expression.

"If anyone knew, I would think it would be his secretary. She's worked for him for a few years now, I believe." Mom shrugged. "Gerald liked to keep secrets, but maybe not from her. Not if her knowing made his work easier. He was always secretive, but Gerald was lazy too." She winced a little and then shook her head with a little laugh. "Bad to say such things about the dead, but it's true, nevertheless."

That should have been obvious. Why hadn't we asked Paulette about the symbols? I doubted the chance was high that she'd know as much as Mom seemed to think, but even if Gerald hadn't trusted her with it, perhaps she knew him well enough that she'd be able to decipher some of their meanings.

TWENTY

"Really, Winifred? It's after eight and you're calling me. You really need to get a life." Susan's bored voice answered the phone, while familiar music played in the background. "Don't you have a boyfriend or something?"

"I had a life *before* I was in a relationship, thank you very much. Besides, he's working. The moonlight hikes are really popular this season, and..." Irritation at myself entered, as I realized how that sounded. In the pause, I recognized the faint music on the other end of the phone, and I couldn't help myself. "I don't know if you're one to judge about having a life if you're sitting there simply watching *Golden Girls* reruns." As soon as I gave into the impulse, I regretted it. Susan's and my relationship was much better than it used to be, but she could still get under my skin and make me act like a middle schooler.

"How do you know I'm watching... oh." There was a click, and the background noise vanished. The bristle in Susan's voice increased. "Not that it's any of your business what I watch or do during my off hours, but for your information, I'm working. I just happened to have the TV on for background noise." Susan might be working, but the second part was a lie, I had no doubt. I'd been utterly floored when I discovered Susan had a penchant for cheesy old sitcoms. "I keep going over the paperwork we got this morning. Not that there was much there, but I feel like the answer is in there someplace, or, more so, in what's not there."

"That's why I'm calling you." After dinner, I'd stopped by the Cozy Corgi and snagged a few of the remaining pastries, then called Susan as soon as Watson and I returned to the car. "I don't know how I didn't think of it before, but if there's any way to decipher Gerald's symbols, I bet Paulette is our best shot."

Susan groaned. "I don't think I have it in me. I don't do well with prissy and persnickety. I also don't do well with a lot of crying. Put them together and you're holding my kryptonite."

I was tempted to point out that someone who enjoyed *The Golden Girls* should have a little more empathy toward elderly women, but I refrained. "Paulette is a little... serious, I'll give you that, but cut her some slack. It's clear she put Gerald on a pedestal, and add that to the fact he died the same way as her husband—or at least Paulette thinks he did—and that's a lot for anyone to handle." I heard Susan start to protest and rushed on. "Besides, I'm not asking you to do anything about Paulette. Just calling to see if you knew where she lived, thought I might swing by on my way home and see what she says about the symbols."

"Number one, as I told you before, I am *not* an information hotline. *Especially* when I'm off the clock." As many times before, I thought I picked up the slight enjoyment in Susan's voice, as if giving me a hard time was the best part of her day. "And two, it's getting kind of late, don't you think? I doubt she's in the mood for guests. Who knows, she's probably already asleep."

I had considered the last part but was too driven to care. "I have a box of pastries to help her get over my rudeness, and she seems to have a soft spot for Watson. I'm hoping between the two she'll give me a few minutes."

"Better you than me. I have her address in the file here somewhere." Susan sighed. "Besides, maybe you'll get a new angle. I'm spinning in circles. It's right at my fingertips. I just can't—"

"Did you notice the appointments with Jonathan Beaker?"

There was a pause in the flicking of pages. "In Gerald's schedule? No, I didn't. Honestly, I've barely glanced at it. I've been more focused on trying to trace the trails of money that weaved around his list of investors. Not to mention, I also got the information on Gerald's cases from the courts, so I'm working on going through those as well." She didn't pause to consider as she changed directions. "That is interesting, though. Maybe I'm going the wrong way with that. Ethel wouldn't like the idea of her son meeting with Gerald. But... as unpleasant as Ethel is, I don't think she's a murderer."

"But she might pay to have someone murdered." I stole Percival's idea.

Susan laughed. "You're right. *That* I can see. Still, that's a weak motive, although I've seen weaker. I think the money angle has more of a chance of playing out. I keep coming back to Angus. How you mentioned he claims to have gotten Gerald started in the investments and then Gerald went rogue. Maybe Angus had enough."

"That wasn't exactly how I put it, and while I

don't think Angus is the kind old man I thought he was, I can't believe he'd kill Gerald. Their friendship was real. You saw Rocky's reaction yesterday, and you know how close your brother is to those three."

"Thanks for that reminder." She made a disgusted sound. "On that note, I'm going to get back to this list and see if I can make sense of it. Figure out what Gerald *didn't* say in his paperwork. Let me know if Paulette has any insight into the symbols, that is if you can even get her to answer the door. In fact—" She paused as if considering, and then almost sounded like the words were forced out of her when she spoke again. "—why don't you come here after you meet with her? Going through the court cases will go faster with two of us."

Paulette did answer the door, in a neat but worn blue flannel nightgown under a green housecoat, pink foam curlers in her hair, and a stern expression over her face. "Honestly, Ms. Page. It's nearly bedtime. I was just getting ready to put on my night cream. Besides that, it's common courtesy to call instead of arriving unannounced at one's doorstep."

"I know. I'm sorry. I won't take much of your time. I just wanted to know if—" I switched directions midthought, hoping to soften her up, and held out the box of pastries with the Cozy Corgi logo on top. "*Watson* and I wanted to bring you something yummy. We know today has been rough."

Her intelligent gaze narrowed on the box, but then softened as it traveled down to where Watson sat stonily at my feet. As soon as she bent down to pet him, I knew she'd let us in.

That certainty was threatened when Watson looked like he was about to pull away, probably afraid he'd get strangled in another sobbing embrace, but he sat stoically as she stroked over his head and muzzle. I had to admit, he'd gotten much better at faking social niceties during his time as the Cozy Corgi mascot.

"Such a sweet boy." Seeming more relaxed, she stood and moved aside, ushering us in. "Thank you for whatever baked goods you brought, though it's much too late at night to indulge in such things. While I appreciate them, and the visit from Watson, I'm certain you have another ulterior motive on why you showed up at my doorstep, so let's get to it."

As Paulette shut and locked the door, I did a quick scan of the small house. I hadn't considered what it would look like, but it suited Paulette. Nothing fancy or expensive, and most of the furniture was worn on the edges. But everything was neat and tidy and intentional. The walls were a soft faded yellow, and the furnishings mostly done in pastel blues and creams. While not frilly, the space felt overtly feminine.

"Even though you arrived unannounced, would you care for some hot tea?" She took the pastry box and headed into the kitchen. "I'll put on the kettle. I don't know if I have anything dog friendly. There may be some crackers in the cupboard."

I nearly told her no, that I didn't want to bother, but the act of eating together always seemed to help a situation. Chances might be higher Paulette would be willing to spend more time going over the symbols. "That would be lovely, thank you. And Watson will be just fine with a cracker or two."

Whether it was because he was truly a dynamite detective or it was just natural dog instinct to know when he was about to get a treat, Watson's disposition brightened, and with a little hop, he trotted after Paulette.

She instantly began to coo at him, and I knew I'd made the right decision. Pastries and puppies could soften anyone up.

Though I was tempted to follow, I forced myself to be patient and settled in on the threadbare sofa.

From the new position, I could see into the rest of the house. It was roughly the same layout as Gerald's. A hallway led to two open rooms, and another doorway that was closed. The lights were on in the bedroom and bathroom, and they matched the living space—the same soft yellow, the same feminine feel. Only then did I remember Paulette had moved after her husband died. Gerald had helped her get this one. "How long have you lived here?" I made an effort to simultaneously raise my voice so she could hear me in the kitchen and to not yell, then realized it sounded like I was starting an interrogation. "It's charming. The yellow makes it very relaxing."

"Nearly three years ago." Paulette's voice drifted in from the kitchen, unrestrained, even over the sounds of dishes clinking together. "And I lucked out with the color. There wasn't money to paint or redecorate, but I liked it well enough." She walked back into the living room and placed a small chipped plate on the coffee table. Saltines were arranged in a circular pattern, but there was nothing else accompanying them. She'd also not put out any of the pastries I'd brought. It seemed she'd been serious about it being too late for such indulgences. "It's smaller and not as well-maintained as the house Walter and I had, but it's enough to be thankful for and more than I feared I'd be able to have."

Watson sat at the end of the coffee table, staring at the spread of crackers, and looking between the two of us in offended disbelief that he had yet to be offered one.

The rest of her story came back to me, and I couldn't imagine going through it. Your husband killing himself, only to lose your finances and nearly becoming homeless. No wonder she was so loyal to Gerald. I would've been too. "You've done a good job with it. It's soft, feminine, and inviting."

"Feminine." She chuckled, for the first time that I could recall. "The other house was as well. I think it drove Walter a little crazy. He insisted on some 'manly touches' here and there, as he called them." The brightness left her instantly, and she motioned down the hallway. "All his things are in the spare room. I couldn't bring myself to unbox them when I moved here. They would be a constant reminder..." She dropped her hand and shook her head. "Don't even go in there anymore. Not in ages. But... it helps knowing they're near. It's like his presence is still with me, but yet not screaming at me all the time that he's gone."

Having been through the death of my father and

watching my mother go through the death of her husband, I knew there was nothing to say. Trying to distract, I took one of the crackers and held it out to Watson.

He huffed out an annoyed chuff, snagged it, swallowed it whole, and stared openly back at the tray.

It worked. Paulette laughed again, almost in relief. "He's a man who knows what he wants, isn't he?" She handed him another cracker and turned to me in all seriousness. "While I don't want to be rude to company, even uninvited company, the kettle will be whistling soon, so maybe you should start telling me why you're here."

"These." I pulled Gerald's photocopied planner pages from my purse and laid them between us on the coffee table. "There are drawn symbols beside most of his appointments, but there's no key that I can find to explain what they mean. I hoped you would know."

She leaned forward slightly, though from her lack of surprise or curiosity, I was certain she didn't really need to inspect. She'd obviously seen them before. "No, I'm sorry. I don't."

I studied her for a heartbeat. I wasn't sure, but I thought she was lying. "Really? I know how much

Gerald... Mr. Jackson meant to you, and I know he must've trusted you greatly. You don't have any idea?"

She sat back. "I'm afraid I don't."

Watson looked back and forth between us, then pointedly at the saltines.

I ignored him. "Then maybe could you take a guess? You probably knew Mr. Jackson better than almost anyone outside of his small circle of friends. And after the years working for him, being his trusted secretary, you must have insight into what they could mean."

At her narrowed expression, I realized I was pushing the flattery a bit too far. "The answer is still no, I'm afraid."

Watson gave up and began to explore the room, sniffing the edges, probably looking for a snack or a place to nap.

I tried another angle. "I noticed Jonathan Beaker met with Mr. Jackson and had an upcoming appointment. Any chance you know what they were discussing?"

"I'm afraid you have the wrong impression, Ms. Page." Paulette's hands folded primly in her lap. "Mr. Jackson did not take me into his confidence. I was his secretary. Not friend. Just an employee."

"But..." For the first time, there was coldness behind her austere response, and it threw me off. "It's clear how much he meant to you. And obviously, you were important to him. He helped you with housing, gave you a job."

Paulette softened again, though it looked like it took some effort. "It's true that Gerald went out of his way to help me after... everything that happened. I was grateful, but that doesn't mean he took me into his inner circle."

Just as she predicted, the kettle began to whistle.

"I'll be right back. Do you prefer honey or sugar in your hot tea?" She stood. "I'm afraid to insist that our teatime be short. I must get to bed."

"Plain is fine, thank you." I never drank my tea plain, but I wasn't paying any attention to what I was saying, more focused on something Paulette had just said. When she disappeared into the kitchen, I realized what had stuck out to me. She'd referred to being grateful in the past tense, as if she wasn't grateful anymore. But what would've caused her to suddenly feel so different?

Watson continued to sniff around the room, clearly not finding anything of interest, though he did sniff for an extra-long time at the doorjamb of the opposite end.

I assumed it led to the small attached garage I'd parked in front of. Whatever he smelled didn't capture his attention for long, and he continued sniffing, around the silver oxygen tank that sat beside the door, then around a basket filled with different pastel-hued spools of yarn, and then, as if giving up, returned to sit by me.

Relenting, I offered him another cracker, then nibbled on one myself as I considered the change in Paulette.

The answer hit as she walked back into the room, holding two steaming mugs of hot tea. "Forgive me for prying, but with Gerald gone, and your job, are you...?" I should've paused before I'd started speaking, come up with a polite way to ask. "Are you in danger of losing your home again?"

After handing me the tea, she returned to her seat. "I should be good for the next three or four months. I've built up a little bit of savings this go around. Hopefully by that time, I'll find new employment."

This go around. It was obvious, and I couldn't blame her. As far as Paulette still knew, Gerald had committed suicide. Which meant that the two men she depended on in her life had both killed themselves and left her floundering and almost homeless.

Even in the midst of grief, there had to be anger about that. "I'm sorry, Paulette."

Surprise crossed her features. "No need to be sorry. I'll find a job."

"I know you will." I smiled reassuringly. "I'm just sorry you have to go through this again. I know it's not exactly the same, but it's got to be bringing up all sorts of memories and probably feels a little like déjà vu."

Her surprise morphed into confusion. "I don't know what you mean."

Why had I said anything? But I had no idea how to stop at that point. A lot of the time my tendency to stick my foot in my mouth happened automatically, but this was one of those rare occasions where I could feel it getting shoved in bit by bit, but still couldn't stop it. "If it was me, Gerald's suicide would be reminding me of my husband's. And with both of them leaving you in the lurch... I can't even imagine. You've got to be so heartbroken and yet so angry as well."

As if proving my point, irritation flashed over her face and bit into her tone. "I have *never* been angry at Walter, not for a moment. It broke my heart to lose him, and that he felt he had no other way out, but I never blamed him, not at all."

Watson paused in his demanding of crackers, his ears perking up at the sound of her voice.

Paulette didn't glance his way. "Walter was so sick, and in so much pain, and no one would help him, no one could do anything. The insurance was laughable, wouldn't even pay for in-home care. What choice did he have? I had no idea he was going to do it, but he did it in the best way possible, and he even went to the effort to make it look like an accident. I still don't know how he found the strength to put his oxygen tube underneath the leg of the chair, but he did. A last valiant effort, his last show of love to me. He didn't want to put me through years of watching him die slowly, of making me nothing more than just a nurse as our finances dribbled away. He made it where he ended things on his terms and left me in a position where I would've had more money than we'd ever had in our lives. I wouldn't have been wealthy, but I wouldn't have had to work until the end of my so-called golden years."

"You would've had more money? Because of how he died?" More of Paulette's story came back to me, and her anger that I'd thought I'd understood switched directions suddenly and made even more sense. Her husband trying to make his death not look like a suicide. Because of life insurance, clearly. She would've been able to live off her husband's life insurance.

Paulette bristled, but didn't respond, a sour expression across her face.

... He even went to the effort to make it look like an accident...

Doubtless the life insurance policy was null and void in cases of suicide, as was common.

"Sorry. I didn't mean to pry." Realization after realization slammed into me. The insurance hadn't paid, and I was willing to bet Gerald had lost the case, costing Paulette everything.

At the next realization, I tried to keep my expression frozen. It wasn't the Irons family, wasn't Ethel, wasn't Simone. Gerald didn't die because of his bad investments or his dealings with underground organizations. He died because he'd ruined the retirement years of the little old lady sitting across from me in a flannel nightgown and curlers.

"I'm so very sorry." I thought my voice sounded normal and sincere. It was the best I could do. It was those words, said more than any others, when someone you loved died. So I repeated them. "I'm so sorry, Paulette. I lost my father suddenly. It was horrible, and watching what his loss did to my mom made it even worse. But I can't imagine having to witness your husband die slowly in front of you. No one should go through that."

"No, they shouldn't." Still the anger lingered, though her voice seemed to tighten at the memory.

I needed to keep her talking, distract from any more mention of Gerald, drink a little tea, eat some saltines, and leave as fast as I could. "He..." A Rolodex of names spun through my mind "Walter. You said Walter was sick." I glanced toward the oxygen tank by the doorway. "What was he sick from?"

Paulette was slow to answer. "Cancer. Stomach cancer. By the time we found out, it was too late to do anything. It was just a matter of time. Walter's best friend was a doctor, and even he missed the—" Her gaze followed to where I'd looked, and she missed a beat, but she cleared her throat and continued as she turned back at me. "Even he missed all the signs. It had already metastasized everywhere. Like I said, I don't blame Walter. No one should be forced to endure such pain."

"I'm so sorry." I couldn't think of what else to say. If I wasn't careful, I'd slip again. Instead I reached for a cracker, started to chew, but choked on the dryness and then gulped from the hot tea, burning my mouth, and choked again.

Watson shoved against my leg.

Paulette flinched and blinked rapidly. "Goodness, do be careful. You've had saltines before, haven't you? I don't think I'm strong enough to give you the Heimlich."

Still coughing, I was able to wheeze out that I was okay. My klutziness had done what I'd been unable to do for myself—offering a distraction and altering the conversation. After a few moments, I took another sip of the hot tea, slower that time. As I set the cup down, fear sliced through me for a crazy moment. What was I doing, drinking tea prepared by the woman who'd killed Gerald? Mentally I shook myself. There was no reason for Paulette to try to hurt me. I hadn't done anything. I didn't think she'd noticed my reaction at her anger about the insurance money, and even if she had, she'd prepared the tea before then.

"Better?" She lifted her brows questioningly and sounded sincere enough.

"Yes. Thank you." I started to reach for another cracker, to offer it to Watson, then paused halfway, that fear returning. Even more irrational than the first one. No way had she poisoned the saltines. Nevertheless, I put it back on the plate, unable to make myself give it to Watson. "We've encroached on your time enough. I am sorry we barged in so late. Thank you for your input on the symbols." I stood and glanced toward Watson as I patted my thigh. "Come on. Let's get you to bed."

He didn't even spare a glance at the crackers, confirming he was as uneasy as me.

I snagged the leash on the couch and hooked it to his collar. From the corner of my eye, I noticed Paulette lean down and pick up the photocopied papers, inspecting them. She made a small humming noise. "You know, I may have some insight to these after all. Or at least be able to give you a lead. I brought home the papers I was working on, one of Mr. Jackson's recent cases. There are some similar drawings on that paperwork. Maybe seeing how he used them will help narrow down their meaning." She gestured toward the hallway. "Let me go get my satchel."

"No, that's okay. I don't want to take more of your time." I took a step toward the door.

"It won't take a minute. I insist." Paulette turned, the green housecoat fluttering behind her as she disappeared down the hallway. A door opened, followed by the sound of something being moved and papers rustling.

I glanced toward Watson, whispering, "Do we just leave? Run away?"

Watson whimpered and headed toward the door.

More clattering came from the back hallway. "Sorry, I chose the wrong folder. Let me check this one."

Whether Watson understood my question, was simply picking up on my unease, or could feel something I couldn't, I followed his lead, regardless of how it looked. I started to follow him, then realized I was leaving the paperwork I'd brought over and turned back. Almost instantly I spun around once more. Like the photocopies even mattered!

We'd just about reached the door when Paulette emerged from the hallway.

At her appearance, I winced, though I wasn't sure what I was expecting her to do.

She didn't seem to notice, only continued, and held up a large file in her hand. "Here we go. Let's compare the symbols."

I debated for a heartbeat. I was being silly. All she had was a stack of papers in a folder. Even if she did attempt to hurt me, I could easily overpower her. But every instinct I had was suddenly screaming to run. "Sorry. We really need to get going." I turned toward the door and grasped the handle. "I promised Watson a treat, and I have to get up early tomorrow."

Even in his stress, at his favorite word, Watson let out a yip, though not as frantically happy as it typically inspired. As I twisted the handle, there was the sound of scattering papers behind me, followed instantly by a sharp jab below my neck, and Watson began to bark.

I should've yanked the door open and bolted, but at the pain, instinct forced me to turn around. "What in the world..." My foot slid on one of the papers just as Watson lunged back across the room, yanking the leash that was hooked around my wrist. I had to throw my hand out to grip the wall.

Paulette scrambled backward out of Watson's reach, and when I looked up from steadying myself, she was pulling a handgun out of the pocket of her housecoat. Aiming it at me, she took a few more steps back. "Close the door."

If someone had painted this picture for me—an old woman in a nightgown, housecoat, and pink curlers in her hair, holding me at gunpoint—I probably would've laughed at the sheer lunacy of it. But it wasn't funny, not at all.

"I said close the door." Paulette's voice trembled, as did the gun in her hands.

In my near fall, I managed to pull the door halfway open. I'd not even noticed. It was enough, I could fling it the rest of the way open and rush out, dragging Watson behind me.

"Don't even think about it. I'm aiming at Watson right now." Her voice still trembled, but regained some of her cool primness it possessed before.

Feeling defeated, I did as she said, then turned to face her. Though her voice sounded more in control, the shaking gun wasn't. While in one way that made it even more unsafe, it also made me hope that all wasn't lost. That if I could distract Paulette enough, there'd be a moment where I'd be able to disarm her.

She took a few more steps back so she was in the doorway of the kitchen. The debate of what she should do next clear on her face. She obviously hadn't been planning on this. It had to be impulse.

Of course she'd not be planning this. She hadn't known I'd show up on her doorstep. "Paulette, I can tell you don't want to do this. You don't have to."

A sardonic smile curved her lips, a sad one. "No, I don't want to do this, but yes, I do have to."

Watson continued to growl and bark, straining at the end of his leash at his attempt to get to her. If Paulette had the gun trained on me, I could risk it, release Watson's leash and let him be the distraction. But the gun was still aimed at him, and I knew what would happen if I released him.

Still pointing the gun at Watson, she gestured with her eyes across the room. "Tie him up on the leg of the couch." When I hesitated, her voice grew louder, slight panic sinking in. "Now, Ms. Page. Tie him up."

Though I hesitated again, I saw no way out of it. Not yet. It wasn't my first time at gunpoint, and that helped a little, knowing there'd likely be some moment where I'd be able to disarm her. That moment just hadn't arrived. "Watson, come on."

I headed toward the couch, but Watson remained focused on Paulette, barking, growling, and trying to get to her.

"Please, Watson. Please." I didn't think she'd shoot him just for barking, if for no other reason than she would've lost her leverage, but I couldn't risk it. "Please."

At the pitiful sound of my voice, Watson glanced over at me and then adjusted so he could face Paulette, still growling, while backing toward me, keeping himself between us.

When there was enough slack in the leash, I looped it around the leg of the heavy couch and tied it in a knot.

"A double one, Ms. Page." More control had seeped into Paulette's voice, which worried me. "I don't want to hurt Watson, but if he breaks loose and comes at me, I will."

I double knotted it and faced her.

To my surprise, though her expression was stony, I could make out pity on her face, and when she spoke, there was even a little softness as though she was somehow asking for forgiveness. "I promise you,

I will not hurt your dog unless he tries to hurt me. Even after..."

I met her eyes and lifted my chin. "Even after you kill me?"

She took a breath, nodded, and widened her stance. She made no movement like she was going to come any closer. "Sit down. On the couch."

I did.

"I am sorry. I know you don't deserve this. But..." She shook her head.

"Then don't do it." Even though I knew I was wasting my breath, I had to try. "There may be some leniency for you. A jury would understand why you killed Gerald. After what he cost you. There won't be any leniency at all if you add me to the list."

She didn't answer, and the shaking of the gun stopped.

After a few silent moments, Watson stopped barking and straining at the end of his leash, and came to sit at my feet, fangs still showing and his pointed ears at attention.

In the relative calm, I realized my shoulder at the base of my neck was throbbing. I forgotten that initial pain and found the source instantly. A syringe lay partially buried under the scattered papers.

Without thinking, I lifted my hand and touched the spot. "What did you do?"

Paulette shook her head again, but still the gun remained steady. "It won't hurt. You won't be in any pain. None." Again, I could hear that apology in her tone.

Terror washed through me, rushing in as cold as ice. "What is it? What did you do?"

"Nothing. I promise." Ridiculously, she sounded almost plaintive. "I promise, it won't hurt you."

I almost laughed at that. The woman had a gun pointed at my face, told me I was going to die, but yet promising she wasn't going to hurt me. Then I got the nuance. *It* wouldn't hurt me—the whatever she'd injected me with. I met her eyes again. "What was it?"

For a second, it looked like she wasn't going to answer. "Just ketamine. Walter's doctor prescribed it to him a couple of months before he died. It was the only way he could get any relief, any sleep. He was in so much pain all the time. The pain pills they started with were getting harder and harder for him to swallow, so the doctor gave us the injectable version. He made an exception, didn't make Walter go into hospice or spend his last days in the hospital. He was a good man, a good friend."

As she spoke, I could see her retreat into the past.

This was the moment. I threw myself forward, sending the plate of crackers scattering over the floor. I attempted to lunge at her, but with getting up so fast, the room spun.

Paulette stepped farther into the kitchen, well out of reach, and though for a second she'd swiveled the gun in my direction, she aimed it back to Watson, who was barking even more madly. "Don't try it again. I will shoot him."

As I attempted to right myself, the room continued to spin, and I realized it wasn't because of how quickly I'd thrown myself from the couch, but the ketamine. I had no idea what effects the drug might have. Again, that rush of fear. But whatever might be coming, it wasn't so bad in that moment that I couldn't function—I could still try to disarm her, it was now or never, as every second that followed would make it that much more impossible to do.

When I refocused on her, doing my best to make the room stand still, I knew it was pointless. She was too far away. The couple of yards between me and where she stood in the doorway of the kitchen might as well have been miles. Even if the room wasn't spinning and I could make a full-out leap, there was no way she could miss me, even if she was the world's worst shot.

"Couch!" Paulette didn't scream it, but with the ferocity in her whisper, she might as well have.

I returned to the couch and sat back down. I laid a reassuring hand on Watson's head. He didn't stop barking. The sound gave me another shot of hope. Maybe someone would hear. I tried to remember how close her neighbors' houses had been when I drove up. I couldn't quite picture it. They definitely weren't side by side, but *maybe* they were near enough to hear?

At that moment, my cell phone buzzed in the pocket of my skirt. Paulette couldn't hear it, but neither could I stick my hand in and answer. Even so, it brought a second rush of hope. Maybe it was Leo, although he wasn't scheduled to be done with the hike yet... but perhaps more time had passed than I thought. Maybe it was Katie. Though what good would either of those calls do? They didn't know where I was.

Either way, I clung to any hope I could find, whether it was a neighbor hearing Watson or whoever was calling my cell. I just needed time. I needed to keep Paulette talking. "Did you set Gerald up for Birdie's death?"

"Be qui—" Paulette's directive died as I finished the question, and though the gun stayed steady on Watson, she looked at me confused. "Birdie? No. Why would I have anything to do with that?"

Maybe it was the drugs beginning to have effect, but I struggled to see how that wasn't obvious. "To frame Gerald for murder. For payback." Even as I spoke, I decided the drugs *were* having an effect, because it didn't fit. Paulette wouldn't have killed Birdie just to set up Gerald, only to kill him before he could really suffer from the fallout.

"Of course I didn't. I'm not a murderer." Paulette truly sounded offended. "Besides, I had no idea what Gerald had done when Birdie died."

That didn't make sense either. "What do you mean you didn't know? About what? Gerald's insurance schemes? The article was already published. Birdie spelled it out perfectly."

"I didn't believe it. I trusted Mr. Jackson completely." Anger flicked across her features at that. "It wasn't until you came to visit him in the office. He was talking to you when I called on the intercom. I heard him admit the whole thing to you. His deal with the insurance companies. And I knew. I knew he'd done it to Walter and me as well. Walter had been careful. He didn't overdose on ketamine like he could've. He'd known that would cost me the insurance payout. He didn't even rip the oxygen from his nose. Despite his pain, he managed to get the oxygen cord under the chair leg, making it look like it accidentally got pinched off. Gerald promised it was an easy case, open and shut. It wasn't." The fire had started to rise in her tone, but by the end, it was cold, utterly cold. "But maybe it was, for him, and the insurance company. Gerald received whatever percentage he made from the insurance company not having to pay me. And then he had the nerve to approach me and make it seem like he was doing *me* a favor. Helping me get this dump, getting me to work for him for less than anyone else would've agreed to settle for. But... I owed him, and I needed the money."

Though I didn't move, the room spun again, making a spike of nausea cut through my belly, making me sway. I lurched forward, having to catch myself on the coffee table.

Both Watson and Paulette reacted. Watson barking and then hopping on the couch beside me, trying to help. Paulette yelling for me to sit still or she'd shoot.

It was bad enough that I couldn't follow her

directions and had to keep hold of the table to keep from sliding to the floor.

"Oh." In that one word, Paulette's tone reverted to apologetic. "It's working, isn't it?"

I couldn't answer, not that I needed to or wanted to for that matter. After several deep, long breaths, I sat a little straighter, and when I was sure I wasn't going to throw up, leaned back on the couch.

Watson whimpered frantically and began lathering my face with his tongue.

"It's okay, buddy. It's okay." The lie almost brought tears to my eyes, but I held them back, needing to be as strong for him as I could.

His wet nose shoved against mine.

What was I doing? I couldn't think that way. *Needing to be strong for him*, like this was the end. I couldn't give up. I just needed time, more time. I needed to keep her talking.

But how? I tried to think through Gerald's murder, through the paperwork, the symbols, but nothing came. Just flashes and images of those things, but no real thought that I could string together into words.

Then Paulette was sitting in the chair opposite the coffee table, the one she'd occupied earlier, though she'd pushed it back to be out of Watson's reach.

I thought I was seeing things—how could she have moved from the kitchen to the living room like that?

And Watson wasn't against my face anymore but curled up on my thigh, his head on my lap, chocolate eyes looking up at me desperately.

Then I realized. I'd gone away. Passed out or fallen asleep. Maybe for ten seconds, maybe ten minutes.

What had woken me? Had my cell buzzed again?

I couldn't feel it.

"You're back." Paulette stood but didn't come any closer. "Okay then, it's time."

I looked at her but couldn't find it in me to form words.

"Get up, Ms. Page." She gestured upward with the gun, returned the aim to Watson. "Stand up!"

With monumental effort, I steadied one hand on the coffee table again and somehow pushed myself into a standing position. The room still spun, but I closed my eyes and forced myself to stay standing.

"Now, walk through there."

I opened my eyes again at her voice, confused, and then saw her gesturing with the gun.

Looking to where she pointed confirmed I'd missed more than I realized. The door beside the oxygen tank was open, revealing that the room was a garage, as a car sat inside, the driver's side door open as well.

Even so, I didn't understand.

"Move, Ms. Page. Get in the car." She gestured with the gun again.

What a strange request. Why in the world...? The answer came through the fog that roiled in my mind. "This is what you did to Gerald?"

She didn't answer. "I will keep my promise to you, Ms. Page. If you do what I say, I won't kill Watson. I'll drop him off in Loveland or maybe drive to Greeley, find a shelter there. I swear it."

I believed her. And really, even if I didn't, what choice did I have? I couldn't fight her, not like this. If I tried, she'd shoot me and maybe Watson as well. And then time would've run out. Time was the only weapon I had. If I complied, maybe there'd be more.

With a lumbering lurch, I made one step toward the garage, then stopped, steadying myself again.

Watson hopped off the couch, offering his weight against my leg.

"It's okay, Ms. Page. Be careful. Don't fall." Paulette made no move to come closer. "Although the longer you take, the more difficult it will become."

"Why not just shoot me?" I hadn't meant to say the words. How stupid.

"Gerald won't be the only one who committed suicide."

Surely it was the drugs making me hear things. That couldn't be her logic. "I'll be in *your* car, in *your* garage."

"No, you will be in *your* car, in *your* garage. I'll drive you there once... once you've..." Unless I was hearing things, her voice wavered again. "That's where they'll find you."

"I don't have a—" I barely caught myself. Maybe I was imagining all this, as it didn't make any sense, but in case I wasn't, telling her I didn't have a garage might make her pull the trigger and be done with it.

"Move." She pointed with the gun again and brought it back to Watson.

I don't know how long it took, or even how I managed. Every single step was harder than the last, and each one brought me closer to falling and being sick. All I knew was that Watson started barking again as he was at the end of his leash and I was out of reach. Then my hand was on the doorframe into the garage. I stumbled over the single step down and crashed into the opening of her car, gripping the edge of the door to keep from falling on the concrete.

"Good, sit inside." Paulette's voice was behind me.

I turned slowly to look at her, standing in the doorway, finally within arm's length. Watson, barking and straining at the end of his leash behind her. If I could just push off the car, fling myself at her, knock her off-balance.

Paulette swiveled the gun toward Watson again. "Get in the car, Ms. Page. Leave the door open. I'll close it after you've passed out and I've started the engine."

Even without the gun, even if Watson wasn't there, I wasn't launching myself anywhere. It wasn't physically possible.

I collapsed and just happened to land in the driver's seat, or at least that's how it felt. Time blacked out for a little bit, and then she was demanding I pull my legs inside. I managed to do so, one at a time. When I was done, I couldn't even lift my hands.

This was it. I'd pass out and she'd start the car, and that would be that.

Time. We needed more time.

I tried to form a thought but couldn't. I just needed time.

Watson was barking. So desperate.

I needed time.

The thought came, offering a little gift—a piece of the puzzle that didn't fit. There'd been no traces of drugs, other than the marijuana from his kombucha in Gerald's system. It didn't make sense. "Is this what you did to Gerald? Drugged him and made him get in his car?"

I didn't know if it took her a long time to answer, or if it just felt like it in my hazed-out state. "No. I went to Glen Haven early that morning, parked the car over two miles away and walked to Mr. Jackson's house." She snorted in disgust, and I couldn't tell if she still had the gun trained on Watson or not. "He had me water his plants anytime he was out of town, so I had a key. I waited in the back seat of his car with my supplies until he got in the driver's seat to head to work." There was no quaver in her voice now, no apology, and though the world was growing dim around the edges, I could hear triumph as she spoke. "I put the gun to the back of his head as soon as he shut the door, made him wrap ropes around himself, and even secure the bungee cords at his chest. I was able to use my free hand to pull them so the release was in the back of the seat and out of his reach. I had him turn on the car—I wore Walter's oxygen mask—and then I just waited. It took longer, so much longer, than I'd imagined. But he finally passed out. I removed the ropes, the bungee cords, got out the other side of the car after I locked it, and left him there, the car running. I walked back to my own car, which took forever again, and drove home, cleaned up, and went to work."

I blinked, trying to keep her in my vision, but she swayed like a mirage.

"I was over an hour late. It was the first time since—"

Then there was blackness. Again, I don't know for how long.

The noises were loud enough to bring me back, the pounding on the door, Watson's frantic barking, and the bang of a gun, and then yelling.

I tried to call out for Watson, but couldn't.

I tried to jerk myself out of the car, but couldn't. At first, I thought it was the effects of the drugs, but then realized ropes bound me to the seat.

My mouth wouldn't move, or my tongue; I didn't know which. Nothing worked.

The world began to fade, the little garage growing dark as a figure stood in the doorway again. I thought it was Paulette, then realized it was much too big.

Hope shot through me even as the darkness encroached further. Leo. Leo had come. Just in time. Leo had come.

His big body hurried toward me as he flung open the car door and leaned in, already ripping away at whatever bound me. "I swear you're more trouble than you're worth, Winfried Page. You and the fleabag."

I blinked, trying to make the face and the voice match. "Susan?"

"No, I'm Nancy Drew." She hoisted me out. "No, wait. That's you, isn't it? Though Nancy Drew would never let herself get trapped in a car without even being tied up. This is just embarrassing."

TWENTY TWO

"You've got to go." I squeezed Mom's hand from where she gripped me beside the hospital bed. "Your plane leaves in five hours. It takes nearly two to drive to the airport in Denver, and they want you there three hours early for international flights."

Mom simply shook her head, the remaining auburn streak in her silver hair catching the morning sunlight pouring through the window. "I thought I could, but I can't. I just can't."

"That's why I agreed to stay in the hospital last night, so you'd be assured that I'm okay. And I am." I wasn't even lying. I was tired, and I had a headache, but considering... I was more than fine.

Mom tightened her grip. "How am I supposed to go off and enjoy caves filled with healing crystals when my daughter was nearly murdered?"

"Judging from all the healing crystals you stuffed under this pillow, I doubt there's any left in Scotland at all." I shot a pleading glance to Barry where he was kneeling on the floor, beside Leo. Between the two of them, Watson was in seventh heaven and wasn't feeling the least bit of residual strain from the night before.

Casting me a wink, Barry stood and came nearer to put an arm around Mom's shoulders. "Fred is safer now than she'll ever be. She just solved the murder, and that murderer is in custody." He kept going when Mom started to protest. "Verona and Zelda are going to drop by before Fred's discharge, and they're bringing their whole collection of healing and protecting crystals and gems, just like you asked."

I'd been about to point out that I hadn't solved the murder, not really, but gaped at Mom instead. "They're bringing *more*? Mom, I'm not strong enough to carry all of them."

"See, I should stay." Mom sniffed. "Help you get them to your house."

Chuckling, Leo stood, earning himself a longingly pitiful stare from Watson. "I promise, Phyllis, I can carry all the crystals for Fred, and I'll keep her safe, not that she needs me to."

I nearly pointed out that apparently, I did need someone to keep me safe, but once more I stopped myself. "Mom, I love you. Have a wonderful time.

Text me when you board and let me know when you land in Scotland. Bring me back a stone for increasing book sales. Oh, better yet, one that will allow me to eat all of Katie's pastries that I possibly can and not gain an ounce."

"I do wish there was a crystal for that." Mom sighed, and began to smile, then a protest started to rise again.

"Leave!" I yelled it, laughing, and barely suppressed a wince from the shot of pain through my head. "Take lots of pictures. I can't wait to hear all about it. I'll be here when you get back. Safe, happy, and whole. And a few pounds heavier if Katie has anything to do with it." I gestured to the huge box filled with assorted savory and sweet pastries Katie had brought in on her way to work that morning. It was practically enough for the entire hospital staff.

"Fine." Though Mom scowled, she pressed a kiss to my forehead. "But no more murders, not until we get back at least."

"If that's the rule, stay gone longer." I squeezed her hand a final time before releasing her. "Three weeks isn't nearly long enough. No more murders, not for a long time."

Mom and Barry said their goodbyes to Leo and Watson and with the final wave toward me, walked out the door. Instantly, I turned to Leo. "The second Barry texts and says they're through security, we're getting out of here. I'd do it now, but I don't trust that some gossip won't see me leaving the hospital and call Mom and she'll turn around and come back."

"Are you sure?" The concern he'd apparently been hiding in front of my parents arose. "There's no reason not to stay here longer. Just for observation."

I pulled him down for a kiss and hid my wince that time as well. "Don't you start. I'm fine. Even the doctor said so."

He didn't look convinced. "Then at least let me take off this evening's shift. There's no reason for you to be alone."

"Honestly, I love you, but I need to be alone, just for a little while. When I'm *at home*. You leaving the room for a few minutes doesn't count. I need to get a grip on everything that happened last night, and what it all means." I took his hand like I had my mother's before. "You'll be back in time for dessert, I'm sure. Which is fine, I don't think I'll figure it out in one night, but I need to start sifting through everything. Barry was wrong, and you and I both know it. I didn't solve this murder. Paulette wasn't even on my radar. And I don't expect to be right all the time, but I can't help but think there's a reason I was suspecting the people I did."

With his free hand, Leo brushed his thumb over my cheek. "And by that, you mean the Irons family."

"Mainly." Why try to deny it?

There was a knock on the door, causing Watson to yelp, and Leo and I both looked over.

Angus poked his head in. "Up for a visit?"

I wondered if he'd heard the comment about the Irons family. He'd clearly thought I was a fool for still being concerned about them. "Of course, come on in." I forced a smile that I didn't feel. Though I needed time to myself, I didn't mind the visitors. But Angus wasn't one I would've chosen. At least not right then.

I hadn't had a chance to fill Leo in on my conversation with Angus, and he shot me a quizzical glance at my less than enthusiastic response, but seemed more than willing to go along with it. "I got a text from Paulie a few minutes ago. He and Athena"—he cast a quick grin down at Watson—"*and* Pearl, are on their way. So we probably shouldn't have too many visitors in the room at once."

"No problem." Angus stepped the rest of the way in, holding the largest bouquet of gerber daisies I'd ever seen. Their multitude of bright colors were whimsical and happy, two things I didn't feel about Angus Witt anymore. "I won't take long. But I owe Fred a—" He'd been speaking to Leo and snorted out a breath before focusing on me. "I owe *you* a thank-you and thought I should do it in person."

While I appreciated that he didn't talk about me like I wasn't in the room, after our last conversation, his gratitude made me queasy. "You don't owe me a thanks, actually. I didn't figure out Paulette killed Gerald until a few moments before she was trying to kill me."

He shrugged. "The end result is the same." He set the flower arrangement on the counter across from my bed and offered a hand to Watson.

Watson approached, a little more tentatively than he normally would with Angus, sniffed, and allowed a solitary pat on his head before turning and trotting back to sit beside Leo's feet.

Angus refocused on Leo. "Do you mind if we have a little privacy?"

"Whatever you say can be said in front of Leo." I surprised myself with how strong the sentiment came out. Even that I minded being alone with Angus at all. "I'm... not quite myself yet. Still a little fuzzy. There's a good chance I'll forget half the things that are said to me right now."

Leo looked my way, and while his expression was steady, I could see the question in his eyes, but he went with it.

"I regret that I've fallen a few pegs in your esteem, Winifred. Or maybe more than a few." Angus approached the bed but didn't attempt a hug or anything, thankfully. "I do want to thank you, whether you solved this or not. I admire and respect your sense of justice, your bravery, and intelligence. While we may not see eye to eye on everything, I want you to know, if you need anything, anything at all, you simply need to say the word."

I studied him, and if there was any haze left over from the drugs from the night before, I didn't feel it. I tried to find a threat to the words but couldn't. "The same blind, unconditional help you offered to Gerald and probably your other friends?"

Something like a smile played at the corner of his lips. "Most people would say that's a good quality to have in a friend."

Though I could feel Leo studying me as I studied Angus, I didn't look his way, nor did I respond to Angus's point. "Does your help extend if I come up against the Irons family again?"

His hint of a smile didn't waver, nor did his tone turn judgmental. "I'm afraid I don't share your concerns in that area." Once more he shrugged, as if it was inconsequential. "Like I told you before, you really are something. Quite spectacular."

Something about the way he said it made me squirm. I couldn't quite label why. His words could have been interpreted as dismissive in a way, like I was an object. Or even misogynistic, as I was willing to bet he never spoke to a man that way. But it felt more like... more like...

Then it hit. Like I was a possession, like he owned me. Or maybe a collectible, and he was proud to have me in his display case.

"Are you part of the Irons family, Angus?" I hadn't meant to say the words, hadn't even finished thinking them.

Beside me, Leo stiffened, coming to full attention and ready to defend. Even in that moment, though I remained focused on Angus, it meant the world to me that Leo didn't question or look at me like I was crazy. That he trusted my instincts enough, even if he didn't agree with me, to know something was off.

Angus did smile then, gently. "I can see it in your eyes, Winifred. You think I am. Is there anything I could possibly say to help you believe otherwise?"

Before I could reply, or even answer his question to myself, there was another knock on the door, but before anyone came in, Watson let out a happy bark and rushed across the room, hopping like a puppy. Pearl had arrived, and the two humans with her.

And whatever was going on between Angus and me was over.

I planned on having grilled cheese and tomato soup, then curling up on the couch with a book—partly reading the story and partly letting my brain follow the funny trails on its own regarding everything that happened with Gerald and the assortment of people who'd changed in my estimation of them. Before I'd even retrieved the skillet, I changed my mind. I didn't want to stay in the house, as comfortable and cozy as it was. That's what I thought I'd wanted. Leo was at work, though he'd return in a few hours. Katie had asked to come by, promising more pastries, and I'd even told *her* no.

After Athena and Paulie had left the hospital, my uncles, the twins, their husbands, and all my nephews and nieces had come to visit. It was enough to make me nearly want another dose of ketamine. I could go without seeing another person for a week. And for whatever reason, the walls of my beautiful little log cabin were starting to close in.

"Walk?"

With me heading to the kitchen, Watson had known what was getting ready to happen and was excited about it. At my question, he looked at me as if I'd lost my mind.

I motioned to the door. "Come on, let's go on a walk. Get some fresh air. I'll make you..." Saying dinner could be nearly as dangerous as saying the word *treat*. "We'll eat later."

He allowed me to affix his collar and leash, albeit grudgingly, and followed me out the door.

Once locked, we barely made it down the steps of the porch before the engine of a car sounded, and then a police cruiser came into view. *So much for a long, solitary walk.*

Susan's shadowy form was identifiable through the windshield as she parked. I didn't think I'd ever forget her silhouette again.

She got out of the car and walked toward me. To my surprise, I realized I wasn't disappointed. I didn't mind her presence.

Susan lifted a large hand in greeting and halted in her steps a few feet away. "Holy cow." She gaped at my neck. "Do I even want to know?"

I didn't have to look down to remember, the amount of crystal pendants Mom had forced on me had to weigh nearly five pounds. "They're protection and healing. Mom made me promise to wear them. One more concession to get her to go on vacation."

"Really?" She cocked an eyebrow. "My estimation of your mother just went up. She gets to go on vacation *and* gets to make you look like a moron." She glanced down at Watson. "Hey there, fleabag."

Watson didn't growl, but he did offer her a show of his fangs.

"Oh yeah, tough guy. I got it. I'd be afraid if I was a doughnut or scone or whatever it is you live off." Susan refocused on me. "Nothing's wrong. I just wanted to... process. Let's go inside."

It was so Susan to not bother to inquire if I had time or the desire to process. And once more I realized that I didn't mind. Instead of turning back to the porch, I gestured toward a small gap in the forest that led to our makeshift trail. "Actually, I need to be outside. Want to take a walk?"

She looked over her shoulder to where I pointed and scowled.

"There's a meadow a little way up. A herd of elk have been hanging out there lately. There are several babies that still have their spots. They're pretty cute."

"Oh!" Susan clapped her hands and cheered in a

fake excited voice. "Wow, if there's a bunch of Bambis, count me in. Goodness knows I haven't seen enough since Estes is filled with just as many of them as tourists."

I couldn't help but laugh. "Bambi was a deer, not an elk."

"I'm sorry, do I look like your park ranger boyfriend? And *why* do I keep having to ask you that?" Without waiting for a response, she turned on her heels and headed toward the trail. "Well, come on."

I did, Watson trotting by my side. When the trail was wide enough, we fell in step beside her. To my surprise, Susan didn't speak for a while, as we walked through the thickness of pines and aspen trees, with the mountains towering overhead. I realized that despite her grumbling, she loved it all as much as I did.

Sure enough, when we came to the clearing, the herd of elk was present, and the babies were frolicking in the early evening light.

Susan didn't say anything more about Bambi, just leaned against a tree, her arms folded, and watched.

For his part, Watson sniffed the air occasionally, clearly enjoying the scents, but was much more captivated by the sounds of chipmunks rustling through the underbrush.

"How did you know?" I hadn't seen Susan since the night before. And I didn't remember the parting. Everything was a blur until the wee hours of the morning.

"After you called, I gave up on looking at the list of Gerald's investors and the court cases and checked out the day planner like you'd said." She hadn't needed any clarification, and she kept her gaze focused on the elk in front of us. "And there was Jonathan, of course, and a bunch of other clients, along with a whole host of Gerald's stupid symbols, and I just kept wondering why anyone still used that man as their lawyer. I'd thought it even before I knew he was *intentionally* losing." She looked my way. "But I chalked it up to him being Gerald Jackson, just part of the good-old-boys club."

"Of course." I gave a combination shrug and nod. I'd thought the same and dismissed it just as easily. The good-old-boys club was real and strong. And as much as I'd experienced it, I was certain it was nothing to the stories Susan could tell, given her chosen field.

"But all those names, all the clients he must've had over the years, couldn't just be chalked up to the good-old-boys club. Not all of them." She returned to the elk. "And while I still don't know why people were seeing him, though from his planners, it seemed like clients were getting fewer and farther between, I started considering the likelihood that the murderer was someone whose case he'd lost. Approaching at it from that point of view, it barely took five minutes before it hit me smack in the face. Seriously, it was so obvious, I don't know how it didn't hit both of us."

"Because of Paulette's husband's suicide?"

"That was one part, sure. And double-checked and found that particular case in the court files, as well." Still she didn't look over. "In and of itself, that might have been enough to make me wonder, but then all the pieces started clicking into place. Why had there been money in Gerald's getaway case at his home, but not at his office, not to mention the file cabinet was unlocked."

I breathed out a gasp and felt the pieces click for me as well. "Paulette had been through Gerald's things after she killed him. She needed money."

"And maybe the beef jerky as well, who knows, since it wasn't there for fleabag." She gave a dark chuckle. "There were also a ton of missing files. At least it felt like there were, so I started cross-refer-encing the cases Gerald lost over the past several years and the insurance companies involved." She turned to me again, her expression quizzical. "Care to guess which insurance company had all their files missing?"

I tried to remember the name of any of them, then realized that wasn't what she meant. "I bet the insurance company that Paulette and Walter used."

"Bullseye." She gave an irritated shake of her head. "I have no idea what Paulette was thinking, if she was doing her own research, going to let other victims know, or just trying to hide evidence. But either way, stupid. It was clear enough that I was nearly one hundred percent certain, but the nail in the coffin was when I tried to call you and you didn't answer."

"Thank you for that, by the way." I waited until she looked at me again. "For saving my life."

Susan made a gagging sound. "Oh, good Lord, can we avoid the hysterics? I was just doing my job. Does anyone ever stop and thank you for selling books after they sign the credit card receipt?"

"Yes, actually." I smiled at her. "But I'd say I'm even more fond of my life being saved than of selling books. So, thank you."

She waved me off and looked back out at the scenery. We fell into silence once more. Long enough the sunset turned from a dusty pink to a deepening purple.

"I made detective."

Susan's whisper was so quiet, so out of the blue, that it took me a moment to process it, and then I gaped at her. "What! Detective?"

"Don't sound like that. I'm not the police chief or anything." She sounded gruff, but she couldn't hold back a smile. "It was already in the works, I'd taken all the tests, jumped through all the hoops, but that was back with Briggs. He kept finding reasons to... whatever..." She grunted, though the smile still didn't completely fade. "Chief Dunmore cleared it today. So now you'll have to call me *Detective Green*. No more of this Susan junk. I don't know how I let you get away with that to begin with."

"Susan! That's wonder—" I moved like I was going to give her a hug.

"Don't you even think about it." Susan put a hand between us. "We're in the woods, and no one can hear you scream. And didn't I *just* say no more of the Susan junk."

"Yes, sir, Detective Green, sir." I saluted.

"That's better." Chuckling, she leaned back against the tree. "It is nice out here."

It was, more than. After a few more moments, I

sat on the ground. Giving up on whatever chipmunk or bug he'd been scouting, Watson trotted over, curled up beside me, and placed his head in my lap as he sometimes did. And as always, that little bit of magic made an already perfect moment even more so.

PRECARIOUS PASTA
COZY CORGI MYSTERY BOOK FOURTEEN

Halloween creeps in, bringing costumes, carbs, and a corpse or two...

Estes Park is bustling with fall tourists as Winifred and Katie deck out the Cozy Corgi Bookstore and Bakery, while corgi mascot, Watson, helps in his own special way—snacking, napping, and being his adorable grumpy self.

When Fred and Leo's date at the romantic restaurant, Pasta Thyme, leads to an invitation of a murder scene, instead of ghouls and goblins, Fred is haunted by ghosts from the past. Death might lurk around every corner as Fred investigates motives of infidelity, jealousy, and the dark shadow cast by a crime syndicate.

By the time Halloween night arrives, not everyone will get out alive...

Out Now - Precarious Pasta

Katie's Empanada recipe provided by:

2716 Welton St Denver, CO 80205

(720) 708-3026

Click the links for more Rolling Pin deliciousness:

RollingPinBakeshop.com

Rolling Pin Facebook Page

KATIE'S EMPANADA RECIPE

Filling:

    ¾ lb pork roast

    ¾ lb beef roast

    2cups prepared/jarred minced meat

    ½ cup pine nuts

    ½tsp allspice

    1 tsp nutmeg

    1 tsp salt

    3 cups sugar

Directions:

    1. Boil pork and beef until tender - let cool - then grind fine (Meat must be ground)

    2. Optional: add 4 oz of suet or beef fat for added flavor

3. Add mincemeat, sugar, spices and nuts until mixture is well blended and moist. If too dry add a little corn syrup.

Dough:
    6 cups flour
    5 Tbs baking powder
    5 Tbs shortening
    1 1/2 tsp salt

Directions:
    1. Sift flour, baking powder and salt together.
    2. Cut in shortening.
    3. Add enough water to make a dry dough.
    4. Refrigerate for about 30 minutes.
    5. Roll about 1/8 inch thick.
    6. Cut circles about 6" in diameter.
    7. Spoon about ¼ cup filling in each circle and fold in half.
    8. Crimp edges to seal.
    9. Place in 375 degree oil about ½ to ¾ inch deep.
    10. Fry until deep golden brown on each side.

AUTHOR NOTE

Author Note

Dear Reader:

Thank you so much for reading *Meddlesome Money*. If you enjoyed Fred and Watson's adventure, I would greatly appreciate a review on Amazon and Goodreads—reviews make a huge difference in helping the Cozy Corgi series continue. Feel free to drop me a note on Facebook or on my website (MildredAbbott.com) whenever you'd like. I'd love to hear from you. If you're interested in receiving advanced reader copies of upcoming installments, please join Mildred Abbott's Cozy Mystery Club on Facebook.

I also wanted to mention the elephant in the room... or the over-sugared corgi, as it were. Watson's personality is based around one of my own corgis, Alastair. He's the sweetest little guy in the world, and, like Watson, is a bit of a grump. Also, like Watson (and every other corgi to grace the world with their presence), he lives for food. In the Cozy Corgi series, I'm giving Alastair the life of his dreams through Watson. Just like I don't spend my weekends solving murders, neither does he spend his days snacking on scones and unending dog treats. But in the books? Well, we both get to live out our fantasies. If you are a corgi parent, you already know your little angel shouldn't truly have free rein of the pastry case, but you can read them snippets of Watson's life for a pleasant bedtime fantasy.

Precarious Pasta, book fourteen, will be coming Fall 2019. Thanks to some health issues and life changes, there will be a larger time between books, but Fred and Watson aren't done. Not even close! In the meantime, again, please continue to share your love of the series with friends and writes reviews for each installment. Spreading the word about the series will help it continue. Thank you!!!

Much love, Mildred

PS: I'd also love it if you signed up for my newsletter. That way you'll never miss a new release. You won't hear from me more than once a month, nobody needs that many newsletters!

Newsletter link: Mildred Abbott Newsletter Signup

ACKNOWLEDGMENTS

A special thanks to Agatha Frost, who gave her blessing and her wisdom. If you haven't already, you simply MUST read Agatha's Peridale Cafe Cozy Mystery series. They are absolute perfection.

The biggest and most heartfelt gratitude to Katie Pizzolato, for her belief in my writing career and being the inspiration for the character of the same name in this series. Thanks to you, Katie, our beloved baker, has completely stolen both mine and Fred's heart!

Desi, I couldn't imagine an adventure without you by my side. A.J. Corza, you have given me the corgi covers of my dreams. A huge, huge thank you to all of the lovely souls who proofread the ARC versions and helped me look somewhat literate (in completely random order): Melissa Brus, Cinnamon, Ron Perry, Rob Andresen-Tenace, Anita Ford, TL Travis, Victoria Smiser, Lucy Campbell, Sue Paulsen, Bernadette Ould, Lisa Jackson, Kelly Miller, Eric Thornton, Cecelia Stroessner Clark, Deni Winter Breitenbach, Sue Wilson Keefer, Arlene Leonard, Brandi M. Nolan, and Judi Stankovic. Thank you all, so very, very much!

A further and special thanks to some of my dear readers and friends who support my passion: Andrea Johnson, Fiona Wilson, Katie Pizzolato, Maggie Johnson, Marcia Gleason, Rob Andresen-Tenace, Robert Winter, Jason R., Victoria Smiser, Kristi Browning, and those of you who wanted to remain anonymous. You make a huge, huge difference in my life and in my ability to continue to write. I'm humbled and grateful beyond belief! So much love to you all!

CPSIA information can be obtained
at www.ICGtesting.com
Printed in the USA
LVHW112242230920
666963LV00001B/105